NEW YORK *Nights*

By
Brandon J. Harmer
Cover Art By Deborah Allison

NEPTUNE PRESS

WWW.NEPTUNEPRESS.ORG

NEPTUNE PRESS

Printed in the U.S.A.

Publisher's Cataloging-In-Publication Data

Harmer, Brandon J.
  New York nights / by Brandon J. Harmer.

  pages ; cm

  ISBN: 978-0-9906103-0-4

  1. College graduates--New York (State)--New York--Fiction. 2. Reunions--New York (State)--New York--Fiction. 3. Friendship--New York (State)--New York--Fiction. 4. Man-woman relationships--New York (State)--New York--Fiction. 5. New York (N.Y.)--Fiction. 6. Domestic fiction. I. Title.

PS3608.A764 N49 2014
813/.6   2014947052

For my loving family:
Joan, Keith, John, and Carol
And for my dear friend:
Mike

Part One

1

Lana, David, Amanda, Aaron and Hunter are the names of the friends in this book. There's also me, Will, your narrator, and Emily. She and I have become so inseparable that to divide our names by a single sentence would cause me alarm. Now, I just give a banal smile when I'm asked at parties, *Where's your other half?* As pun-loving Hunter liked to say, *Where there's a Will, there's an Emily.* But enough about happy couples. Let me start with Lana.

I've been told that the use of physical description can stand as a reliable substitute for a quality beginning. So instead of anatomy, let me begin with her name: *Lana. La. Na.* No matter how many times I say those two syllables, they are still just as enchanting as when, on that initial morning at Columbia, I said them for the first time. *A Zola-Nabokovian fusion*, Hunter would always insist. Without them, a man is tongue-tied. He heaves out rough utterances until stumbling across the union of *La* and *Na. L* melts off our top row of teeth. With an orthodontist's delight, we open for *A*. We strike the palate with *N*, only to open again. If Emily ever reads this (and I'm certain she will) she'll call me insane for writing this way about Lana. It's true though, I've always thought her beauty begins with her name.

It was Lana's parents who gave her winning numbers for the genetic lottery. The father, a dapper lawyer, and the mother, a former model, raised three daughters in Darian, Connecticut. Lana was the youngest, preceded by her two sisters Jacqueline and Sarah. She loved her sisters and they loved her. Growing up, Lana had many friends and admirers. Often, they were indistinguishable from one another. As those juvenile romantics made themselves known, she slowly realized that their interest was sparked by nothing less than the changes in her physical appearance. Vanity was not in her emotional repertoire. Even still, she was not upset to catch her reflection in a mirror.

Is this me? Is this what they see? Is this what makes them look at me the way they do?

Naturally, many boys competed for her attention. A handful met with success. The most memorable of them all was a boy named Tim Simmons, a popular athlete and an exceptional student. For a while he made her happy. Their relationship came to an abrupt end when, on a chilly Saturday night in October, Lana, uninvited, opened a forbidden bedroom door during a house party, finding Timmy with Billy…and *Jane* in-between. The discovery, a mortifying shock to Lana, was anticipated by practically every one of her friends. In retrospect, she probably took it much harder than she should have. Yes, it was a vulgar display of betrayal. But if Tim was the type of guy to indulge in the circumstances of their breakup, was he really worth all of Lana's tears?

Needless to say, the experience left Lana with a less than favorable outlook on the male sex. When her mood did not improve, her father decided to have a talk with her. One day, a few weeks after the breakup, he knocked on her bed room door. Lana was resting her head on a pillow, looking out a window at nothing in particular. He came in and sat on the edge of her bed. For his daughter's sake, he tried to be calm, but truthfully, he was just as angry as she was. Lana had always been his favorite. After hearing the details of the breakup from Jacqueline, he was ready to forgo his years as a prosecutor and tear straight through Tim's front door.

"We men," he told her, "are damn bastards. We only think of ourselves and we hardly give a thought to what the love of a woman actually means. But there are some who are better than the rest and, well, that's the kind of man I've tried to be for you and your mother. Just know you'll find the right guy someday, and don't let one little prick ruin it for you. On second thought, you might as well avoid boys altogether. That would be best, don't you think!"

Lana had heard these kinds of talks before. She knew her father's words were merely compliments to the indescribable love he felt. She looked up at him from the pillow. Rubbing her eyes and forcing a smile, she said, "OK."

It occurs to me that, aside from name games and one invasive story, I have not said anything about Lana at all. I apologize for that. I honestly cannot remember much else about her pre-university days, even though she's told me much more than what has already been written. To the one that lives it, childhood is a singularly unique experience. To me, Lana's past signifies the lives of New England's most privileged daughters. Although I may be forgetting a few details, her history is really quite typical. Thankfully, I've arrived to where Lana went away to college in New York. There, she met the second name we have introduced.

David is a true New Yorker, for whatever that title is worth. Born at Mt. Sinai Hospital, he was raised by his parents until the age of seven when family life collapsed. I do not know the exact reasons for the divorce. David never really brought it up. It's so common for children to blame themselves for the problems of their parents. Yet, for whatever reason, I do not believe David ever did blame himself. By the time he turned twelve, he was shipped off to Armory Prep in upstate Connecticut. There, he shared the same fate as many renowned politicians, entrepreneurs, and self-made men. He was placed in a well-established boarding school by parents who had the money to afford the best education for their child, but not the love that is most essential.

With each year at Armory, David grew closer to manhood. The school was single sex, encouraging a strong bond of brotherhood between him and his peers. In the absence of women, that fraternity was left unchecked and unchallenged. From an early age, he learned the value of strength and courage. As his mind became equipped for leadership, so did his body. While undressing for a morning shower, the mirror became his sole companion. Surrounded by steam and tile, he grew taller, stronger, and hairier. If, by chance, he found the showers empty, he spent at least ten minutes admiring his body. Mirrors do not lie. Angled under the right light, his imagination found equals in Classic heroes like Achilles and Aeneas. Other times, it was some forgotten 90's star.

Sometime during his freshman year at Armory, David experienced what he would later call a biological compulsion towards the opposite sex. Through self-perpetuated rumors, he was known as the highest authority on girls. In reality, he was a novice on the subject. Like most boys, he lied to gain the respect of his friends. Rather than being deterred by his inexperience, becoming more familiar with girls became a personal mission for him. On visits from Armory to the nearby town of Mayflower, David did not return to school without the number of at least one potential romance. He even became somewhat of an ambassador for the other boys in his class. By trial and little error, he learned methods that worked with girls. He discovered words that turn them red and words that keep them at a comfortable distance.

David's first romance, as he told us in a fit of drunken dorm room hysteria at Columbia, was a cashier who worked in a grocery store. They met on one of his first visits to Mayflower. He was fourteen, she was older. For the life of him, he could not remember her name. After the exchange of some not-so-heartfelt words, they arranged a rendezvous at *Heaven's Gate Cemetery*. It was a rather presumptuous title, David reflected. The location was the midway point between school and town. In the shadow of a red cedar, David, for the first time, felt the ephemeral spasms of curious love. Occasionally, two heads leaped above a gravestone, inspecting the sound of a faraway hearse or a solemn group of mourners. What seemed like an eternity could not have been longer than ten minutes. When the meeting had gone its natural course, both parties decided to go home. They adjusted their clothes, shook the twigs from their hair, and left each other.

Despite all appearances, girls were not David's only priority at Armory. He rose to the top of his class, surpassing his rivals in both academics and athletics. David learned that the price of success was well worth the energy put in. He also learned that, if channeled the right way, that amount of energy could be very minimal. David carried his ambition with him to college. On two separate occasions, it could have gotten him expelled.

The first incident took place during our first finals week at Columbia. He was enrolled in a calculus class. It was a tedious requirement for the core curriculum. David hated the class, partly because of the professor: a tenured teacher gone bad. But the real reason David hated calculus is because he was never any good at it. After studying until 2:00 in the morning before the final exam, he decided his time would be better spent devising a way to cheat. He probably underestimated the consequences he would face if caught. However, he had received a *B-* on the midterm and would not permit his grade to be jeopardized by one professor's dotage. He cheated on the exam...and did not get caught. With homework and class participation factored in, he received an *A*- in the course. It was the only blemish on his otherwise perfect semester.

David never told me how he actually cheated. Cell phones, cryptic notes, the inside of a water bottle: none of these suited him. They were far too risky. However he did it, cheating on the final brought his average up to a 3.93, which caught the eye of the administration. Once the spring semester began, David continued his Armory legacy by positioning himself at the top of our class. His success only increased his brimming self-confidence.

The second incident happened a year later, in the spring of our sophomore year. David was already on a pre-law track, intent on going to law school. As the student with the highest GPA in his concentration, he was asked to write a paper on a legal topic of his choosing. If it was exceptional, the paper would be published in our undergraduate legal journal. Having developed a keen fascination for philosophy in matters of legal justice, David wrote on the classical form of utilitarianism. He critiqued several well-known and long held criticisms of the doctrine. I never fully grasped the heart of his argument. To give a poor summary, David said that *the greatest good for the greatest amount of people* can infringe upon the rights of individuals. However, so long as a person could accept violating the rights of others, David thought utilitarianism could still be used to achieve great deserts despite its moral ramifications. As with many of his arguments, he seemed to draw his proof not from truth, but from the clouds.

However David composed his paper, it must have been very persuasive. The Chair of the pre-law department took great interest in it. Hearing about David's work, the Chair squirmed his way into overseeing his research. Once the paper was finished, David submitted it to the Chair in order to receive feedback and the necessary approval for submission to the research journal. He did that one month before the submission deadline. A week passed and David received his paper, bloodied with corrections in red ink. At the end of the paper, the Chair demanded a re-draft before he would give his approval. More time passed and a trend developed. David submitted the corrected paper, only to have it returned with more comments than on the previous draft. The first time, David did not suspect a thing. The second time, he thought the Chair was just being picky. The third time, he knew something was wrong. The submission deadline passed and, much to David's anger and confusion, the paper was never presented publicly. A few months later, he learned why.

Looking over a second tier legal journal, David found an article written by the very same Chair who had thwarted his work from publication. On closer inspection, he discovered the article was the same one he had submitted to him months before. How the man expected to plagiarize the work of a student without being caught, I'll never know. He probably figured that the likelihood of David ever reading the journal was so remote that he could get away with it. The problem for David was that, even though the administration knew he was working on a research paper, he never shared it with anyone other than the Chair. No one could corroborate his story. It would be his word versus a professor with nine years in the department. David understood that this was a battle he could not win by conventional means. Instead, he took an alternative measure that, in hindsight, was more rewarding than publication in any journal.

As a sophomore, David needed to start perfecting his application if he wanted to be accepted by the country's top law schools. His LSAT score needed to be the best. It just so happened that the Chair of the pre-law department was a part-time employee of the Law School Admissions Council with the job of proof reading each copy of the test for logical fallacies. David saw his opportunity to turn an unsavory betrayal into something beneficial. He took it. Instead of reporting the Chair, he confronted him one day in his office. David revealed that he knew about the plagiarized paper and had the evidence to prove it. As proof, David showed him the drafts of his paper alongside a copy of the plagiarized article. He also revealed a chain of emails with the Dean of his class informing her of the progress of his research, with copies of each draft in the emails. This last piece of evidence was completely fabricated. There were no emails, none from the Dean, anyway. Startled by the overwhelming evidence, especially by the emails, the Chair admitted he plagiarized David's work.

Instead of reporting the Chair, David offered him a deal. In return for failing to report the incident to the academic integrity board, David demanded private tutoring for the LSAT, free of charge. He also demanded that the Chair reveal every detail of the test. If he refused, his reputation as a professor would be ruined. Understanding the circumstances of the situation, the Chair reluctantly accepted. If anyone ever discovered he not only plagiarized a student's work, but then agreed to hand over everything he knew about the LSAT, his career would be finished. On balance, the threat of being fired from the university was more pressing. So long as he gave David what he wanted, he saw no reason why the student should make an enemy of him by reporting both transgressions. So through the most unusual means, David won himself a mentor for the LSAT. Evidently, it was worth the price of not publishing his paper. He earned a near perfect score.

David always saw life under a Machiavellian lens: *the ends justify the means* and, so long as no one gets too hurt, those ends can be reached by any means necessary. But what exactly were these *ends* to which David so religiously devoted himself? Even David, with all his interest in philosophy, could not answer that question. All he knew was that his eventual goals would be met under the satisfaction of two conditions: connections and wealth.

All his life, he had been building towards them. Now, in the greatest city in the world, he would distinguish himself in order to first acquire connections and soon thereafter, wealth. Everywhere he looked, those were the things that mattered most to people. So, he reasoned, they must be terribly important to have.

He was a boy of rare intelligence, entering college with a common appetite for girls. But when he saw Lana, something changed. Ironically, they met in an ethics class. David impressed her by the way he was able to rival the professor's knowledge. That people were ends in themselves, worthy of so on and so forth, was just one of the innumerable metaphysical carcasses he had scavenged through years of self-reflection. Their routes to class intersected, at first by chance and later by design. One time, Lana passed him on the way to the cafeteria. David, surrounded by a group of friends, watched as she crossed in front of a glass building. Before the opportunity passed, Lana turned her head and looked at her reflection. David smiled. It pleased him to know that he was not the only one who could not resist her looks.

Like in high school, Lana's beauty attracted fierce competition. David never guessed that his rival would be his roommate, Aaron. My knowledge of Aaron's pre-college life is hazy, to say the least. He attended a conservatory for the arts and had a passion for theater. His father had always been against his son's decision to pursue acting. This was likely due to his deep conviction that a respectable man must earn a living not only for himself, but for his family, an impossible task given an actor's salary. Accompanying this belief was a certain ever-present, well-hidden, homophobic anxiety towards any poofda activities that detoured Aaron's path to manliness. Despite his father's old-world bigotry, the tuition bill was paid. With his mother's support, Aaron began his studies at Columbia.

As a tall, well-toned, good looking young man and

with his love of the performing arts, people were bound to make assumptions about Aaron's sexuality. These people bothered Aaron, especially when he could never find the right words to set the record straight. Even his father began to worry when, by his senior year in the conservatory, he seemed to show utterly no interest in women. But that was not true. Aaron was interested. It was his lack of self-confidence that made forming friendships with girls nearly impossible.

All that changed when he met Lana. She drew him from the shelter of his childhood. New to the city, Aaron became a complete recluse during his first week at college. While David explored the streets, Aaron stayed in the dorm room. Communication became so difficult that David began filing for a room transfer. Just when Aaron had given up all hope of friendship, Lana came into his life. She probably was compelled by pity and a desire to be friendly, rather than any feelings of physical attraction. Nevertheless, Aaron must have made a good impression. Two weeks after our first day of classes, they went on a date.

I do not know what happened during their brief time together, or if anything occurred immediately afterwards. What I do know is that Aaron never went on another date with Lana. The strangest thing was that, after the date, they were still the best of friends. It was like they had reached an agreement that their friendship could never be anything more than just that.

I should mention, although David did eventually win Lana over, the steps along that road were not easy. It was not because of any prudishness on Lana's part, nor because of any hesitation by David. Believe me, he became more emboldened with each rejection. In reality, Lana was as eager for David as he was for her. Still, her past told her to be careful. She was afraid of getting hurt again. Moreover, she loved her independence in New York. For the first time in her life, she felt completely free. She was young and wanted to live her first year of college to the fullest. So, if David wanted her, he simply had to wait.

For David, the idea of waiting for any girl amounted to a personal offense. With Lana, however, he made an exception. The more forbidden the fruit, the sweeter the taste. At least, that's what he thought at first. But while David waited, he began to feel what you or I might describe as the first feelings of love. There was no denying it, she was changing him.

After Aaron and Lana's friendship was established, David started seeing more of Lana. He checked her *Facebook* religiously, became friends with her friends, and even made sure to attend every party where she was invited. One time, David tried explaining his sudden devotion towards Lana.

"Under normal circumstances," he told me on some dreary afternoon between Chemistry and Nietzsche, "I would never consider anchoring myself to one girl. But with Lana, it's different. There's something strange about her, a mystery, you know? She's one of those rare girls that doubt the very looks that others crave. Those are the type I like. Just knowing how much she's the object of other men's desires, can you imagine it? To know that she is mine, and that I am hers."

With that as his motivation, after a year of persistence, Lana became David's girlfriend.

His victory could not have been accomplished without the help of the rest of the group. Amanda became Lana's best friend. After spending time with David, she encouraged her to start seeing him. Despite their connection to Lana, David and Aaron became good friends, with David as the leader and Aaron at his side. As long as you didn't know too much, David was extremely hard to dislike. He was the kind of guy you just could not say no to. I lived in the same building as David and Aaron. With increasing

12

regularity, I found myself in their dorm room with a beer in my hand. Yes, it can be said that David and Lana were brought together by the rest of us: Aaron, Amanda, Emily, myself, and eventually, Hunter.

Together, the city was ours. No Saturday night was ever spent alone. No Sunday morning was ever seen. We always had one or two outsiders drift into the group, but when 4:00 A.M. rolled around and *Dominos* called, it was always us seven. Despite having two couples in the group, the others never felt out of place. Landmark bars, cramped apartments, and the inside of toilet bowls: we saw it all. Except for the clubs, that is. We never went to the clubs. The memories we created will likely be the happiest of our lives. But even in those immortal moments, I still felt that secret fear which tells us that our best years have passed us and that any recreation of them will be hollow and in vain.

After college, everything began to unravel. It started with Lana. After graduation she started seeking work outside university walls. Still financially dependent on her parents, but determined to make it on her own, she needed a place to live. After not too much thought, she went to David with the idea of moving in together. After all, they had been seeing each other for more than three years. Her innocent proposal changed David. He began distancing himself from every aspect of her life. His visits to her became less and less frequent. At first, David's dwindling presence did not worry Lana.

He's just busy with school. This isn't college any more, he knows better than to waste his time partying. He's too stressed to think about looking for apartments with me. If I give him time, things will get better.

But things did not get better. Two visits a week became one. One became once every two weeks. By April, Lana had gone without seeing David for over an entire month. Even when he started to reschedule promised dates, Lana did not mind so much. At least he was speaking

13

with her then. But by the beginning of spring, they had a complete communication breakdown. Their relationship was suspended in limbo. Since graduating from Columbia, Lana had been staying with Amanda. She hoped it would be a temporary stay before a lifetime of happiness with David. And did she seriously intend to spend the rest of her life with him? She probably had not thought that far ahead. All she knew was that her happiest memories were with him. She wanted to create more of those memories by sharing her life with his.

Lana and David were not the only ones to take on distance at that time. Although Amanda and Lana remained good friends, Aaron became just as reclusive as he had been during his pre-university days. He struggled to find work as an actor, especially given the state of the economy. Perhaps Hunter had been hit worst of all. A year out of college and he was still unemployed. He refused to accept a job that was *beneath him*. I worried that, if he did not find work, he would be evicted from his apartment.

Even my relationship with Emily was vulnerable to the changes that followed college. We had known each other since the fourth grade. We had never been separated by more than a fifteen minute bike ride. We were even lucky enough to attend college in the same city. But while living out my four years at Columbia, I harbored a secret fear that my NYU girl would one day look beyond her childhood beau for a new beginning. Over ten months had passed since college and I started to have the agonizing, heartbreaking, and completely unwarranted premonition that my best friend was slipping away from me.

Now the introduction ends. It was the night of May 4th that things took a turn for the worst. It started at a diner in Harlem, our Seinfeldian retreat from the demands of college. Emily had the idea to stage a reunion after we all had spent a year in *the real world*. The actual reason for our get-together was to bring Lana and David under the same roof. We hoped that the company of friends would help them work out their problems, maybe even return them to the way they once were.

Looking back on the misfortunes of our past, we sometimes wonder how events that seemed so insurmountable ever made us so miserable. That goes to show just how forgetful we can be.

2

Rain in May. It fell on the city, cooling the hot asphalt and evaporating into a thin layer of steam that stretched over the streets of New York. Just as the first drops splashed against my forehead, I rounded the corner of 114th and saw the neon lights of the diner. I turned to Emily and saw her looking ahead. Her cheeks were wet and she was smiling. The rain picked up and I felt her hand clench tighter to mine as we ran across 115th. She went ahead underneath the maroon canopy of the diner. She took off her stylish tan raincoat, revealing a yellow summer frock. I forgot the rain and was transported to all the times I had seen her in that dress before. It could have been the hundredth time she had worn it, but I always looked at her with the same amorous eyes.

"Are you coming inside?" she asked, still smiling.

It was then I realized I was still standing in the rain. I stepped underneath the awning and my hand fumbled with the door handle. Leaving the night behind, we walked through two sets of heavy doors until a tall waitress greeted us.

"Hello, how many?" she asked without looking at me, using her keen sense for customers.

"Seven," I said.

She grabbed two menus and led us to a booth in the corner of the diner. Sitting by a window, I imagined I was inside a submarine staring out into the wet street. A string of cars waited impatiently behind a red traffic light. The rain fell steeply with the strong wind. A newspaper blew across the sidewalk like tumbleweed. Street signs fought against the storm.

"You'll fit fine here," the waitress said, wiping the table with a damp rag.

"Does a waiter named Roy Lipton still work here?" Emily asked, sliding into the booth after me.

"His shift doesn't start for another ten minutes. When he comes in, I'll tell him you asked."

Roy was a senior at Columbia, a year younger than us. Although most of my memories of him are from forgettable parties, he was still a good guy. It would have been a shame if we didn't at least say *hello*.

The clock above the bar hit 7:50. The place was packed. Evidently, everyone in the upper Westside had the idea to visit the diner while the storm passed. Conversations filled the room, accompanied by the clang and clack of silverware. There was music, barely audible above the noise. Waiters, busboys, and an occasional cook frantically weaved through the aisles. One of the grills in the kitchen had malfunctioned, creating a backup of food orders. Emily and I listened as a family next to us, a mother, father, and two daughters, was told their food would not be ready for at least another fifteen minutes. The waiter apologized for the inconvenience.

"Inconvenience!" the mother shouted in a shrill Long Island accent. "We come here expecting a decent meal, and that's all you can say? Do you still expect us to pay for our food? Aren't you ashamed for having made my girls starve? They just got out of gymnastics, you know. Aren't you…"

She went on like that for a while, embarrassing the rest of her family. The father, after failing to calm his wife, sunk into the corner of the booth and lowered his head. The

17

girls retreated to their *iPhones*.

"Poor guy," I said.

"The husband or the waiter?" Emily asked, ritually unfolding her paper napkin and placing it on her lap.

"Both. They're both helpless."

"I've always hated how people give waiters a hard time."

"What do you mean?" I asked.

"I mean, it's not the waiter's fault that your food isn't ready yet or that it tastes horrible. He's just trying to do a job he probably despises in the first place."

"Yeah, but that's what they're paid for: to bear the brunt of lousy customers like you and me."

"Are you familiar with the expression: *Don't shoot the messenger?*" she asked. "Well, the same thing applies here. Waiters are messengers. I would understand if the guy made a mistake, like getting the order wrong, or if he was just plain inattentive. But when there's nothing he can do? It just doesn't seem fair to me."

"They spit in our soup anyway, so it evens out in the long run. It's the way the business works. That guy probably has kids to feed, working a crappy job and taking food from the kitchen to bring home to his family. If listening to Drescher is the price he pays, then that's the way it is."

"All I'm saying is that people should put themselves in other people's shoes more often."

"I feel worse for the husband. He has to go home to that. Look."

The husband was in act six of an endless Italian opera. His hands covered his eyes, mouth, and nose, making him look like a frightened turtle. At one point, he lowered his hands to try to calm his wife. When she snapped at him with her sharp fingernails, he withdrew to his shell. Eventually, the woman quieted down and the family was forced to wait a little longer for their food.

18

"Poor guy," I confirmed.

"The only reason people harass waiters is because they've got nothing to talk about with the people they are with. If they had something interesting to say, they wouldn't care that their food wasn't ready. But these people have nothing to talk about. They would rather stuff their faces in silence. It's really kind of sad, if you think about it."

True, it was sad. But I could not resist smiling at Emily's observation. She really had a talent for seeing things from another person's perspective.

"We've sometimes gone entire meals without saying a word to each other," I added, knowing just how she would respond.

"That's different," she said. "We have comfortable silences. We don't pollute the air with nonsense because we know each other so well. In the beginning it wasn't like that. You would talk and talk for hours. Sometimes I would zone out, and when I came back, you'd still be going on and on."

"I always say couples should just skip from date 1 to date 965."

"The fun is getting there," she said with a wink. "Only, don't talk about comfortable silences. It's so cliché."

Before I could tell her that she had raised the subject, my eye caught the light from the outside street glinting off of a passing umbrella. It was plastic, translucent, with a dome that insulated a head of smooth red hair. The rain washed over the clear bubble. Layers of thin waves ran towards the ground, bending and shaking the light. When the umbrella went by, another, a black one, followed in its wake. They entered the diner and collapsed, revealing two girls. As they stood side-by-side, I remembered an observation Emily had made years before, about one having to struggle to achieve her looks, while to the other, they came naturally.

Amanda and Lana approached our table. Amanda

wore red lipstick that stood out against her light skin. Her eyes were blue. As she walked towards us, her small hips swayed in rhythm with her step. The only feature that was out-of-place was her small nose. It always seemed to have a bend or slope that did not align with the rest of her face.

My eyes moved away from her and towards Lana. Shaking some drops of rain from her hair, she came to our semi-circular booth. It had been so long, I had almost forgotten what she looked like. Even Emily admired her looks. Like she always said, *there's no shame in admitting a beautiful thing is beautiful.*

"Hey you two," Lana said, cheeks red, eyes bright. "We're not late, are we?"

"Nope. We're just early," Emily answered, standing from the booth and embracing first Lana, then Amanda. I followed her lead.

"Is Aaron here yet?" Amanda asked, removing her bashe rain jacket.

"Not yet," I said, returning to my seat. "He's coming alone, isn't he? The weather's probably slowing him down."

"It's always exciting when a storm comes to the city," Lana said. "Electricity in the air! It's the way New York should always look, covered in rain. Amanda, remember when we had that huge storm back in college and the power went out and they had to cancel classes?"

"The power never went out," Amanda corrected, following Lana into the booth. "A few tree limbs fell on campus so they said it wasn't safe to go outside that day."

"Ah, right, I remember. So fun, too exciting..." Lana paused for a moment, smiling to herself, remembering our university days.

"How is work?" I asked Amanda, trying to generate some small talk.

"*Comme ci, comme ça.* We're opening an exhibit on British pop art in two weeks."

Amanda worked in a modern art museum in Queens. It was the reward for her labors as an art history major. The job paid well and allowed her to associate with some of the most financially well-off art enthusiasts in the city.

I noticed Emily give a coy smile and knew what it meant. Emily had always been convinced that Amanda's prime motive for the museum job, as with many things in her life, was to position herself around various types of men who could provide her with various types of material things. She knew Amanda had no great love of art, nor any real appreciation for its history. One likely source of Emily's disapproval came from the fact that Amanda had attended a top private school on the Upper East Side. She heard rumors of the school, as well as the kinds of girls it generated. *They come out of factories!* she was fond of saying. Honestly, I always thought she was a little jealous of Amanda. Not jealous of her talents or abilities, but of the wealth and benefits that had been bestowed upon her by the accident of birth. Emily had worked all her life to get where she was. She could never stomach the thought of anyone being entitled to what she worked so hard for. At its core, their relationship was edgy. Although Amanda never gave her any precise reason, Emily still did not trust her. It was like Amanda had broken some dear promise she had once made to Emily, or had lied to her at some important time. Only, there were no broken promises and there were no lies. I could never see why Emily was so skeptical about Amanda. In the five years we had been friends, Amanda never treated me badly. How could I say I disliked her?

"That sounds interesting," Emily said in a very uninterested way.

Amanda could not tell whether Emily was mocking her or was simply making a trite comment. She chose to ignore her.

21

"My how this place *has* changed," Lana said, mocking a line that I guessed had come from an old actress. She took a minute to compare her memories with her surroundings.

New booths had been added to replace the cracked, sticky, simulated brown leather of the old ones. A few fans hung from the ceiling, vastly improving the air flow. A sparkling glass refrigeration case hummed near the front counter. It had cakes and pastries in a wide spectrum of delicious colors.

At that moment, I noticed a tall man enter the diner. He started looking around. He moved awkwardly to the left and to the right. He was trying to maneuver around an elderly couple slowly approaching the exit. As the man looked in my direction, I saw Aaron's handsome face.

"Some things never change," I said, waving to him. He smiled and waved back. His short fine hair clung to his forehead. Drops of water ran down his thick neck, settling on his sturdy collar bones.

"I'm sorry I'm late," he said apologetically. "Have you been waiting long?"

"Just got here, actually," Emily said, happy to see him.

"Here, *assieds*," Amanda insisted, patting the booth.

She sat on the outside of the circular bench, with Lana seated immediately to her left. Aaron hesitated for a moment, waiting to see if Amanda would get up. Seeing her merely slide over, Aaron took his seat. Lana saw this little exchange and knew what it meant. She moved towards my end of the table, putting more distance between her and Amanda. Aaron pretended like he didn't notice anything.

"I would've been here sooner," he said anxiously, adjusting the trunks of his legs underneath the table, "but I had an important call."

Lana took the hint.

"About what?" she asked.

With pride in his voice, Aaron explained how he had been called to audition for a feature film produced by *Black River*. We were all genuinely impressed and congratulated him on the opportunity.

"It's no time to celebrate," he said, mistaking our enthusiasm for celebration. "I haven't got the part yet."

"When's the audition?" I asked.

"A couple of days from now. I've got to spend some time with the sides they gave me."

"What's your character like?" Emily joined in.

"He's some young up-and-coming politician, or an aid to a politician. I don't really know. The story is fueled by the American dream and centers on how my character loses touch with reality. It's dramatic and over the top, but it would be a step in the right direction for my career."

"Well, *bon chance*," Amanda said, "I know you'll be great."

A momentary silence. The ring of Amanda's atrocious French lingered in the air. Two years of college level language and a study-abroad trip to Paris apparently endows one with the right to sprinkle random foreign phrases throughout their sentences. It was a pompous habit I thought only authors gave to their characters, until I had the misfortune of meeting a person who had acquired it. No matter how many ways you can say *connaissance*, you will never get more of it, as *mon amour* always dreamed of saying to Amanda. After some time, I thought back to what Emily said about comfortable silences. Undoubtedly, this was not one of them.

"Well," Aaron began, "should we order now or wait?"

"We should wait," Emily said resolutely. "They should be here any minute. You told Hunter to come at 8:00, didn't you?"

"I told him 7:45," I said. "I tried to make sure they

would be here on time."

Lana's face became worried. Her thin eyebrows furrowed together and the corners of her mouth sunk inward, causing her to frown slightly. Seeing that I had seen it, she made the look disappear.

"No worries," I said to everyone, but meant for Lana. "They'll be here."

Soon, two conversations began simultaneously between Emily, Lana, myself, and Aaron and Amanda. Lana told us about new music artists, the latest celebrity gossip, and the finale of some famous television show. It seemed obvious to me that nothing about what she was saying was of any interest to her. Meanwhile, Amanda continued to question Aaron about his audition. Emily, blessed with a keen appreciation for social graces, tried to draw Aaron and Amanda back into the general conversation. Amanda said two or three words of acknowledgment and immediately returned to Aaron. On his part, Aaron tried posing some questions to Lana, asking her to repeat what she had just said or to clarify certain words. After a few minutes, both conversations came to a stop. We found ourselves in the same silence with which we began.

The question on all of our minds, although no one dared pose it, was *where in the hell could David and Hunter be*? I had talked to Hunter the day before and had even confirmed earlier that they would meet up and come to the diner. About fifteen minutes had passed and they still had not arrived. Emily sent both boys a text message asking them where they were. Those texts received no reply.

"I don't think they're coming," Lana said at last, forcing a smile. I took a welcomed sigh of relief, only to feel Emily's elbow prod against my ribs. Aaron opened his mouth as though he wanted to say something to comfort Lana, but no words came out.

"Do you remember," Lana resumed softly, "when we came here for Hunter's birthday a few years ago. How he smiled when the waiter brought out that big chocolate cake. I don't remember ever seeing him smile like that. And then, what did David call him? The way Hunter looked, he said *he looked like a–*"

"*Like a sorry version of the big bad wolf, trying to blow out birthday candles,*" Emily completed, remembering Hunter's balloon face.

"That's right!" Lana said with infectious laughter.

Although the happy moment was fading, I was determined not to let the mood fall. I kept the conversation going with stories from the past, throwing in bits of news about Emily and me when appropriate. Whether or not the stories were real made no difference. All that mattered was we were laughing. The conversation was a welcomed distraction from both the present and the future. It was painful to think that David and Hunter had abandoned us, let alone the fact that the only way we five could speak was if we spoke about the past. I remember thinking we had reached that certain stage of friendship where history is the only thread that unites a group of people who changed long ago. The sad thing was I thought we had more time before we got to that stage. Behind all the stories, laughs, and happy memories, it was all very depressing.

Perhaps the most upsetting thing of all was Lana. While the reunion was a failure for the group, it also meant that she was now further from David than she had ever been. The hope of reconciliation slowly died in her eyes. With each revolution of the minute hand on the diner clock, she felt more and more certain she was being forgotten.

Eventually, Roy came to take our orders. He was elated to see us. He shared all the latest news from Columbia: who had been fired, who had been expelled, what changes had been made to the school, and so on. In this way, the evening dragged on. We all managed to get through dinner without too much anxiety over our missing guests.

When the time came to say our goodbyes, Lana was lost in thought. She did not know whether to count this failed reunion as just another stalling tactic of David's, or as a resolute sign that he had left her behind. Amanda led her out of the diner, with Aaron close behind, followed by Emily and me. The weather was less-severe. The wind was quiet now and the rain fell slowly. Aaron gave a lingering hug to Lana. He asked to see her again and assured her that everything would be alright.

Lana pretended that his platitude consoled her, but even Aaron could tell he made no great impression. Saying goodbye to Emily and me, then finally to Amanda, he left us. I called out, "good luck!" to which he raised his right hand, the only sign that he heard me. He kept walking along crowded Broadway until he rounded the corner of 112th and was gone. Amanda and Lana said goodbye. They went in the opposite direction as Aaron.

"We should go," I said, looking towards the sky.

"Not yet," Emily said seriously. "Didn't you see Lana tonight? She was acting so weird. Go to Hunter's apartment. Find out what happened—why he didn't bring David."

"What about you?" I asked.

She started to walk away and I smelled her yellow hair when she turned. "Some people have work in the morning!" she called back.

"Hey, I get up earlier than you!" I ran to her and we kissed. "I'll see you back at the apartment. Be safe."

She smiled and her eyes looked into mine. Then, she placed both her hands on my chest and shoved me in the right direction. I found the 1-train. After a seven minute wait, I was on my way to Hunter's.

3

    While riding along in the prison of self-expression that is a New York City subway car, now would be a good time to introduce a person who has already been the subject of much conversation: Hunter Ricci. He was always an outsider in our group. While the rest of us solidified our circle by the end of freshman year, Hunter was a transfer student who entered in the middle of sophomore year. I do not know the details about why he transferred. He never told us much about his old college or even his high school. He was five feet, nine inches, with a slender body devoid of any real muscle tone or upper body strength. Apparently, he had once been good at track and field, but he threw the sport away when he came to Columbia for a more intellectually inclined lifestyle.

    Hunter was not as handsome as other boys. His dark and curly hair sheened with a mixture of oil and sweat. There was a large birthmark towards the far side of his left cheek which he always looked at with disdain. His deep brown eyes were puffy, as if he suffered from constant allergies. Hunter's problem was that he could never put these physical imperfections aside in order to be the person he wanted most. He was not as good looking as David or Aaron, but he was certainly not ugly. People always sensed he was uncomfortable in his own skin.

    In class, one of his restless limbs would never

fail to convulse. He rearranged his posture almost every minute and had the gross habit of biting his nails to the quick. While walking, he hurried like he had some place terribly important to be. The worst was when we seven tried smoking together. His paranoia killed the mood. From then on, whenever we smoked, we made up some lie so that he would not follow us. At first, no one treated him poorly. He was not ridiculed for his awkwardness, nor did anyone attempt to provoke his odd behavior. But from the first day he crossed the black gates on 116th Street, Hunter was isolated from his classmates. It was like he hated everyone around him, but at the same time, was insulted that no one befriended him. Because of this paradoxical trait, people were inclined not to abuse Hunter, but to build a wall of indifference towards him.

There was one exception to Hunter's otherwise perfect record of severing himself from human contact. That exception was me. Whatever the reason, Hunter broke his seclusion in the spring of sophomore year. By its end, we were friends. I could never tell what drove him to reach out to me. Maybe he was just tired of being lonely all the hours of the day and needed some level of companionship. Whatever the reason, I'm glad we became friends. God knows what would have happened to him if he had stayed alone. I'm quite possibly his best and only true friend. Even for a misanthrope like Hunter, that must mean something. Still, I could not help but feel that, to him, our friendship was nothing more than a casual acquaintance. Most days, it seemed like he merely tolerated my company as opposed to enjoying it.

The reasons Hunter used to justify his grandiose sense of self-worth are complex. For one thing, he always had a deep love of learning. For the most part, however, that love went unreflected in his college academics. He must have done well to transfer to Columbia, but when he arrived, he fell into the tail end of the pack. His transcript was spattered with mostly *Cs*, occasionally *Bs*, and hardly any *As*. His intellectual appetite was incited outside the classroom, in his writing and reading. A complete bookworm and insomniac, Hunter spent entire nights with his mind synchronized to the pages of his favorite novel. He read mostly classics, but was fond of comics too. Becoming engrossed in works of fantasy became his escape. His favorites were Jules Verne and Robert Louis Stevenson, but he delved through many other genres other than science fiction. Books were his greatest sense of accomplishment and self-worth. The lessons are what he valued most. He would have gone his whole life without them, had they not been recorded solely for his personal benefit.

Hunter's pride was never more apparent than when an argument broke out between David and him over literature. They fought over the first American novelist to win a Nobel Prize. David said it was Sinclair Lewis. Hunter insisted it was Upton Sinclair. *Google* proved David the winner. Hunter claimed he had only been mistaken, that he really meant to say *Lewis*, but it was no use. He was sullen and pouty for the rest of the evening. We all were forced to bear his mood until the night was over.

With his passion for literature, English was a natural choice of major. But even though he adored the subject, his grades rarely broke beyond *Cs*. Teachers appreciated his enthusiasm and clear knowledge of the subject, but his inattentiveness and the frequent absence of both the student and the assignment made it impossible to give him a high grade. When he did submit a paper, professors most often remarked on the eloquence of his writing. It had a seamless flow and a captivating structure. As opposed to crudely throwing out a thesis and dissecting it like some lab rat, Hunter's style was to lead his readers along a journey, revealing his meaning at the height of the paper's intensity. Although unconventional, his style was accepted by most professors. It earned him their respect, but also their pity. They wondered what kind of writing he would be capable of, if only he applied himself a little more.

While reading was Hunter's retreat, poetry was his most treasured mode of self-expression. He liked the beatniks: Jack Kerouac and others like him. His typical daydreams consisted of wandering the rough roads of America in search of nothing more than himself—a rebel in a strange land. It was all very erudite to Hunter, but for those who actually heard his poetry, his writing sounded more like the abstract ramblings of an idealistic boy, as opposed to that of the next Allen Ginsberg.

That consensus was confirmed one night during a university poetry reading. The audience consisted of the neighboring NYC community as well as several distinguished poets with ties to the school. A portion of the event featured Columbia's student poets who recited their pre-approved poems. Hunter submitted one of his poems and was chosen to read at the event. His selection was not one of his favorites. It followed the journey of a young man on a train, admiring a man in the opposite seat. In his opinion, it did not take enough risks. He found the language flat and uninspiring. It was beyond the point of salvation through redrafts. He concluded it did not represent his best poetic potential. I would tell you how the poem was received, however, Hunter never read it.

Instead, he wrote a new poem especially for the event. He finished it just five minutes before he went on. He switched the two poems at the last minute, telling no one. The new poem was disastrous and left the audience completely dumbfounded. He wrote of ancient Greek gods and goddesses, of formless flowers and shapeless nights. The metaphors seemed grossly ordinary, as if intended to mock the very act of writing poetry. The effect was sickening. After the reading, David remarked it was not poison that Claudius poured into old Hamlet's ear, but instead, a line from Hunter's poem.

By the end of the reading, the audience was visibly uncomfortable. Some grumbled in the front, angry at Hunter for forcing them to sit through such drivel. Some snickered and others heckled, receiving cheers of encouragement from the crowd. In short, the poem was just bad writing. Hunter left the stage watery eyed and bitterly embarrassed. To this day, I do not believe he has written a single verse of poetry since.

Considering I have made a point of mentioning the love life of my once-friends, Hunter should be no exception. There is nothing more pathetic than seeing a person search high and low for the right person, only to end up alone. Unfortunately, that was the sum of Hunter's 453 days in college. Within the span of two and a half years, he went on a total of maybe three dates. Not once did he find what he was looking for. But the reasons for Hunter's failure are in many ways his own fault. After much thought, I have found many holes in Hunter's approach to love.

For one thing, he was absurdly selective about who he would even consider getting to know. With his looks, I never thought he could be that picky in the first place. He was also an extremely harsh judge of character. He always found a fault in every person that showed him any kindness whatsoever. He looked for the worst in people to save him the trouble of knowing them. He lived with the assumption that ninety-nine percent of the human population is rotten. Anyone who challenged that bias was disregarded completely. He never considered that it takes time to know a person and that, if everyone followed his way of thinking, human relationships would not exist at all.

Like with finding a job, Hunter did not tolerate any girl he deemed *unworthy* of his presence and conversation. So in the end, he drove away anyone intelligent with his harsh judgment and all the rest with his conceit. His criteria for romance kept the entire population away. Two examples come to mind. The first and more humorous occurred in the summer of sophomore year. Hunter told me the story himself, with a mixture of smugness and pride on his face.

At the time, his interest was raised by Kimberly Beech, a smart girl at Columbia. I do not know what she saw in Hunter. Maybe he simply fascinated her. Kimberly was direct. She chased him when he bolted from class or left her circle of friends to join him in the quad. She surprised Hunter. He was unaccustomed to anyone paying him the attention that she did. By some miracle of communication, the two scheduled a dinner date at *Rosa*, an Italian place on the Upper West Side. It took about twenty minutes to get there, giving the two ample time to become better acquainted. They commenced awkward, "*getting to know you*" conversation until they got to the restaurant. Everything was going smoothly with the exception that, from the beginning of the date, Hunter noticed a particular habit of Kimberly's that pestered him very much.

Kimberly was having a genuinely good time with Hunter. However, whenever their conversation lulled, she always turned to her phone as a means of distraction. Like any normal person, Kimberly checked her messages and went on *Facebook*. As the evening went on, Kimberly's constant phone checking got on Hunter's nerves. He was offended that she would rather be on her phone than with him in the moment. Kimberly would have gladly put the phone away had she known it bothered her date, but Hunter never said anything. Instead, he let his anger boil until it blew up when the entrées were served. While eating her veal Marsala, Kimberly kept her phone on the table beside an unused napkin. Hunter was in the middle of relating some book when Kimberly's phone flashed. He lost it. Before she could answer her phone, Hunter snatched it from the table, held it above her plate, and let go. There was no second date.

Next, there was an Irish girl named Bridget-something. They met when she was a sophomore, and he a junior. Like Kimberly, Bridget developed a strong fascination towards Hunter. She wanted to know more about this mysterious boy. In addition to her honest intentions, she was also genuinely attracted to Hunter: a rare occurrence for him. For his part, Hunter was also intrigued by Bridget and ranked her as one of the most intelligent girls he had met in college. To ignite the initial flames of a relationship, Bridget became increasingly involved in all aspects of Hunter's day. A time came when we all thought the next natural progression of events would be for them to become a couple. Then, the strangest thing happened.

While at first Hunter went along with Bridget's advances as if he truly wanted to be her boyfriend, one day he simply cut her loose. Bridget thought something terrible had happened to him when, after over twenty texts, she had not heard from him in over two weeks. When she waved in the halls, he looked the other way. When she approached him at a distance, he turned the corner and was gone. She was convinced she had done something wrong, or had offended him in some way she could not see. It was like Hunter suddenly decided that nothing good could come from Bridget, and so he chose to forget her existence entirely.

Doing my amicable duty, I asked him why he so abruptly severed his relationship with Bridget. He gave me no credible answer. He only said that she was not the right girl and that there was nothing else to discuss. I tried explaining that behaving like he did—intentionally leading a girl on only to drop her—was not the right thing to do. Even still, nothing I said was getting through. It occurred to me that he might have been gay. It would have explained a lot. But when I even hinted at the subject, he stared at me as if disgusted I could draw that conclusion. From our brief talks, I got the impression that he simply became indifferent to Bridget's affection. It was like the moment he knew he could obtain her, he no longer felt the need to have her. The whole thing was senseless to me. It only supported my general theory that whatever issues Hunter had bottled up inside, I could be of little help resolving them.

Hunter, the troubled soul of our group, was the one I needed to see in order to know what went wrong with the evening's plans. Ascending the stairs of the 137th Street station, I found myself in a pleasant May night. The rain had stopped. Water dribbled down traffic signals and street signs. I crossed onto Amsterdam and started walking downtown towards Hunter's. I had visited his apartment twice before, but that was during the day. At night, the neighborhood had an unfamiliar edge. The loneliness of the street made me walk faster. My usual city sounds were gone and time seemed eerily suspended. In the distance, I heard the wail of an ambulance. The noise faded and I felt the eyes of a thousand tenants staring down at me. When I saw the sign for 132nd Street, I realized I had gone too far. Retracing my steps, I recognized a vandalized awning that read: *Food, Deli, and Delicatessens.* To the left of the closed shop was the entrance to Hunter's building.

As I approached, someone came out of the front door. It slammed against the wall with a loud clang. There was no light over the doorway. The only objects that caught my eye were a pair of golden squares on each of the stranger's shoes. I motioned for him to hold the door and I ran to the stoop. Passing through the entrance, I went to the elevator. I pressed the button and waited, but the doors did not open. Finding the stairs, I climbed four flights until I came to a long corridor. Each time I had visited Hunter's apartment, the hall had a new smell. The first time, it was beer. Next, it was sweat. Now, it was rancid meat.

I stood in front of the door to apartment 4B. Knock. Another knock. The light underneath the door flickered. There was the sound of rustling papers. I knocked a third time.

"Well, what is it?" a gnarled voice let out. "Leave me alone!"

"Hunter, it's me."

"What?"

"It's me, Will."

Silence. I heard footsteps approaching from the other side of the door. There was the clank of a bolt being released. The door started to open, but before I could step inside, it was caught by the chain lock still fastened to the inner wall.

"So?" Hunter asked, his face half covered by the door, "what do you want?"

I saw his black hair and one agitated eye. Light shined on the corner of his mouth, revealing a dab of red blood on his swollen lower lip. With the door ajar, I glimpsed the inside of his apartment. The floor was littered with newspaper and books. A stingy armchair seemed to grow from the filthy back wall. It was like the physical space suffered a raging fever.

"Jesus, Hunt," I said, looking at his lip. "Are you alright?"

"Go away," he replied obstinately.

"Can't you open the door?"

"No-I, well, no, not now. I'm busy."

"What happened tonight with you and David? You were supposed to bring him to the diner."

At the mention of David's name, Hunter's right nostril flared. His mouth trembled into a scowl.

"Fool…" he muttered.

"What?"

"Go away."

"Not until you tell me what…"

He slammed the door shut and suddenly I was alone. I knocked again and again, but I knew he was not letting me in. After only two steps down the corridor, I heard what could only have been the sound of a voice coming from inside Hunter's room. I had not seen anyone inside while the door was cracked open. There was only Hunter. He must have been talking to himself. I began to feel a sinking feeling that my presence was no longer welcome in the building. Instead of braving another attempt, I went to the stairs, placing one foot in front of the other as quickly as possible without actually running. I did not look back during my exit. I was afraid to see the monsters of my childhood that lurked at the bottom of my basement after I had switched the lights off, turned my back, and fled upstairs. Crossing onto Broadway, I hailed the first cab I could find.

4

"Fifty-five minutes past curtain, right on time," David said with a smirk. He held a bundle of roses as he came to the entrance of the *Jecoy Theater* in SoHo. Exactly twenty-four hours earlier, he had stormed out of Hunter's apartment in a fury. Now, he visited the theater to see the opening night of *Cymbeline*, and also to check on a particular investment he had in the company. She was a young actress named Carrie O'Reilly, playing the part of Helen, an attendant to the lead, Imogen. She was a member of an upstate Shakespeare company before moving to the city in the winter. She was also one of the girls David was seeing behind Lana's back.

David walked into the lobby of the small theater. It was intermission and there were crowds of people all around him, some by the bar, others by the restrooms. Weaving his way through, he came to a glass booth and gave his name to the receptionist. Then, he went to the bar. There was a woman in a maroon dress in front of him. A man in a navy blazer had his arm around her waist. David looked at the woman and could not decide whether she was pretty. Motioning to the bartender, he ordered a drink and took out some money. Looking again, he decided that the woman was indeed pretty, and so the matter was settled and he no longer had a reason to look at her. He left the bar and went inside the theater. There were fewer people and the

37

air smelled of dry wood. He went down an aisle and found his seat: Row CC, # 9. On his way, he stopped an usher and handed him the bundle of roses.

"Make sure these find their way to Carrie O'Reilly," David said, placing a folded bill in his hand. The usher took the money and the flowers, walked away, and rolled his eyes.

David sat down. After five minutes or so, the lights faded and the second act began.

Admittedly, David had not come for the play. Acting, above all other careers, was the most laughable to him. Like Aaron's father, David held the deep seeded conviction that a man cannot support himself with the meager earnings of an actor. Unlike Aaron's dad, however, it was the artist David decried, not the art itself. Actors, according to him, were selfish people. They mistook work for leisure. He adamantly believed that acting was a job best suited for the daughters of wealthy parents, mothers and fathers who could support their princesses as a fixed crutch, a wellspring of financial aid. He thanked those parents with all his gratitude. They gave him an endless supply of evening fun. Consequently, Carrie, and the night to come, was the main object of his focus.

As *Cymbeline* unfolded, however, David was drawn into the plot of the play more and more. He had read Shakespeare many times. His favorites were the staple tragedies *Hamlet* and *Macbeth*. This was his first time seeing *Cymbeline* though. As the action picked up, he was even sorry he had deliberately missed act one. In particular, he was captivated by the speech of Posthumus, where the misinformed lover curses women. David acknowledged that much of the dialogue went over his head. Even still, the speech had a profound effect on him. He agreed that all men are bastards. He agreed that women restrain men of lawful pleasure, *with a prudency so rosy the sweet view on't might well have warm'd old Saturn*. He accepted that

38

any faults in him could be retraced to a feminine weakness. The jealous ravings of a deceived man came as no great shock or surprise to him. Somehow, Posthumus confirmed David's innermost convictions on the nature of women.

If Shakespeare thought as I do now, then I must really be right.

In the end, David could not decide whether to call *Cymbeline* a tragedy or a comedy. As the house lights came up, the audience stood and applauded. His attention turned immediately to Carrie. When she came out for curtain call, her red hair shimmered under the hot lights. Scanning the audience, her eyes found the boy they searched for. Her cheeks became bright red. To hide her blush, she turned her face to the other side of the theater. Avoiding the crowds leaving through the front, David found the stage door and went into the side alley.

After ten minutes, Carrie came out of the same door. She held David's roses in her hand. The air was cool and she took a deep breath to relieve her warm lungs. Below her and to the right, David was leaning against the brick wall of the theater.

"Can you spare an autograph?" he teased, not moving.

"Thank you so much for the roses," she said, looking down into the bundle and then at David. "It was so sweet of you."

"Pleasure. You were remarkable tonight."

"Spare me, it's a small part. The show goes on without me."

"Not true! Who was it that said: *There are no small actors, only small parts*?"

"Very funny, David."

She moved closer to him and leaned against his chest. David kissed her. With his eyes closed, he smelled the mixture of roses and Carrie's perfume. He placed his hands on her hips. He let the kiss linger until Carrie drew her head back. Brushing a few strands of hair from her cheek, he looked into her eyes.

"Well…where do we go now?"

One subway ride and a short walk later, David was with Carrie in the lobby of his apartment building on the Upper West Side. The building was 60 stories and his apartment was on the 53rd floor. The elevator took just over thirty seconds and, on the way up, Carrie felt her ears pop with the altitude changes. David had grown accustomed to the feeling, but for Carrie, it was the first time she could remember ever going so high. Unlocking the apartment door, David invited her in.

They passed through a bottle-neck corridor that opened into the living room, kitchen, and dining room. Each was furnished with white carpeting, pink tile, and solid wood respectively. There was a black piano in the corner of the living room, facing a wall of cabinets and shelves. When Carrie would revisit the scene that is about to unfold in her mind, it always surprised her to recall that David had no pictures of himself, friends, or family placed on the shelves. Towards the back of the apartment, a large window stretched from the living room to the dining room. Outside, she saw practically the entire upper half of Manhattan, with a good view of the Hudson and part of New Jersey as well. It was far into the night and the city below was alive with strips of color. Suddenly, Carrie was ten years old again on her summer trip to Bermuda, three miles from shore and looking down on a fantastic coral reef: red, yellow, pink, and white against an expanse of dark water. A stream of light shot out from beneath her and rose like a golden staircase in the sky. It was Broadway.

"Incredible!" Carrie said, looking down with both hands on the cold window. "It's so different from the top."

David appeared from the kitchen with two drinks.

"About now, with you standing where you are,

40

I suppose I should say something like: Now the view is perfect."

Despite David's shameless flattery, Carrie could not hide her blush.

"Come here," she said to him. "You've got to see this."

David went to Carrie and handed her a drink.

"I see it every day," he said.

Carrie sighed. "That's your problem. Nothing excites you."

"You excite me," he said, walking away from her. "On the whole though, you're right. Nothing excites me. But what's there to be excited about? I've seen today. These days, once you've seen today, you've seen tomorrow too."

Carrie laughed at David, even though she knew that he probably did not mean for her to laugh. His urbane speech was something she had only heard in books. There was something strange in his voice. You felt special when you heard it, but also distant. It was a gate that kept you out and made you wonder what was inside. You loved to listen, but you could not help but feel that, for him, any listener would do. Was it all an act or did he really keep his most veritable self locked away for only those that dared to love him?

"Why haven't you brought me here before?" Carrie asked.

"I can't just bring anyone here," David said, looking at his drink before taking a sip.

"All of it is yours?" She returned her attention to the window.

"My mother's *pied-à-terre*," he answered. "She lets me use it when she's not in the city, which is practically year round." He paused for a moment, looking at Carrie in the window. "You really were good tonight," he went on. "You've got a natural stage presence. And you don't overplay the part like most actors."

"Thank you," she said, turning to him. "I'm pleased myself. Even if this part in that theater is as far as I go, it would all be worth it."

"You mean you'd be happy acting for the rest of your life?" he asked in an unassuming voice.

"Of course! What a silly question. It's what I love."

"That kind of commitment is commendable. You don't see many people doing what they love these days. You're doing a hell of a lot better than the life-long waitresses and waiters of New York, that's for sure. So acting is it then, that's your passion?"

"Yes, obviously. Not the only one, but the one that makes me the happiest."

"That's good, that's very good. It's just, well…"

"Go on," she said.

"It's just I've always had this one thought about the life of an actor. I never could shake it."

"Out with it," Carrie said with guarded playfulness. She could not tell if David was being sincere or else was setting her up for one of his usual traps.

"Well, I've always felt there's something so philosophically and psychologically wrong with acting."

"What could you possibly mean by that?" she asked.

"Well, can you think of anything more hopeless than pretending to be other people for your whole life? Wouldn't you rather just be yourself?"

"It's not pretending," she said defensively, "I am being myself."

"Ok, sure…you've heard that one before, but how about this. I think acting is a selfish profession."

"Selfish! I've been called a lot of different things by boys—who all want the same thing, by the way—but never selfish."

"It is!" he said. "Don't deny it. What could be more selfish than going on stage each night in front of a crowd and demanding their attention for two and a half hours?"

"No one demands anything. Not all actors have an ego the size of yours."

"Most do. Have you ever had a conversation with one? What can they talk about? They don't know anything. They have no skills, no hobbies, no real knowledge. All they know are themselves. So what do they do? Talk about themselves. Incessantly."

"We're talking now, aren't we?"

"You, darling, are the exception that tests the rule."

Carrie scoffed. She moved to the black piano on the opposite end of the room. It was obvious she was in no mood to continue the conversation. She sat at the piano bench and opened the cover, revealing the black and white keys. She pressed them randomly, the way small children often do. The sound filled the room with an air of chaos and disharmony. David became irritated.

"Do you play?" she asked, eager to change the subject.

"Only *Heart and Soul*, unfortunately. It's mostly there for show. My mother bought it for when we have guests, but she couldn't play. So its presence is totally impractical, if you ask me."

Carrie stopped playing. The room was quiet. She adjusted her posture and lifted her hands above the strand of keys. Then, her fingers dove into the bars. Music came out of the piano. The sound was slow and heavy at first. It started building on itself. It stirred David and he sat up straight. Once he recognized the sound, his eyes became fixed on Carrie. It was Beethoven's Piano Sonata No. 14, the *Moonlight Sonata*. He had heard it many times before. The most memorable instance was as a young boy at Carnegie Hall, visiting his mother from Armory. In fact, he had heard it so many times that he wondered if he had ever truly listened to it at all. Sitting on the couch, he closed his eyes and concentrated on the heavenly music. Each note carried a fragment of a thought that he could not wholly grasp. Before he knew what he felt, a different sound poured forth, making him sense something new. He heard two sounds now, one high, the other low. He took a deep breath and opened his eyes. There was Carrie. He followed the bottom of her green mini dress to her lush red hair.

Now here's something I didn't expect. What art. Such beauty. Yes, she certainly is beautiful.

And as David listened to Carrie's music, he felt that primordial urge begin to stir in his blood. He knew the feeling well. He had felt it many times, always in the presence of girls like Carrie. Yes, the feeling was good. It was the greatest good of all. Red lips. Tight hips. Bare thighs. Closed eyes. Aching veins and throbbing loins. Dizzy brains and tangled joys. A gentle touch along naked skin. Kisses on a hot neck. The moon hanging in the night, obstructed only by a soft cloud. Bodies pulsing. Senses brimming. All leading to a moment of euphoric bliss. It was carnal in essence, mixed perhaps with a semblance of what David called *love*. Yes, for David, it was love.

He returned from the hazy spell of his inner thoughts to the tranquil music. He stood from the sofa and walked slowly to Carrie. Standing behind her, he placed his hands on her waist. The music trickled into silence and the room became still, expecting something.

"Where did you learn to play like that?" he whispered softly in her ear.

"I've been playing since I was a little girl. Do you like it?"

"I do."

He moved his hands along the curves of her body. He felt the folds of her dress and imagined the skin that waited underneath. He felt the rise and fall of her shoulders and heard the gentle rhythm of her heart. Placing his lips to the nape of her neck, he gave her a soft kiss. Once, twice, then many more, each time, pausing to see how far he could go. Carrie leaned her head back, looking towards the ceiling. She felt faint, so she closed her eyes. With effortless strength, David slipped his hand underneath her legs and lifted her in his arms. He walked with even steps from the living room, through the narrow corridor, and into the dark bed room, distinguishable only on account of the lights of the city below, and the pale moon above.

Hours later, David lay awake in bed. He could not sleep. Carrie was at his side, holding him with her arm on his chest. Their bodies were covered by a soft white sheet. David's arms were bent behind his head, supporting the weight with both hands. Restless, he shifted his position by rolling onto his side. Looking out the window, he saw the peaceful lights of the New York skyline. His mind was clouded and murky. Scenes from previous days drifted in and out of focus. Eventually, the thick stream of memories unwound and he felt sleep coming on. He closed his eyes as he prepared to drift off. Then, he thought about Lana.

Full consciousness returned at once. She appeared in his imagination just as vividly as if she were in the room with him. Suddenly, without any clear cause, he replayed a moment from one of their first dates. It was at Bryant Park and they were ice-skating. She had just gotten onto the ice, when a young boy with blue mittens was gliding towards her on a collision course. Reaching towards him, Lana grabbed the boy's hands and they spun around. After two full circles, she let the boy go. He raced away, looking back at her and laughing. David could not tell why he had chosen that particular scene to recall among the thousands of others in his head. It had no more significance than the rest. He wondered why it alone was more impressionable than the other nearly forgotten moments of their date.

At some point in his thoughts, he must have woken Carrie. When he turned to check on her, she inched closer and placed her head on the pillow beside his. The air conditioning, along with the night air, gave the room a slight chill. Carrie drew the blanket from the bottom of the bed and covered David and herself. She tossed a little, finally resting on her back with her head on the pillow.

"I think everyone just wants to feel important," she said, chewing her words.

"What's that?" David asked in a groggily voice. Having been immersed in his own thoughts, he had not heard her.

"I said, I think I just want to feel important. It's the reason why I act, I mean. I know you were just playing, but what you said earlier got me thinking and, well, feeling like I matter is the best answer I can give you. Maybe you'll say it's selfish, but even a *selfless* person likes to feel important. Otherwise, what would be the point to anything? Animals, you know, dogs and cats, they're different. They don't need to feel special, or spend a life time convincing themselves that they really matter. But we're not like that. I think it's the curse that we all must bear. With each line, we try to make ourselves immortal in the eyes of our audience. That way, we'll never die. It's not as funny as you might think... kind of depressing really."

David did not reply. He heard everything Carrie had said, but her words made no great impression on him. He wrote them off as the philosophical musings of a naïve and inexperienced girl. With that brief interruption over, he returned to his inner thoughts, which became more and more distant as he drifted to sleep.

That morning, David was due downtown by 8:30 for work. On any other day, getting up would have been a routine nuisance. On that day, however, it meant he did not have to spend the morning with Carrie. That pleased

46

him immensely. Slipping on last night's khakis, he moved out of bed without waking his sleeping beauty. He went to the kitchen where he made himself a quick breakfast. Grabbing a pen and paper, he jotted down a note that read: *Sorry for leaving so early. Didn't want to wake you. Food in the kitchen, use the shower. Expect to be out of the city for a while. – D*

After gathering everything he needed, David quietly left the apartment. He even held the latch back on the door handle so that it would not clack against the frame. At work, he thought about the previous evening. He felt neither guilt nor shame over what he had done. Carrie was not the first and she would not be the last. He counted them on his fingertips, tallying the girls that were away, the girls that were in New York, the girls that were single, and the girls that were claimed, but could be compelled otherwise.

His phone chimed and his concentration was broken. It was a message from me asking him to lunch. I knew he had enough time to meet me in midtown and, considering the restaurant was his favorite and that I would be paying, he would not likely refuse. David probably knew he was walking into an interrogation, but that did not intimidate him. He accepted my invitation. At around 12:30, we met at Gabriel's Restaurant off of 43rd and Broadway.

5

Inside Gabriel's, the usual lunch crowd was surprisingly absent. The section where I sat was nearly empty. A couple of men in suits sat at the bar, nursing drinks. An older man and a younger woman sat a few tables to the right of mine. To pass the time, I tried to guess their relationship. The woman wore a wedding ring, while the man did not. They could have been daughter and father, however, the old man placed his hand on top of the woman's and began caressing it, suggestive of a certain nasty degree of intimacy. The woman smiled, flashing her perfectly white row of teeth. She was a sharp contrast to the old man. He had a triangular grey beard and a halo of fine hair on his head. My little game was interrupted by David. Having told the waitress he was looking for a friend, he was shown to my table.

"Sorry I'm late," he said, removing his blazer and hanging it on the back of his chair. "Have you ordered?"

He sat down across from me and took a sip of water. The heat from outside had caused him to sweat, giving his skin a light sheen.

"No," I answered, "just got here a few minutes ago. I haven't been waiting long. You look thirsty."

"You know what I haven't had in a while? A nice lemonade. It's spring after all. Excuse me," he called a tall waiter over, "a glass of lemonade, no ice. And for my friend?"

"I'm fine with water, thank you."

The waiter left the table. David unfolded his napkin and placed it on his lap, rearranging the silverware as well.

"Thanks for bringing me here," he said. "It's been so long. My favorite is the Reuben. I don't know how they do it, but it's the best in New York. Though, I guess people aren't busting down the door for a Reuben. Not like chicken soup or whatever."

"Don't mention it," I said. Although I had not seen him in months, he spoke like no time had passed at all. "I've wanted to see you for a while. It's been…well, I don't know how long it's been since I last saw you. I know school normally keeps you busy, so I figured your schedule would clear up near the summer. Then you land this impressive internship and no one sees you anymore."

"It's nothing special. Just something to make connections and throw onto the resume. You know the deal. Besides, it's nothing compared to…remind me where you work again?"

"Senator Jill's office," I said.

A different waiter came back with David's drink.

"Are you both ready to order?" he asked.

"I think so," I said. "I'll have a Caesar salad."

"And for you, sir?"

"Just a Reuben," David answered.

The waiter took our orders and went away.

"A Caesar salad?" David asked, smiling. "It really has been a while. The Will I know would never trade a good piece of steak for some lettuce."

"Too hot outside," I replied. "I need something light."

"You must be picking up bad habits from Emily. You're a Leo, aren't you? No? I knew a guy who once told me that your Zodiac sign determines what kind of food you need. If you're a Leo, you eat meat. If you're a Pisces, you eat fish."

"Sounds like bullshit to me."

"Yeah, but those things are always interesting. Speaking of which, how are things with you and Emily?"

"Going well. The usual."

"Well that doesn't tell me very much!" He gave a short laugh. Leaning back in his chair, he began fidgeting with the silverware. He twirled a knife between his fingers and studied his reflection in the curve of a spoon.

"How long has it been now?" he asked, looking up at me.

"Seven years and four months."

"But who's counting, right?" David winked, which bothered me. "That's excellent," he went on. "Very heart warming. It's always fascinating to hear of couples like you."

"I don't know, I think relationships like the one I have with Emily are more common than you think. You just don't give people enough credit."

"Maybe," he shrugged. He thought back to Posthumus' line about how all men are bastards. His impression of the line had not changed since last night. He sat in quiet approval.

Conversation ceased. David drank his lemonade in large gulps, which refreshed him on account of both the heat and the amount of talking he had done. Seeing my opportunity, I ventured to discuss why I invited him to lunch in the first place.

"You were in a hurry when you left Hunter's apartment the other night. We all missed you at dinner."

"Oh," he let out calmly, as if my reveal was as agreeable to him as talk of weather. "I almost forgot about that unpleasant event. How could you tell it was me?"

"You just did," I said. "You and those gold squares on your loafers."

"Hah!" David let out, crossing his legs and

inspecting his right shoe. "Well detective, who showed up?"

"Me, Emily, Aaron, Amanda, and Lana."

"Sorry I missed it. Unfortunately, your little friend left me in no mood to socialize."

David took another gulp of his lemonade.

"We didn't want it to be an intervention or anything like that," I said. "We just wanted you and Lana to talk, to try and work things out. Even to have fun, like we used to."

"You should stop living in the past," he said bitterly. "You're like Lana. All she talks about now is the way things used to be."

"Not that you would know. You haven't seen her in over a month." He said nothing, so I went on. "She's hurting, David. She cares about you so much and just wants to work things out."

"You don't have to tell me that," he said. "And don't you think I care about her?"

"Well, that's what I want to talk to you about."

"A lunch can never be just a lunch with you. You've always got to complicate things."

"Drop it, David," I said, leaning in. "You brought up Emily. You wouldn't have done that unless you were willing to talk about Lana."

"Fine, smart ass, ask me what you want. It won't matter anyway."

"Why did you hit Hunter?"

"How do you know I hit him?"

"I saw his swollen lip right after you left the apartment."

"Maybe he did it to himself. Masochists like Hunter get off on that."

"That's not funny," I warned him.

David readjusted himself in his seat. I thought he would have been more defiant. Despite all appearances, however, things were going smoothly. He was beginning

51

to tell me what I wanted to know. With any other person, the surprise would have been pleasant, but with David, it put me on edge.

"We had a little disagreement," he said casually. "It wasn't anything serious. Besides, it doesn't matter now."

"What was it about?" I pushed further.

David was silent for a while, composing his thoughts.

"Look," he said at last, drawing his eyes level with mine. "Instead of asking me all these questions, why don't you just cut the shit and ask me what you already know."

"What's that?"

"You know damn well what it is."

"I want to hear it from you."

He stopped again, this time, gathering even more of his resolve.

"You think I'm cheating on Lana. You've had your hunches and guesses, but with everything that's happened between us, combined with the Hunter incident, the only reasonable conclusion you've drawn is that I must be seeing someone else. Is that about right?"

"Yes, along with the fact that we've been friends for the past five years, so I like to think I have a good handle on your character."   "Humph" he scoffed. "What could you know about me?" He leaned back into his chair.

"Prove me wrong then," I said.

"Unfortunately… I can't."

His eyes went away from me. He looked over his right shoulder, then his left. Meanwhile, I sat at the other end of the table, trying to absorb what he had so easily confessed.

"Let me try explaining something to you," he said in a low voice, leaning forward. "Do you see that couple over there? The one on your right." It was the same pair I had been observing before his arrival. "The woman in the orange dress, do you think she's pretty?"

"Yes," I answered. "Without a doubt."

"Prettier than Emily?"

He caught me off guard.

"That's a loaded question. I won't answer it."

"The fact that you won't answer only proves that you acknowledge she's more beautiful than Emily."

"See, now you've changed the question. She might be prettier than Emily, but she's certainly not as beautiful. Beauty is many things. It's physical, sure. But it's also personality and character. Those are things you could only know if you spent time with her, not just eye her like a creep from across the room."

"Yes!" David agreed. "But suppose you did know her and you found out that she is, in all respects, a better girl than Emily. What would you do?"

I knew where he was going with this.

"Your question means nothing," I said. "I'm happiest when I'm with Emily who I love. And I know what you're doing. You must have found another girl, one who is *superior* to Lana?"

"Not yet," he answered. "Don't jump to conclusions so soon. My only point is that for every girl you are with, there is, somewhere in the world, a girl who is better than the one you have. And my next point is that you would drop your relationship in a heartbeat if the opportunity came along for you to have the *superior* girl, as you put it. The only reason that a person like you wouldn't go through with it is because of fear."

"Fear?"

"You're afraid of the consequences. You're afraid of splitting with the noble traditions that you so desperately cling to: loyalty, faithfulness, the list goes on. If I wanted to, I could be faithful. I'm the best thing that happened to Lana, or any other girl, for that matter. I could be the best boyfriend, hell, even husband, any woman could ever have. The only thing that stops me is that I know better. Do you honestly think someone should spend their entire life with one person? Imagine this. A man will spend a lifetime with a partner he's known for how long? A few years? People change, Will. The woman you love now won't be the same in ten years. Over his life, a man will encounter many other women—women who are more attractive, intelligent, and decent than the nagging one he's ended up with. So what stops him from ditching the load? Simple. He prefers to deceive himself into thinking that he's a good and honest person. Imagine that! He'll endure years of suffering, if only to hold onto his own misguided self-image. You're no exception, Will. You would fly to a girl who proved herself superior to Emily, if only you weren't afraid of the consequences."

"You really think this?" I asked, amazed.

"In fact," he went on, "I bet you want to do it. You want to find that girl who will satisfy you in every way, the perfect one. You may say that Emily is the best, but you know that's a lie."

I sat quietly and listen to David's theory.

"Take me seriously. You know I'm right. Think about it. You walk down the street and you see some gorgeous girl. Your eyes meet and then bam! Connection. As if, in that single moment, you say to one another, *Why be so shy? Don't look away, look at me! You're beautiful, I'm beautiful. You're young, I'm young. I want you, you want me. So why not get together?* But no…you pass and you'll never see each other again. You're alone on the subway, sitting all by yourself, when a girl gets on and sits across from you. The doors close. You're alone with her. The car races down the tracks and you imagine how good it would feel to sit next to her, to hold her hand, to touch her. The car screeches into the station. She gets up and walks to the door. You turn your head, trying to steal one last look before she's out of your life forever. You want this girl. Everyone does. The only thing I've done is act on what

I know is true in order to prevent the suffering that comes when a man is too involved with a woman."

The waiter brought us our food. David had taken my appetite away. The thought of eating anything became almost repulsive to me.

"Enough," he said abruptly. "Let me at least have a few moments of peace while I enjoy my lunch."

Silence ensued and my appetite slowly returned. David, always a fast eater, consumed his sandwich with wide, voracious bites. My salad was quite good as well.

"You see," he muttered, shoving a piece of corned beef into his mouth. "It all depends on how hungry you are."

I looked up from my salad, confused by his statement.

"I mean—a person like you—you don't get hungry very often. You'd be content with, I don't know, a hot dog. Cram it in your mouth and done. But me, I prefer a good piece of steak. Loads of it. Real high quality stuff." He took another large bite of his sandwich. "So," he said, chewing with his mouth open, "I've only got one question for you, Will. Are you a hot dog man or are you a steak man?"

His question was so callous that to have answered it would have made me sick.

"That's what I thought," he said with a satisfied smile, wiping away some Russian dressing that had dribbled down his lower lip.

"We shouldn't blame ourselves," he let out, just when I thought he could not say anymore. "Men, I mean, shouldn't be blamed for rebelling against a life of monogamy. If you want to blame anyone, blame biology. Humans are animals. As animals, we have a biological imperative to ensure the survival of our species. So it makes sense that we men would want to have as many partners as we could, to make sure our genes—the next generation—lives on. It's just like how parents have an instinct to protect their young. It could be because of love, but it's also to make sure the next in line is able to survive and, in turn, protect their offspring."

"There are plenty of bad mothers and fathers," I said, "who hit their kids for no good reason, who aren't there for them when they're needed most. Just because it may be biologically suitable doesn't mean it's hard wired into our very essence. And just because our ancestors were apes doesn't mean we should go around throwing shit at each other."

David was silent and returned to his meal. On my count, I thought I had won that last round.

"It's all a matter of location," he said under his breath. "Nothing else."

"What's that?" I asked, thinking I had not heard him correctly.

"I said it all has to do with your environment—who you meet and who you fall in love with— everything. We love who we love because we are near them, because we are acquainted with their patterns of social and environmental interaction more than anyone else. Choice has nothing to do with the equation. It isn't a matter of preference, taste, or even destiny, for that matter. All that love amounts to is a simple coincidence of proximity, two people sharing a common location, who otherwise would never have become anything more than strangers. You think love is a thing of fate, two stars crossing in the night, but you're wrong. You can love anyone given the right amount of time and location. But do you understand what that means?"

I looked at him blankly.

"It means love is arbitrary! Your Emily could just as easily have been a Rachel, or a Sarah, or anyone!"

"So," I began after a short silence, "what is Lana to you? Just another girl to be replaced by a better one that comes along?"

"No!" he said angrily, slamming his palm to the table. "Don't you realize? If love is arbitrary, then…then why love at all?"

I stared at him with unaffected eyes, immune to his appeals.

"Pah," he said with disgust, "I knew a person like you could never understand. You're blinded by your life with Emily, ever since you were young. Growing up with her has spoiled you. You can't see love for what it really is."

"I understand what you're after," I said. "They call it *hook ups and friends with benefits*. In college, you wanted something more. Now that you have it, you're running away. You're in a relationship…or were, in this case."

"It's more than just the sex, you idiot. You could never understand. Besides, being with Lana provides me with certain benefits I wouldn't have otherwise."

"Like your internship?"

"That and her father. But things being the way they are, I doubt those connections will last me much longer."

"You're really something, you know that? What the hell happened to you?"

"I grew up," he said with a voice unshaken and resolute. "One day you will too."

Having finished our meals, David signaled the waiter for the check. I had my answers. There was no doubt. He was cheating on her. Whether or not Lana knew was another thing. She must have known. And Aaron, lord knows what he would do if he found out. But what exactly did Hunter say that caused David to split his lip? Still, I knew very little. And worst of all, there was very little I could do to help.

"Your parents are divorced, aren't they?" David asked abruptly, disturbing my train of thought. It was a sore subject for me. I did not intend to spend much time on it.

"Yes, they split when I was very young."

57

"My parents are divorced as well. I think you knew that. That gives us something in common. You, more than any other person, must see the logic behind what I've said. The constant fighting, the slammed doors—running to a corner of the house where you can't hear the yelling—all that takes a toll on a kid. After going through what we both have, how can you honestly say that spending your life with one person is the right way to live? Maybe, for some sliver of the population, love ends in happiness. But for most, it ends in anger, disappointment, and regret. Just think about what I've said. I don't need your forgiveness, or anyone else's. In the end, I will be the man on top. And what will you have? Well, you know the answer to that question already. Thanks for lunch, Will. I've got to get going." He stood from his chair and put on his blazer. "Everyone settles…but I'm not everyone."

He left the restaurant without looking back. I sat in my chair and watched him leave through the front entrance, out into the heat of the New York afternoon.

6

Later that day, Aaron entered building 500 on 8th Avenue between 36th and 35th Street. His stomach churned, a reaction from either the forthcoming audition or the elevator carrying him to the twelfth floor. He clenched the sides he had been poring over the last few days in his sweaty hands. They were marked with strands of pink highlighter and black ink, noting when to breathe, when to take a beat, and the pronunciation of the word *Basque*.

He had felt this nervous anticipation before. It always made his face sweat and gave him the desperate urge to use the bathroom.

Excitement and nervousness are one in the same. Excitement and nervousness are one in the same. Those butterflies are how you know you still care. The worst that will happen is you won't get the role. That's all. His thoughts settled until he turned and saw his reflection in the marble elevator wall.

No, no, no! Wrong attitude. You must have this part. You need this part. It's your time. Remember the lessons. Be in the scene. Don't rush. Don't anticipate. React. Stanislavski, Olivier…none of that matters now. Be free, be natural. Forget what you know. Be Cameron Heart, not Aaron Fletcher.

The elevator made a sharp *ping* when it reached the twelfth floor. He thought of that old line, *Ask not for whom the bell tolls*, but got angry at himself for being so dramatic.

Walking down the hallway, Aaron passed other actors. Some were genuinely confident, while others sat doubled over as if in fervent prayer. He turned a corner down an even narrower corridor, furnished with tall potted plants. Two girls dressed in unitards ran past him. They giggled and almost knocked him over. He passed several doors with signs taped on them, reading: **Recording in Progress. Quiet Please! Trespassers Will Be Shot!** At room 12 G, a blonde receptionist greeted him.

"Hi!' she said with rehearsed enthusiasm, "are you here for American Dream?

"I am," Aaron answered, just a bit too loudly.

"Great. I'll take your headshot and resume. If you wouldn't mind filling out some information, you can go right in."

When all the information was filled, Aaron went in.

The room was square, white walled, with a camera mounted to a tripod in the far left corner. The lighting was poor, fluorescent. Not the most flattering light for his face. A man in his mid-30s with black rimmed glasses and a ponytail stood behind a collapsible plastic table. On his left was the camera man. On his right was a young girl sitting with a script in her hand.

"Nice to meet you," said the man with the ponytail, taking Aaron's hand. "Please stand on the black line right over there and, when you're ready, slate your name for the camera and the role you're auditioning for."

Aaron placed the crumpled sides on the floor.

No turning back now. Moxi, moxi, have moxi! He began the scene.

"Hi, my name is Aaron Fletcher, and I'll be auditioning for the role of Cameron Heart."

Beat. Another beat. *Shit, what's my first line?*

"Look Cameron, you've got to tell your friends what you've been up to."

Oh thank God, that's right, she speaks first.

"No way, Cindy, they can't find out."

What stupid dialogue. A monkey could write better stuff than this. Why hasn't she said anything? Did I mess up?

"You've got to tell them that you've been out seeing Sandra again."

What a relief. Damn that bitch! What lousy timing.

"Not when I'm running for city council."

"About that, I don't like what this election is doing to you."

"Cindy I…" *Wait, what's my line? I just had it. Cindy I…I what?*

Aaron felt a heavy iron ball sink in his throat. It was gradual suffocation. It was like the air in the room was being slowly turned off, leaving his lungs feeble and starved.

"I…um." His mind began to fail as he stumbled blindly for his next words. He started to turn red, desperately looking around for anyone or anything that could help him. "Uh…umm. Look, why don't you just come back home?"

He jumped ahead in the script, trying to veer his chances back on course. The look of the girl in the chair mortified him.

Save me! Save me! The script is in your hands, you idiot!

The camera man removed his eye from behind the lens and stared at Aaron.

They're all disgusted with me. Disgust and pity. I don't need their pity. Come on. Think. Think! What's your line? Relax, stay in it. Stop looking around. Not at the camera. Don't look into the camera. Look at her. Not the camera!

He looked into the camera.

"I, uh, I…" The air slowly returned to his lungs. "I give up…"

61

As Aaron walked up 8th Avenue, sunlight beamed off of the surrounding buildings. The glare nearly forced his eyes shut. His temples throbbed from the heat and fumes of the city. The sun hung between two skyscrapers, allowing no shade on his side of the street. The gross humidity, the draining temperature and, above all, the botched audition, put Aaron in a particularly low mood.

I practice and practice and look what happens...I fail. Practice makes imperfect. Why did I put the script down? I could've held it in my hands. No one would have cared. Stupid. This is the second time now. The first time was awful enough. Thought I had learned my lesson. Where have my years of training gotten me? No confidence. Father's right.

The audition seemed to Aaron just another entry on a long list of failures that proved he would never amount to anything special in life. When he was younger, he had a certain naïve trust that Fate had singled him out. Despite his shyness, or perhaps because of it, he sensed that he was different from everyone else and that this difference would propel him to a great future. Yet, as each year passed, it seemed like the mere possibility of that future was slipping away. He imagined himself getting older and older, always assuring himself that, if he only waited a little longer, he would reach his goal. He would keep waiting until he died, filled with the hope of a better tomorrow, and no more time to make it a reality.

Looking for a distraction, he took out his phone and slid through his contacts. He quickly realized that there was no one who would want to hear his troubles. He looked up and saw a massive poster on a building a few blocks down the road. It took up nearly the entire wall and advertised a show that had come out in the winter. Aaron studied the poster for a moment and then looked away.

Normally, he would have listened to some music.

At that moment, however, he hated the idea of being like every other New Yorker who walks with wires hanging from their ears. Aaron returned his phone to his pocket and began searching the street. He was looking for anything that could take his mind off of the audition. As he crossed 39th Street, he bumped into a kid wearing loose jeans and a red shirt with a pattern in shimmering gems. Aaron did not notice at first, but the impact caused the kid's sun glasses to fall out of his hand. The boy bent down and picked the glasses up from the sidewalk. He was in a group and a few others laughed and jeered.

"Damn, my glasses," the kid said lethargically. There was a crack running down the left lens. Whether or not he had caused the glasses to break, Aaron had no way of knowing.

"Oh, I'm so sorry," Aaron said, trying to gather his thoughts. "I didn't see you."

"Looks like you jus' violated the number one rule of New York," another boy laughed, seeing his friend's broken glasses.

"What's that?" Aaron asked.

"Keep yo head down, mind yo own business, and keep it movin'!"

"Beat it," the kid with the glasses said to the other.

"I really am sorry," Aaron said, trying to step away.

"Nah man, you gotta watch where you're goin'. Look what you did."

"I thought I was watching. I'm sorry. Here, how much are they worth?"

Reaching into his back pocket, Aaron took out his wallet.

"Oh, uhh," the kid stumbled, "at least fifty dollars."

"Fifty dollars huh?" Aaron looked at the cracked sunglasses again.

"Well, I don't have fifty."

"There's an ATM right over there, man."

Indeed, there was an ATM across the street. But even Aaron knew better than to withdraw cash with a stranger standing by, even if it was only a kid.

"Unfortunately, I don't have a pin number, so withdrawing money wouldn't work."

"Man...well you gotta give me something."

Wanting to do some good after his failed audition, Aaron decided to speak with the boy some more. He started walking and motioned him to follow.

"What's your name?" Aaron asked.

"Dwight," the boy said, surprised by Aaron's cordiality.

"Nice name. Mine's Aaron. Look, I don't have fifty dollars, but how about I get you some new sunglasses, any kind you'd like."

"How you gonna pay for them if you ain't got no cash?"

"I'll use my credit card. There must be a store that sells some sun glasses around here...look! There's one right here."

In the window of a souvenir shop, there was a display-case filled with sunglasses.

"Nah, those aren't any good. Those aren't my glasses. Nothin' you gonna buy can replace them."

"Well how about I treat you to dinner?"

"What?" Dwight asked.

"Food, you know, we can go to *Wendy's* or something. I'll get you whatever you want."

"You think just cuz I'm black, I can't pay for my own food?"

"No, no!" Aaron said. "I didn't mean it like that...I was just asking, you know, trying to be nice."

"Damn man, I've had such a rough week, and these are my favorite glasses. And you tellin' me you can't give me nothin'?"

"What are you talking about! I offered to buy you

a new pair."

"Man, I don't want any of that. I want *my* glasses."

Aaron paused in disbelief. Then, he laughed to himself.

"Well, Dwight…I'm sorry we couldn't come to an agreement."

Aaron grabbed Dwight's hand and shook it. This caught him by surprise. He pulled his arm away quickly.

"Whatever you say. Creep."

He turned and ran down the street, looking over his shoulder at Aaron once or twice. Aaron stood still for a moment, watching him run. Then, he resumed his walk along 8th Ave.

What the hell was that? First tries to get fifty bucks out of me, then calls me a creep for offering to buy him something. Just for trying to do him a favor. What's with people? And did I complain like most would? I didn't break those glasses. Did I tell him to get lost? You try to be nice and look what you get. Head down. Mind your own business. Keep moving.

It was 6:45 P.M. The sun moved slowly behind a large skyscraper, cooling Aaron. He had no plans for the evening. There was no one he had to see. Even still, he did not want to go home. The thought of walking through the front door of his apartment and sitting on the couch humiliated him. He kept walking along the street, eventually cutting over to 9th Avenue. He was moving towards the river. Some time passed and he began to come to terms with his failure.

Always more auditions. Your time will come. Chalk this up to experience. Learn from it and move on. This has been good, in a way. The more you fail, the more you hate the feeling of failing. Blessing in disguise, really. It'll make your success feel even better in the end.

Lana flashed in his mind.

Her? Now what made me think of? So what. Don't

need to be an actor to impress her. Just need a chance to be with her. With her. Four years not enough? Spend so much time with a person. Hardly know them at all. Already a year since college. More time gone. More distance. Wonder, does she think about me as much as I do her? Most likely not. Still, can never tell. One super power? To know what others are thinking, but only if they want you to know. Solve a lot of my problems. Others' too. Huh. What a stupid thought...

While Aaron walked along, he gradually let go of his imagination. He imagined Lana beside him, holding his hand. They went into a store. She pointed to a gift that caught her eye. He bought it for her. She loved him for it. They went to an outdoor café and sat down for dinner. Their conversation was lively, ending with hushed tones and heartfelt words. Night fell and her face grew brighter by the candle light. He leaned over the table, reaching for one endless kiss with his love.

While he daydreamed, Aaron stepped into oncoming traffic. A bicycle messenger shouted. A car horn blew. Just in time, Aaron jolted back to reality and jumped onto the side walk. His heart pounded against his ribs. He sat on the edge of a fire hydrant, trying to catch his breath. Strangers stared at him, guessing he was either drunk or high. He saw their looks and cursed himself for being so absent-minded. His heart beat slowly returned to normal. He longed for the world of his daydreams. Deciding that he was in no condition to wander the streets alone, Aaron went to the 42nd Street subway station. He had to return to his apartment and to his normal life. It was a life without the success of an actor or the money to afford nice things. More importantly, it was a life without Lana.

Just before Aaron swiped his metro card in the turnstile, his phone vibrated. It was a text from Amanda, saying: *Come over to my apartment now.*

On my way home, some other time, Aaron

responded.

It's an EMERGENCY, Amanda replied.
It can wait
It's about Lana…
On my way

7

Aaron rushed towards Amanda's apartment on the 1-train. He was crammed in the corner of the car behind an old woman with a collapsible metal cart. Amanda lived in Chelsea, just three stops from Times Square. Along the way, he reread what few texts he had shared with her. He was searching for some hidden meaning.

She's probably just using Lana to lure me right away. Never calls me when something's wrong. What does she want? Something wrong with Lana? No. Amanda's just trying to trick me, that's all. Up to something. And here I am, despite everything, going to see her. Lioness' den.

His mind ran full circles throughout the journey until he arrived at Amanda's. Just like before the audition, he felt his stomach churn. Suppressing his nerves, he came to her room and gave a hard knock on the door. Moments later, the door opened, revealing Amanda in frame. She had seen him enter the building through her window. She wore a simple black dress that tapered to the middle of her thighs. Her hair was pulled back and her face was touched with light blush and eyeliner. Her earrings were simple but elegant. Judging from her appearance, she had just come from the museum.

Aaron expected her typical playfulness, but she was unusually reserved. Without saying *hello*, she motioned him inside. They crossed through a small hall that opened into the living room. As he passed a closed door, Aaron heard what he thought was the sound of a soft instrument, a violin or a saxophone. Stepping closer to the door, he realized the music was not music at all. Someone was crying in the room. Aaron raised his hand towards the door knob, but Amanda stepped forward and grabbed his wrist.

"Is she in there?" he asked. "What happened?"

Amanda released him and walked into the kitchen.

"Well? What's happened? Is she hurt?"

She moved from the kitchen to the living room.

"I always knew how much you care about her," she said. "I pretended not to sometimes, but I could always tell."

"Quit it," he said, annoyed. "Just tell me…was it him?"

"Why do you think it was him?" she responded.

"Stop it!" Aaron stepped forward, displaying the strength in his voice so rarely heard by his friends. The muscles in his neck were taut. "Tell me. It was him, wasn't it? He did it, he's done this to her. But what did he do? Tell me! Please…"

Aaron was suspended in a state of torture. Not knowing killed him and knowing would crush him. He wanted to end all the horrible hallucinations of David's cruelty he had been suffering in his head for the past five years.

"You know better than anyone else," Amanda said softly, "they were never meant to last." Aaron took in her words. They weighed on him.

"Sure, but how? How did it end? It couldn't have been her, so it must have been him. What was the reason?"

Amanda walked to the farthest end of the living room, motioning him to follow. He hung on her movement like a congregation before a preacher.

"She shouldn't hear us talking. You already know

how it happened. You must know." She paused for a moment and then went on. "He cheated on her, wasn't it obvious? David's been sleeping with other girls. I don't know how long it's been going on, but I found out from Hunter. He said that David admitted it himself. Don't pretend. We all knew. Even Lana knew, although she never wanted to admit it. She just needs time. I honestly expected you'd be happy. Unless…wait." She looked at him closer. "Don't you care? Have you stopped lo…" she caught herself. "Hey, where are you going?"

Aaron moved away from Amanda and towards Lana's bedroom.

"Hey!" Amanda called. "Don't go in there."

Aaron went into the room. He closed the door softly behind him. The room was dark and the blind on the far window was down. A ceiling fan twirled above him. Lana was sitting on the edge of her bed, bent over. Her head was in her hands and she did not move.

"Lana…" Aaron said quietly. Her head came up and she turned to him.

"Oh, Aaron," she said, surprised. "I didn't hear you."

Aaron went closer to her, reaching for something to say.

"Here," Lana said. She shifted to the right and Aaron sat down on the bed.

"How are you?" he asked her. He realized after he asked it just how dumb the question was.

Lana thought for a moment. "I can't tell yet," she answered quite truthfully. Aaron searched for his next words. Although there were many things he wanted to tell her, he could not arrange his thoughts. He sat with his hands clasped together, looking at the floor.

"Lana," he said, breaking the silence. "There's something I need to say. Something I have always wanted to say. I've known you for a long time. I wish I knew more about you. I wish…" he stumbled forward, heart racing, words failing. "I wish you knew how sorry I was. That's all. Because you deserve better than the people around you. David, he doesn't realize. He will never know what he's lost. There are lots of people who love you in the beginning. But watch how much they hurt you in the end. They'll hurt you to show you how much you never meant to them. That's messed up, right? They'll hurt you so that the wound they make will stay with you for your whole life. That's how they remain with you, even though they're not near you. People can be really screwed up like that. But don't you dare let them hurt you. Don't let *him* hurt you. If you only knew what you deserved. I want you to know that…I'm here for you, Lana."

"I know, Aaron," she said, smiling softly.

She leaned her head on his shoulder. Aaron was surprised at first and thought that she would sit up. She kept leaning against him. Slowly, gently, he moved his arm around her waist. Lana brought her arms around his chest. She rested her head on his neck and Aaron felt her smooth hair against his cheek. They kept holding each other. The only sound came from the twirl of the ceiling fan. Then, Aaron drew his head back. Lana did the same. Her cheeks were red and her eyes were clear. Aaron leaned in and kissed her. With his eyes shut, he felt his lips on hers. He ran his fingers through her hair and held the back of her head. They started to lie down on the bed.

"Aaron," Lana whispered.

He was beside her now. He kissed her harder.

"I can't," she said, opening her eyes.

He placed his arms on either side of her. He lifted his chest on top of her.

"Aaron, stop." She pushed against his shoulders.

He could not hear her.

"Aaron, listen. Stop."

He kept kissing her.

71

"Stop!"

She slapped him. Aaron grasped his cheek. He backed away from the bed until he hit the wall. Lana was sitting up. Her arms were behind her and her hair was in her face. She stared at him, breathing hard.

"I'm sorry," Aaron said. His eyes were wide. He touched his lips with the tips of his fingers. Lana did not say anything to him at first. She only kept looking at him.

"It's ok, Aaron," she said finally. "Please go."

"Lana, I–"

"Please go," she said again.

He went to the door and looked over his shoulder. She was sitting on the bed with her head turned away, looking in the direction of the window. The streetlight from between the slits hit the right side of her body, making strips of light in the shade. He left the room.

When he came out of the bedroom, Amanda was waiting for him.

"Well?" she said, raising her arms. "I warned you not to go in."

Slowly, Aaron walked towards the exit.

"Hey! Would you stop walking away from me?"

Aaron walked on. There was a vague mumbling sound behind him, but he could not make out any words. There was a ringing in his ears. He could not feel his feet. He made a conscious effort to bring what had happened in Lana's room into some coherent synthesis of events. But it all seemed beyond belief and impossible to relive. Soon, he felt something tugging on his arm. The pulling bothered him and he wanted to get away.

It was Amanda. She held his wrist and was trying to stop him from leaving. Aaron squared his feet and wrenched his arm away. His pull was so quick that Amanda lost her balance. She fell against the wall.

"Oh, God!" Aaron said, realizing what he had done. "I'm so sorry."

"It's fine," Amanda said, rubbing her shoulder. "You didn't mean it."

Aaron rushed out of the front door, trying to get away from the apartment. Amanda followed him. He pressed the button to the elevator and it came. Before he could step all the way inside, Amanda grabbed his arm again. She was standing between the elevator doors, just underneath his chin. Reaching on her toes, she kissed him. Her lips smelled like cherries. Aaron thought he wanted to move away, but he stayed put. Then, Amanda leaned her head back. She stepped backwards into the hallway. Aaron looked at her and she smiled at him. The elevator doors closed slowly.

8

Aaron burst from the entrance of Amanda's building onto the sidewalk. The night held the heat from the day. There was practically no breeze. He turned his head right, then left, looking up and down the street. There were a few people out. An old woman walked with a young girl who wore jeans and brightly colored socks, visible even in the darkness. The sky was cloudless. Aaron looked up and saw one or two stars between the lighted windows of tall buildings.

He touched his lips again and again. It was like he could still feel Lana's hot mouth against his. He ran his index finger along his bottom lip. It was slick from Amanda's cherry lip-gloss. Once he smelled it, he wiped it away with his shirt sleeve. Then, he ran east towards the subway station. He arrived at the stairs to the downtown line. Before he could take the first step, his phone vibrated. It was a text from Hunter. He asked Aaron to come to his apartment.

Aaron grabbed hold of the metal railing. It was just as slippery as Amanda's lip-gloss and he wiped his hand with the back of his pants. He studied the screen of his phone. Hunter's message stared back at him, waiting for a reply. After some thought, he put the phone back into his pocket. He left the entrance of the downtown line and ran to the opposite side of the street. He did not bother with the cross sign. When he got to the uptown stairs, he stopped again. He was at a crossroad. Aaron had a choice.

The choice was to know or not to know. Neither had a happy ending. If he went uptown to Hunter's, his night would go on. If he went downtown to his apartment, his night would be over. At Hunter's, he could find out exactly what David did to Lana. At his apartment, he could crawl into bed. With Hunter, he could think of his next course of action. Alone, he could forget that he ever loved Lana.

If I know, the result can only be more pain. If I don't know, I'll stay the way I am. And what am I? Miserable.

In the end, Aaron made his choice. He took the downtown line, leading him home to Brooklyn.

Aaron inserted his key into the door of his apartment. He opened it quietly. Inside, the room was dark and static. The blind on the window was still down from that morning. Crossing to it, Aaron pulled the nylon cord. Streetlight came into the apartment. The light covered the room, causing spectacular shadows to stretch up the walls and across the floor. He lowered the blind to its original position and the shadows retreated. Crossing to the sofa, he threw himself onto the plastic wrapped cushions. He picked up the remote and turned on the TV. He started flipping through channels. After several frames, he saw a woman with chique brown hair, marvelous cheekbones, and a poised chin. It was Audrey Hepburn, playing a British art thief in some old heist movie. He stayed with her for a while, until her face began to resemble one more familiar to him and with a striking resemblance, save the short cropped hair. He impulsively pressed the off button. The screen fizzled to black.

Aaron placed his feet on the sofa and rolled onto his back. Even at night, he could make out tiny particles of dust that drifted in and out of his vision. He was exhausted and wanted very much to sleep. He closed his eyes and folded his hands on his stomach. The attempt was broken by his memory of Lana. The moments from their meeting shot through his mind like strands of intense light. Trying to block them out, he rolled onto his side and buried his face into the back of the sofa.

It was no use. He kept seeing her staring at him from the bed, covered in strips of shade and light. The heat and stickiness of the couch irritated him. He rose and staggered into the bedroom. It was even darker than the living room. Once he closed the door, the only sound he heard came from passing cars on the outside street. Aaron threw himself onto his bed. He was relieved to find the comforter pleasantly chilled. He rolled around many times, eventually settling on his side. He tried closing his eyes. Again, he found no peace. His conscience wrestled with the same question that had been laying siege on his mind since he read Hunter's text: to know or not to know.

Rolling onto his back, he stared at the ceiling. He was certain he was not going to get any sleep that evening. Then, out of the silence in the room, he heard a faint ticking noise. Shifting to the edge of the bed, he opened the top drawer of a nearby nightstand. Inside was a shiny wrist watch, a graduation gift from his father.

Still alive? Thought the batteries ran out.

He took the watch out of the drawer and rolled onto his back. He held it above his chest and twirled the metal band in his fingers. He listened to it clank and clack. Bringing the dial closer, he looked at his reflection in the glass. His face seemed plump from that angle. He noticed that the watch had stopped moving. He shook it a few times until it started working again.

Something wrong. Must have been why I stopped wearing it. Can use a phone for everything now anyways.

Finished with the watch, he placed it on top of the nightstand. He jumped out of bed and walked to the bathroom.

Aaron had always been fond of long showers, especially when in a bad mood. The rhythm of the falling water relaxed him. Stripping off his clothes, he turned on the water and stepped into the hot shower. Breathing in the heavy steam, he lowered himself to the tile floor. He lifted his head to the falling water, running his fingers through his slick hair. He folded his arms over his knees and collapsed his chin to his strong chest. He sat like that for a long time, concentrating.

Five years of friendship. Five years of good times and laughs. Five years of regret for not doing what I should have done in the beginning. Should have stopped him. Should have told him, "No, I'm sorry, but she's just too good for you. You don't deserve her." But did I say anything? No. Let him walk over me. I'm no doormat, I'm Aaron Fletcher! And does he ever give a damn about what I want? Supposed to be my best friend. Instead, he took advantage of me. Abandoned me when times got tough. Did he ever think of the pain he caused her and, in hurting her, hurting me? No, David never did.

Aaron turned the water off and stepped out of the shower. The bathroom was filled with vapor. After drying himself off, he stepped in front of the mirror. He could not see his reflection through the fog. He wiped the condensation from the mirror. With each stroke, his face became more visible. He stepped back. As he looked at his reflection, he felt a surge of rage inside him. It came on quick, without any warning.

There was a loud crash. He felt a pulsing heat erupt from his right hand. He checked the feeling and realized he had slammed his fist into the corner of the mirror. The glass exploded from the hit, causing several shards to fall into the sink below. Aaron took heavy breaths. His head was tingling. He held his hand up to the light and inspected the damage. There was no blood, but his knuckles were bright red and in pain.

I must know. Know so I can act. Even if that knowledge only brings me pain, it will bring me closer to righting what has been done. We've all been pushed around enough. We can't just let people get away with hurting each other. They stop hurting when we stop them ourselves...

Avoiding the pieces of glass on the carpet, Aaron left the bathroom and put on a new pair of clothes. Grabbing his wallet, his phone, his room key, and, finally, his wrist watch, he left the apartment.

Hunter. To Hunter, to know.

9

It was Friday, three days since my lunch with David. In the offices of Senator Jill, everything was in disorder. Election season was rapidly approaching and there was still much that needed to be done in order to give the Senator the best possible chance of re-election. The Senator was a two time incumbent for the 28th district of New York. She represented the entire Upper Eastside and a good portion of Midtown. She held a seat on the New York Environmental Committee and was known for her notable contributions in the ongoing effort to improve public health and sanitation within the city. Her opponent was a former defense attorney who ran on a platform of healthcare reform, education reform, and veteran services. Although there were still a few months before the election, the pressure was mounting in our office. As often happens with a rise in expected performance, mistakes increase and tensions build among co-workers. Such was the case that morning.

Aside from the daily functions of the office, which included answering telephone calls, runs on the phone-bank, and collecting survey data, we were also dealing with a typing error that had taken place on the campaign posters. The posters were scheduled to be placed out that afternoon, but now had to be reordered. The typing error was committed by the printing company, so it was not entirely the fault of anyone in our office. However, the intern assigned to ordering the shipment failed to notice the mistake in the sample poster the company sent us weeks ago. This intern was now being subjected to a verbal reprimand by my colleague, and so called office rival, Anthony Hutch.

Anthony graduated from Georgetown University. He had started working in the office nearly three months after I began. He was a chauvinistic kid who always appraised himself at a higher value than those around him. Every responsibility he undertook only served to elevate his misguided sense of self-worth. Any person who threatened to outshine him in the eyes of his supervisors was immediately deemed as a threat. Since his arrival in our office, he had decided I was that threat. At every opportunity, he started fights or used every mistake I made to point out my shortcomings. A few others in the office took notice of Anthony's spiteful behavior. Instead of saying something, they thought it was funny to keep silent and watch me attempt to cooperate with him.

When dealing with the intern who failed to notice the typing error, Anthony was unnecessarily harsh and cruel. As the intern was walking to the water cooler, he pulled her aside so as not to be seen by his superiors. He mocked her for the mistake, warning that if it happened again, she could kiss any letter of recommendation from the Senator goodbye. I thought of intervening, but decided to wait until Anthony was finished. After he walked away, I approached the intern and told her not to worry, it was a simple mistake and no one in the office could have caught it. To make her feel better, I told her of a few mistakes I had made in my first few weeks. My talk seemed to genuinely relieve her.

I always make a point of saying how I don't hate anyone; to hate someone is to pay them more credence than they're worth. Yet, there was no other person who brought out the worst feelings of animosity, embarrassment, and annoyance in me than Anthony. He had absolutely no aptitude for understanding others, a virtue that Emily always held in esteem. As opposed to showing some level of sensitivity to his fellow co-workers—looking at the world through their eyes and figuring out what they want most—Anthony chose the worst possible method of human interaction. His actions constantly centered on what mattered most to him. Not only did this approach make him impossible to deal with, but it also prevented him from working well with others, which, in turn, would have given him the admiration of his superiors he so desperately craved. My father always told me there would be *Anthonys* in the world, and when I met one, it would be the true test of my patience. *Nothing,* he would say, *is as important as the art of human relationships.* Anthony was the rotten, arrogant, and unsympathetic hurtle in our office that everyone had to jump, stumble over, or knock down.

To make matters worse, the Senator was scheduled for a cocktail party with one of her top campaign contributors from the Upper East Side at 6:00 P.M. The elderly gentleman hosting the event had been a close friend of the Senator's late mother. Because of this, the Senator felt obligated to attend the dinner. She went not to repay a debt to a wealthy contributor, but rather, to repay a debt to a good family friend. The dinner would not normally have posed such a problem, but because our staff was given such short notice, we had not accommodated for the disruption in the normal work routine that the event caused.

Aside from the logistics of the ill-timed party, I disliked attending the habitual social functions of the campaign. At every event, it was like I was acting in some great farce of human communication. Like everyone else, I came to parties equipped with pre-rehearsed lines about politics, economics, and of course, the latest mud-slung gossip that surfaced about our opponent. Everyone at these functions wore a permanent smile fixed on their face, like hired clowns. I've read somewhere that very few smiles are genuine and that the way to tell a real one from a fake is in the eyes. If the eyes lift or change in appearance, then the smile is genuine. Such honest smiles are rare at these political parties. Nevertheless, I was obligated to play along with the rest of the staff in the name of good social graces and, like all honest men and women, a healthy fear of losing my job.

After the day's work was completed, the campaign staff took separate cabs to the Upper East Side. The party took place in the lavish apartment of the elderly host, a pleasant change from the typical hotel catered events. The place was extremely modern. Bizarre pieces of art decorated the main room and there was glass paneling that gave the apartment a more spacious feel. When we arrived, the party was already underway. I recognized various faces of Upper East Side society, several of whom had brought their families with them. Children dressed in expensive suits and dresses awkwardly spoke with one another. They seemed out of place among the adults who had decades of experience at saying absolutely nothing of consequence. They were far too young to be thrown into the mundane world of adult social life, and the bored expressions on their faces said it.

The adults spoke with one another in rich tones and large, drawn out, strains of laughter. From the moment we entered, the members of our staff branched out to join the different circles of people that had formed around the room. One circle, the one in which the Senator was located, spoke of the current state of the campaign, where things were going, and what still needed to be done in order to ensure absolute confidence in a re-election. Another group, gathered around an abstract metal sculpture, spoke of their host, the kind of man he was, and his relationship with the Senator. As my fellow staff members moved to one of the many clusters of people, I found myself alone, without anyone to talk to. That pleased me greatly.

Prolonging the absence of conversation, I made my way to the h'orderves table. As I approached, I noticed a small boy reaching for some sliders behind a large tray of grape leaves. His hair was neatly combed and his white shirt was tucked in his small pants like a bed sheet.

"What would you like?" I asked him, motioning to the back of the food table.

"Hamburgers please."

The cordial *please* caught my ear. This was a word that probably had been preached into him by a loving grandmother. A part of me smiled as I remembered back to when I was his age. I smiled even more when I reflected on the fact that, at one time, all the adults in the room were as innocent as him.

I gave him his food and he joined the other children in a world I had grown out of. Just as I was about to walk to an unoccupied corner of the room, the Senator, who was now surrounded by even more people, called me to her circle. Thinking it best to put down my chicken shish kabob so as to avoid talking with a full mouth, I walked over to her. She was in the middle of a discussion with the host of the party, as well as several other guests who floated in and out of the conversation. I noticed Anthony standing a few steps away from the Senator. He was expressing himself with big gestures and his trademark overbearing voice. They spoke about a recent attack on a young apartment owner who lived in the upper east 80s. The attacker was some mentally deranged homeless man, who, totally unprovoked, pulled a knife on a young girl and stabbed her twice in the stomach. The attack was one of several that pointed to the increase in crime in the East Side. The Senator's opponent, using the attack to his best advantage, met with the victim and made a public address criticizing the Senator's lax stance on the rise of crime.

"You shouldn't worry, my dear," said the old host, putting special emphasis on *my dear*, the way old people have a habit of doing, "these stories disappear quickly. There's nothing anyone could have done to prevent that poor woman from coming into harm's way. It couldn't be helped."

"Tell that to the poor woman," Anthony muttered to another co-worker who stood beside him. The two chuckled, but were checked by the silence of the group.

"Thank you, Henry," said the Senator. "Still, the media will have a field day. Oh that rotten man, turning one kind of attack into another. He says he'll string me up by the *Jills* come election time. Can you imagine? What an absurd little slime ball. Will, what do you think of all this?"

"Well," I stalled, gathering my wits, "the more mud you throw, the more ground you lose."

"Say, I like that!" said the old host, revealing his tobacco stained teeth.

"Where did you hear that one?" the Senator asked.

"I read it in a fortune cookie. Who knows, maybe it will bring us luck."

My little line impressed the circle of people. Once the Senator started to laugh, the rest followed. We quickly moved away from the fate of the poor woman. The truth was I had not read any fortune cookie. It was a line I had thought of the other night. I could see Anthony's face grow displeased on account of the favorable impression I had made on the campaign's senior members. It felt good to give him the same discomfort that he gave everyone in the office on a daily basis.

"Henry," the Senator said, stepping towards me and placing her hand on my back. "I don't think you've met our youngest campaign advisor, Will Harrison."

The title *campaign advisor* meant nothing. My true title should have been: *wrangler of interns*. Nevertheless,

I appreciated the Senator's indirect way of parading her employees.

"Say again?" said the old man. His cheery disposition reminded me of my father.

"Will Harrison," I said to him, taking his outstretched arm and shaking it warmly.

"Harrington, pleasure. What do you think of my home?"

"Quite nice," I responded out of habit.

"And what do you think of the art?"

Although I had only just met the old man moments ago, I could tell he was not the kind of person who looked favorably on *people pleasers*. Judging from his wealth and prominence, I reasoned that a man as old as he was must have been tired of people always telling him what they thought he wanted to hear, as opposed to speaking to him honestly. I took a gamble, composed what I wanted to say, and answered his question.

"No disrespect, but I don't understand what any of it means."

At first, I heard members of the group laugh and snicker condescendingly. Even the Senator covered her smile. The old man, however, kept silent. Then, he burst out laughing harder than anyone else in the circle. Neither I, nor the people around me, knew he was capable of laughing so hard.

"You're absolutely right!" he said, raising his hand and putting it on my shoulder. "It's my wife's work. I let her keep it up all year round. I honestly can't stand it. It's, well…it's nothing! These things aren't art. They aren't anything!"

"I agree," said Anthony, nosily making his way into the conversation. "The best art takes the greatest skill. Look at the Duomo or Michelangelo's chapel. Not just any artist could create them. Now look at these pieces," he said, gesturing around the room. "A toddler could have made these."

Although Anthony tried to demonstrate a level of aesthetic refinement, it was not received well. The old man, while he had no personal like for his wife's art, took Anthony's remark as an insult.

I stepped in. "I think you are wrong, Anthony. These pieces aren't bad. They're just trying to make you see the world in a different way. Only, sometimes I can never tell what that way is."

"How true!" the old man chirped. "I can't stand any of that esoteric trash. Where did you find this kid, Ashley?"

The Senator made some casual remark, appreciating my conversational tact. The old man gave me a warm smile. Then, remembering that he was the host and that it was impolite to give too much attention to one guest, he returned to the circle of people and resumed the general conversation. The old man restored my social spirits. I was even going to return to the group with him, but the moment he turned away, my phone went off. I removed it and saw Emily's name on the screen. She knew I was at work and would not have called unless it was something serious. Walking to a corner of the room, I answered the phone.

"What's up?" I said.

"Will, listen, I need you to find Aaron." Her voice was unusually serious.

"Aaron? What's wrong?"

"He's challenged David to a duel."

"A what?" I asked, thinking I had not heard her correctly.

"A fight! I don't know. Who knows what the hell it means. All I know is that he wants to fight David."

"Wha…why? What for?"

"For Lana," Emily answered. "She told me so herself. She doesn't know what to do. Aaron isn't answering his phone, neither is David."

"What do you want me to do?" I asked, realizing I was talking very loudly and drawing the attention of the partygoers.

"Go find Aaron. No…wait. Go to Hunter's. If Aaron isn't home, then maybe Hunter will be, and he's the one who knows what's going on."

"Where will you go?"

"To Aaron's."

"Alright, fine. Just…"

"What?" she asked impatiently.

"Be careful."

"I'll be fine. I'm sure this is nothing. Go when you get off work. Keep in touch. I'll see you later on tonight."

Before I could say *I love you*, she hung up the phone.

"Is everything alright, Will?" the Senator asked. I had not noticed her standing right behind me.

"It's nothing," I said. "Everything's fine."

"You don't have somewhere you need to be?"

I hesitated for a moment, debating whether or not I should attempt to excuse myself from work and explain my situation to her. With her heightened powers of observation, the Senator knew my hesitation meant there truly was something I needed to do.

"Go," she said, smiling at me. "I'm a mother, and whenever I see that face on my kids, I know they're being honest."

I returned her smile. I quickly found the exit and once again made my way to Hunter's apartment, determined to get the answers I needed.

10

Hanging up her phone, Emily tossed on a purple rain jacket and left for Park Place, Brooklyn. Since the beginning of the month, sultry days had led to thunderstorms at night. Not knowing how long she would be gone, she thought it best to have the jacket just in case. When she stepped outside, she regretted the decision. The air was hot and steamy. She could not remember a time when it was so warm in May. She took out her phone, saw it was 6:32, and started towards the F-train to Aaron's.

Emily was watching TV when Lana phoned. She pressed mute and listened as Lana attempted to relay as much information as possible. Aaron was going to fight David. She heard it from Amanda who heard it from Hunter. She guessed that Aaron's motive was to win her over. She might have done something to make him think that he *could* win her over. She did not know how to find them. She did not know how to stop them.

Emily thought to herself. *Alright, so David must have cheated on Lana. And now Aaron knows. Maybe he did say something to David, but to challenge him to a fight? Not possible. Aaron has always felt something for Lana, but he would never act on it. Especially like this. The whole thing is ridiculous. Aaron isn't fighting anyone. He probably said something in a moment of passion and that's all.*

After explaining these thoughts to Lana, Emily ended the conversation. She denied any truth in what she heard and went back to watching TV. However, the more she told herself that the story was impossible, the more plausible it seemed. Yes, in the five years she had known Aaron, there was never an instance of violence. Even still, she always remembered with particular clarity the times when Aaron carried a look of masked jealousy towards David. The more she recalled those times, the more she accepted the possibility of the fight.

How can I know what Aaron really feels? If he loves Lana, what might he do to make her feel the same way? But to challenge David to a fight? What will that accomplish?

Emily decided that if there was even the slightest chance of a conflict, she would do something to stop it. Her first step was to phone me and send me to Hunter's. She knew Hunter had at least some answers to David and Aaron's fight. Furthermore, she had a deeper conviction that Amanda was somehow involved as well. Ignoring Amanda for now, her next step was to look for Aaron, starting with his apartment.

Although she knew the building and even the floor on which Aaron lived, she did not know his apartment number. So, after riding the F-train and then the C-train to Brooklyn, she could not get inside his building because there was no one to ring her up. She phoned Aaron again, but her call went straight to voicemail. Luckily, just as she considered climbing the fire escape, an old man came out of the building. He held the door open for her. Emily smiled at him gratefully and she went inside.

Taking the elevator to the seventh floor, she thought to ask the tenants if they knew Aaron. She started with the first door on the left, but her knocks went unanswered. She tried the next door, but again, there was no answer. Just as she was beginning to lose hope, she tried another door on the right. After a few knocks, it opened. An orange cat scampered out from the corner of the door. Emily tried to stop it, but the cat went between her legs and ran down the hall. Standing up, Emily noticed an old woman in the doorway. She wore a tan night-gown with warn grey slippers.

"Oh, I'm sorry!" Emily said, startled. "I'll go get it." She started in the direction of the cat.

"Don't bother," said the old woman. "She never goes too far." She had on thick glasses that magnified her eyes, making her look like an owl. "How can I help you?" she asked with a hint of distrust.

"I'm sorry to bother you," said Emily, "but I'm looking for a friend of mine. I don't know what apartment he's in."

"What's the name?"

"Aaron Fletcher. Do you know him?"

"Well, I hope so. I'm his grandmother." A look of surprise came over Emily's face. She tried to diffuse the semi-awkward introduction with a laugh.

"Oh, hello!" she said, lifting her shoulders and smiling brightly. "I'm sorry, I thought Aaron lived alone."

"Not likely. He's been living with me since he graduated college. How do you know my grandson?"

"I went to school with him. We're good friends."

"So that must make you—oh what's your name—Lana? Aaron always talks about you. Huh, you are pretty, aren't you?"

"No Ma'am. My name is Emily Foster."

"Oh," she uttered.

Aaron's grandmother became vexed by her mistake. She now had to rethink what she was going to say to Emily, causing her visible annoyance. Emily saved her from the small talk.

"Is Aaron home?" she asked.

"No dear, he's not. He left just a while ago, after

we had supper. Would you like to come in?" Aaron's grandmother stepped to the right and motioned Emily inside. Emily smelled the diffused scent of lavender and dust drift out of the apartment.

"No thanks," Emily answered politely. "Do you know where he went?"

"I'm sorry, but he didn't say. Is he in trouble?" Her voice became worried.

"Oh no, not at all. I just came by to say *hello*. I'll come by some other time."

"Good. I'll tell him you stopped in."

"Thanks."

Just as Aaron's grandmother was about to return inside, she paused in the threshold of the door. "Foster… Foster. Oh! Now I remember." A spark lit in her eyes and her voice became warmer. "You're Aaron's friend. Of course, of course you are. We've met before, when Aaron preformed at Columbia. I remember meeting you after a show."

Emily thought back to when she attended one of Aaron's plays. She did recall meeting Aaron's family, although she could not specifically remember meeting his grandmother.

"Ah, of course!" Emily said. "How forgetful of me. I remember."

"I always saw so little of Aaron then, even though I was right here in New York. He spent all his time at college. Whenever he visited, he always told me about all his friends. You're name came up once or twice, I remember. How nice…" Her voice became more concerned. "Do you still see much of Aaron these days? He never leaves this place. He's always cooped up in the apartment. Don't misunderstand me, I like the company. But at my age, I can tell when a boy needs to get to living, as opposed to looking after some lost cause like me." She laughed softly.

"We still see each other," Emily said reassuringly.

"We're still good friends."

"Oh that's good. Good to hear…" Unable to think of anything more to say, her voice trailed off. "Well, I suppose that's it. Sorry I kept you. Goodbye!"

She shuffled inside the apartment and closed the door softly behind her.

"Goodbye," Emily said after she had gone.

She stood in the middle of the hallway, not knowing where to go or what to do. Suddenly, she felt something pushing against her right leg. It was the orange cat. It rubbed its ear against her jeans and stretched its butt in the air. Bending down, Emily stroked the cat. It purred with its eyes closed. Standing up, Emily went to the elevator. Before she got inside, she looked back into the hallway. The cat was sitting in front of Aaron's apartment, watching her leave. Once she got outside, Emily took out her phone and dialed my number.

11

"Hello?" I answered.

"Aaron's not at the apartment," Emily said. "I just spoke with his grandmother."

"What was his grandma doing there?"

"It's her apartment. Aaron's been living with her since he got out of college."

"I didn't know that."

"Neither did I."

"Should we be worried?"

"Not yet. Just go to Hunter's and find out what he knows."

"I'm already here."

I hung up my phone and walked underneath the familiar *Food, Deli, and Delicatessens* awning towards Hunter's building. The place looked different in the day. The concrete stairs were chipped and cracked. The front door was vandalized with strands of black graffiti, some in sharpie, others in spray paint. Looking up the side wall, I saw a grid of gray windows stuffed with teetering air conditioners. Satellite dishes dangled from window ledges. Pigeons gathered on the railing which bordered the roof top.

The front door was ajar and I went inside. The elevator was still busted, so I climbed the wooden staircase until I reached the fourth floor. In a far off room, I heard the whine of a small child. It was matched by the ferocious yelling of a man and a woman. The air in the hall was stagnant and old. It was a dank odor, like mildew on water. The ceiling was speckled with tiny black dots and there were brown stains in the corners. The floor boards sagged a little with each step. My senses told me to leave and I longed for the sanctuary of my apartment.

At last, I was at Hunter's door. Before I knocked, I heard a faint voice coming from inside the apartment. Leaning closer, I heard whispers. They were angry and brooding and I could not make out any of the words. Stepping back, I gave the door three hard knocks. Just like last time, there were footsteps. I sensed him approaching. He must have been on the other side of the door, watching me through the small peephole. Suddenly, the door swung open.

"Will!" Hunter burst out. "I expected you would show up."

I looked at him and was stunned. I remembered it had been several months since I had actually seen him in day light. His physique had changed. He was skinnier, with sunken cheeks and clothes that fit loosely on his body. His tight lips had lost their redness. They were now limpid pink, just like the rest of his skin. Judging by the length of patchy facial hair around his jaw, he had not shaved in weeks. It made him look feeble and sick. There was a discord between his voice and his body. It was like his eyes had no idea just how bad the rest of him looked. Those intelligent eyes were dim like the light of a pale fire. His black hair was unkempt. Curls and chunks of it sprung out of his head. The cut on his lower lip had started to heal, but it was still swollen. When he greeted me, I tried to conceal the shock and pity I felt. Despite my efforts, I could see him give a slight frown after he finished his first sentence, as if to say: *"Yes, I have become uglier. So what? Will you leave because of it?"* I said *hello* and he brought me inside.

Entering the room, I was struck by the orange glare of the sun. I looked down, avoiding the intense light. There were particles of dust floating around my legs. They stirred in the air with each step I took. Soon, the floor disappeared under an immense carpet of books and papers. Some of the books were very old, the kind that require a penknife to open. Despite their age, they were tossed carelessly on the ground. Their spines were twisted and bent out of shape. A metal trashcan sat in the corner of the room, overflowing with wads of paper. There was no television in the room, nor any other device that would remind the inhabitant that he was living in the twenty-first century. A raggedy armchair with a floral pattern was crammed against the back wall below the window. Immediately in front of the chair was a collapsible wooden table. Despite the folds of paper underneath the right leg, it was noticeably uneven. On the edge of the same table was an open Latin grammar book. Next to the book was a stack of index cards. The writing on the top card was written in red ink and read: *Adultus Adulta Adultum*. On my right, there was a dilapidated kitchen. The linoleum tiles were pealing and were stained with grease and scum. There was no washing machine and the refrigerator gave off a constant din, causing anything on top of it to rattle and jitter. Several pieces of paper and some tarnished pictures were tapped on the door of the refrigerator. In the sink, a mound of dishes rose above the countertop. I looked over at Hunter, who was wrestling a chair from behind a pile of books. The living being and the inanimate space were connected. They were both in a state of dejection. I went to him and helped lift the chair.

"I've been trying to pick up the language," he said enthusiastically. He must have noticed that I saw the Latin book. "It's very formulaic, there's a lot of memorization involved. Overall, I think I'm making progress."

I had not come to make small talk. From my silence, Hunter understood this.

"Well," he said, taking the chair from my hands and dragging it to the other side of the room, "what can I do for you?"

He placed the chair in front of the uneven table. Along with the Latin materials, he had many papers and folders scattered on its surface. Once he adjusted the chair to a suitable angle, he went behind the table and sat in the arm chair. Now he was ready for me.

"A couple of nights ago," I began, "just before I came here, David did that to you." I pointed to the cut on his lip. "Now, I've heard rumors about how Aaron's challenged him to some sort of fight. Emily went to check on Aaron at his apartment, but he wasn't there. You know what this is all about, don't you? You know where they are."

"And now you've come here to force it out of me?" he asked with a grin.

"I'm not going to force you to do anything."

"What a relief," he said blithely. "Otherwise, I'd have to give you my good lip."

His words assumed an air of indifference. The concern in my voice only seemed to increase his amusement.

"Cut the shit Hunter," I said, crossing to him and placing my hands on the table. "It's getting late. I want to go home. Just tell me what's going on."

He took a long pause. He leaned back in his chair, uncomfortable with how close I was. His eyes looked around the room. He was searching for a subject of conversation that would digress from the current one.

"Will, I don't believe this. We haven't seen each other in ages and this is the first thing you've got to say to me? This isn't you."

"We can play catch-up some other time. Right now I need answers."

"Is that so? And you think I've got them? Well maybe your right, but you're going to have to do something for me in exchange."

"Hunter I don't have time to fu–!"

"I won't ask for much," he said quickly. "I wanted to chat a little more, but seeing the rush you're in, perhaps it would be best to get straight to the point." He rearranged himself in the chair, becoming more restless as the silence grew. "There's something I've been meaning to share with you, Will." His lips curled into a slight smile.

"What, Hunter?" I asked impatiently.

"I'd like you're opinion on a little project of mine."

"A project?"

"More like a story, really. Something I've written. I'd like to share it with you."

"Hunter, I don't have the time!"

"It will only take a few moments," he said in a reassuring voice, leaning forward and reaching out his arms to keep me from walking away. "After it's done, I'll tell you everything you want to know. Does that sound fair?" He gestured towards the chair he had placed in front of the table.

I sat down. He was white. I was black. He had the opening move. If I wanted my answers, I had no choice but to play his game for a little longer. I sat silently, which he took as my reluctant acceptance.

"Excellent!" he said. The grin on his face got wider. "I knew you would stay. You're in for a real treat!"

12

"I should preface the explanation of my little story with my general impressions on this whole business of writing. Even though the story is not yet complete, the experience has been a revealing one. I'm sure you, more than anyone, will appreciate my insights. First, I should say that writing this work has shown me the necessary balance between inspiration and routine. By *inspiration*, I mean the moment of creativity that compels a writer to pick up the pen. By *routine*, I mean the practiced discipline of constant writing, even when all sources of imagination are depleted. When I was younger, I always waited for inspiration to come to me. Like a beggar, I let my mind wander unfamiliar places, hoping that some fantastic idea would take shape in the form of a story. I know now that that is not the best way to go about writing. What's needed is equilibrium, a balance between inspiration and discipline. Creativity alone gets no results, for one rarely has the will to finish what one starts. At the same time, routine without inspiration makes for a story that's dry and unimaginative: writing for the sake of writing. Do you follow me so far?"

"I do," I said.

"So, in order to gain discipline, which is what I needed most, I began to keep a record of everything that impressed me in a literary way. Things in nature. Strangers on the street. I snatched up whatever subject the world happened to throw at me. Newspapers proved the best resource for this activity. Stories of murders, corrupt CEO's, government scandals: these allowed limitless possibilities for my writing. I was an English major in college, you know, and even had my turn at some book review columns. Yet, all of it was useless because I had no experience writing of my own free will. It's quite easy to turn out an article when there's a deadline—a gun to your head. It's the fear of consequences, not true creativity, which drives most of our modern writing. In this respect, David is absolutely right. Having a degree in English brought me no closer to writing my book. I knew that if my work was ever to be written, it would have to be done through my own free will, as opposed to a deadline."

"That's an interesting thought," I said curtly. "If a person has something to say, they should just say it."

"Precisely. And it was exactly that *something to say* that compelled me to start my ambitious project in the first place. But I knew I lacked real experience and experience is what I needed in order to make my novel—yes, *novel*, you see how I've been avoiding the word?—come to life. You might say I borrowed a trick from Aaron's bag. I became a method writer. Where would the flash of brilliance that gave birth to *On the Road* have come from if not for the smell of musty car seats carrying wayward travelers along oily black asphalt towards Frisco? Certainly not from the mind alone. Just like them, I aimed to experience all of what I wrote. I admit, I was only partially successful in that endeavor. But any degree of experience enhances the overall honesty of my work, wouldn't you agree?"

By the tone and formality of his speech, it seemed like Hunter was holding something back. His words were loftier than usual. Grandiose, but with precise meaning and intent. He was constructing his sentences cautiously, meticulously. Either he was keeping his distance, or he was preparing me for something quite unusual. Perhaps even both.

"But I see this is boring you," he let out bluntly. "To the point! I'll get there soon. Just one last thought. I've noticed a strange phenomenon occurs while writing. The urge, when forming different characters in the mind, to assign them different parts of yourself is so great. In other words, I couldn't resist dividing up my soul and placing each part in a certain character. I've been told that this phenomenon isn't uncommon for some writers. It is all in *good author fashion*, as they say. But as I slowly began to dissect my mind, I marveled at the many opposing forces that exist within me. How can any person find peace within himself and obtain any harmony of spirit, with all their different natures at war? This is the conflict that stands before me. To resolve it, I have no choice but to complete my work, which will be done soon. Once the final chapter is finished, I'll have my answer, and my mind will be at peace. And that's why I'm delighted you have joined me tonight. You will be my guide as I complete this story of mine. I will share my book with you, and you will give me your opinion. Your opinion, most of all, is what I want."

"Hunt, there's no time! I have to—¬¬¬"

"No, no," he said, amused by my frustration. "I want to hear what you have to say now. But I realize you could never finish the entire book in just one sitting. It would be pointless of me to even ask. Instead, let me describe the novel to you. I'll throw in as much detail as I can, even give you pages out of the manuscript when appropriate."

Seeing as how my previous efforts to stop him had failed, I thought by appeasing him I could get closer to my answers.

"Just hurry up," I said reluctantly.

"You'll get the short version then," he said, satisfied by my compliance. "It will be good enough."

I made myself comfortable in the chair, preparing

for what would follow.

"The novel," Hunter began, "takes place here, in New York. Having spent four years of my life here, I like to think that I've come to know the city quite well. She has a character. Perhaps, if you really think about it, she's the main character of my novel after all. Which reminds me, I've named the principle protagonist of the story John Collins. The name has no literary significance, aside from the fact that it has a decent rhythm to it, something that sounds natural to me. It has resonance, but not so much that it becomes cliché or fictitious sounding. I've made John a college student living in Manhattan. I figured it was what I knew best. He attends such and such University. I say *such and such* because the actual name is unimportant. It's to be artistic, you know. John is dissatisfied with his academic environment, though he does quite well in school. He has many friends, but none who know him for his true self. They don't care to dig deeper into his heart, for lack of powers of observation, prowess, or whatever. John prefers his distance. His happiest moments are often spent in self-reflection. Are you with me?"

Hunter probably noticed my eyes were focused on the floor. It was not boredom, but rather, a sense of extreme embarrassment that came over me as I heard Hunt's description of John Collins. I knew this character. It was Hunter, or rather, the person Hunter wanted to be. I knew it from the moment he began. Nothing he could say would have reversed my conviction. He must have known that too. He should have been a psychology major. I let him go on.

"Pay close attention, Will. This next bit is perhaps the most interesting feature of my story. The events of the novel, the experiences that John undergoes, all take place within the course of one night."

"Say that again?"

"Sunset to sunrise. One vigil. That's the time-span

101

of my entire novel. I describe John's adventures throughout Manhattan, taking place during a single night."

At this point, I thought it best to engage Hunt in more conversation. If silence failed, perhaps by indulging him, I could reach my goal more quickly.

"That's not a bad idea," I said. "Pretty original. It should make your style quite interesting. But you mentioned adventures. What kinds of adventures?"

"The best kinds, Will. From spending time with the love of his life, to visiting the underbelly of the city. My novel will be a breath of New York. I want to write the most memorable night ever lived."

"That limits your options doesn't it? Nights always go by so quickly."

"I've been selective, believe me. Everything fits sequentially, in a logical and timely order. The devil is in the details, you know. I can't have John in the Village one minute and in Harlem the next, it wouldn't be realistic."

"What's the name by the way?" I asked.

"The name of what?"

"Your novel."

"I call it... *New York Nights*," he said with pride.

"Huh."

"What's the matter?" he asked. "You don't like it?"

"It's nothing, go on. Tell me more about these adventures."

"Well, John visits different parts of the city: Central Park, Times Square, even Wall Street, where they worship that bronze bull. There's one scene where he goes to a rave in Queens. That's later though. I even have him visiting strip clubs."

"And you have extensive knowledge of those places I'm sure. Especially given what you said before about the necessity of experience."

"I don't know what you're implying," he said with a sly smile. "I'm puritanical. I've even stopped masturbating."

"God! Hunter–"

"It's true. In order for a man to direct his life, he must first control his life, the impulses. That's what I'm doing."

"A little warning next time would be nice."

"I have been to one or two clubs though," he said, still smiling. "All in the name of research." There was something so unnatural in the combination of Hunter and strip joints.

"John talks to one of the strippers and they get into a conversation."

"About what?" I asked.

"Her life, her profession, how she feels about what she does. By the way, have you passed the strip club outside of Times Square? Where has all the decency gone in this world? Children visit that area!"

"Stick to the novel."

"Well, it goes on like that for a while. John wanders through strange and bizarre places at night, meeting all different kinds of characters. If I were to put a label on it, the book is really a romance novel at its core. More romantic than romance."

Roman a clef is what I would have called it, but I let him go on.

"I want to show the beauty that's in this city, the beauty in all us New Yorkers. Here, let me give you a little taste." Grabbing a bundle of loose pages from the table in front of him, he began thumbing through them one corner at a time. "Here it is, read this." He handed me a page with a few lines written on it. "Read from, "Oh I have…""

The excerpt read: *Oh I have stood atop some of the tallest peaks in the world, but I tell you reader, even the highest do not compare to our mighty skyscrapers.*

"What do you think of that?" he asked. His eyes gleamed. "Does that line capture the beauty of New York, or what?"

I hesitated.

"No one writes like this," I said.

"What do you mean?" he asked innocently.

"I mean no one goes around saying *atop* anymore or referring to the reader in the middle of a sentence. It's all old fashioned."

"So what if it is?"

"No one will understand what the hell you're talking about. They'll think you're trying to be the next Charlotte Brontë or something."

"What's wrong with her?"

"Nothing, Hunt. It's not the point. You know what I mean."

"Why is it my fault if people won't understand what's beautiful?"

"It's not your fault. But when you write this way, it makes you sound like a–"

"Like a what? An asshole?"

"No. It makes you sound pretentious."

"Portentous?"

"Pretentious."

"Hah!" he laughed, leaning back in his chair. "See how much fun we're having? You're very clever. I'll keep your comments in mind for the redraft. Don't worry, the whole novel isn't like that. Only certain parts. Maybe it was a poor example."

"Fine, got anything else?" I asked sarcastically.

Hunter looked around.

"Here, read this scene." Getting up from his chair and crossing to the other side of the table, he picked up a red folder. He removed three or four stapled pages. "I think this is one of the better scenes of the book. It takes place during a conversation between John and the woman he loves."

He handed the script to me, but before I could even

begin the scene, I was struck by the title written on the top of the first page: *John's confession to Lana.* "Hunter!" I threw the bundle of pages onto the table. "This is too much! What kind of story is this?"

"It's only a name, Will," he implored. "I only took the name, nothing more."

"I don't care what you took. Giving your character the name *Lana* is sick."

"If you must know, Lana's character is based on a former relationship of mine."

"Oh well…that's healthier! Hunt, you need help."

"Writing is the way I put form to what's in my soul. There's nothing unhealthy about that. You haven't even read it."

"I refuse."

"You have to read it."

"No Hunter. This is all sick."

"Why do you keep saying that?"

"Because it's all you!" I burst out. "John Collins is Hunter Ricci. This novel is just a way for you to act out whom you've always dared to be: some womanizer like David. Honestly, I don't see why you would ever want to emulate him in the first place."

"John Collins is nothing like David," he said quietly, offended.

"Hunt, enough of this, just tell me where they are."

His dark eyes looked intensely at mine. They were glazed and icy, with a hint of plea in them. Had I known what would follow, I would have picked up his manuscript and never put it down. But I could not then foresee what I now regret.

"So be it," he said, relaxing his stare. "I understand your reaction. If I were sitting where you are, I would act the same way. But no matter what you think of my story, give me your opinion on one final thought of mine. Do it and then I'll give you what you came for."

His game was getting on my nerves. The fake weight in his words annoyed me. He was like some child who, out of loneliness or power-lust, withholds essential information only to prolong your stay. I would have liked to get up and leave the room, but the thought of David and Aaron kept me in my chair.

"Do you remember," he said, looking away from me and towards a broken coffee mug on the table, "that night of our senior year in college when David, Aaron, you and I went to that bar down on Houston."

"After Lana and David broke up. But it was really more of a temporary separation than a breakup."

"Yes, that's right. While we sat at the table, after we had a few drinks, do you remember what David said to us?"

It's amazing how memory works sometimes. The mind can remember moments from our past which appear completely and irredeemably useless. That is, until a time comes when those moments are not so useless anymore, as if some part of you knew all along that they would be of the utmost significance. It's true what they say about the past not even being past.

"He said that love only makes a person weaker," I recited.

"A *man*," Hunter corrected. "Love makes a man weaker."

"Yes, a mix of David's casual sexism and alcohol. So what?"

"I think he's right, Will. I think he's been right all along."

"What do you mean?"

He looked away again.

"I've been thinking this through for quite some time. It's kept me up late into the morning, I swear it. It's a shadow that simply won't quit."

Hunter was preparing himself for something

big now. The corners of his lower lip began to tremble uncontrollably. His head was down and his body became tense, like when standing above a lake and feeling its coldness before you have even felt its water.

"I hate to love," he said at last. "I'm sick of it. I want to get away. I've had my fill of love and can stand no more of it."

All this was becoming too much. I had known Hunter for years, but I had never seen this side of him. It frightened me. He led me down a conversation and would not let go.

"How can you say these things?" I asked.

"Think about this, Will. I'm going to be twenty three years old this summer. I've never had sex. I've never come close to finding a person that I could possibly love. If you could only feel the pain it's caused me. I'm so alone. I see people around me and I want to talk to them, but they don't stop for me. I see them, but they don't see me. They walk by, buried in their lives. I see someone and sometimes I can feel their loneliness. It pours off of them and I feel it and I know that they feel my loneliness too. But I can never do anything about it. For Christ's sake, look around you!"

He gestured past me towards the myriad of books and papers blanketing the floor.

"These stories—these characters—were created so I could learn through them how best to live. So why is my life so miserable? I'm not as ugly as I first seem. Some even say that I'm intelligent, kind, and a gentleman. So tell me! What's the answer? Why haven't I been able to find love?"

Silence. I heard some pigeons cooing outside on the window ledge. It was always such a soothing sound, I thought, the cooing of a pigeon.

"And despite it all, despite everything that's happened to me, every laugh in the shadows or false declaration of ardor, I still remain faithful to my naïve principles. I told you one once. Do you remember it?"

"No, Hunter."

"To place love over sex. What a mad man I must be! To cling to some deformed virtue our mommies and daddies told us when we were young. Completely absurd. Tell me, where have my virtues gotten me? Have they given me someone beautiful? Have they given me trust, commitment, or passion? Tell me, where has love left me?"

"Virginity is a blessing, not a curse."

"Lies, don't tell me any more lies!"

"It's not a lie, Hunter! You will find the right person, you will find your love."

"And what if I never do?" he asked miserably. "What then? Will I end up settling for mediocrity? These questions haunt me, Will. I feel so lost at times. I try dedicating myself to work, as if, through work alone, I'll gain a modicum of happiness in my life. But work is not the answer, it's only a distraction. A distraction unto death. If not happiness, shouldn't I at least be given some pleasure?"

"There's a difference between happiness and pleasure," I said.

"But why must I be forced to have neither?"

"No one forces you to do anything, Hunt."

"I force myself, God Damn it!"

He crashed his fist to the table. Papers and books went flying. I jolted back, afraid.

"Enough Hunter!"

I had no more answers for him. He had dragged me into the endless circle of his conscience. This was only my first lap, but for him, he had been running for a very long time. His resolve shook me. I began to feel myself being sucked into his personal hell. The orange light from the tip of the sun streamed through the dirty window.

"And yet," he said, regaining his composure, "after all this, I still know I will hold on to my principles. I still have hope for myself. Do you know why?"

I was silent.

"It's because of you," he answered. "You and Emily."

Emily. Her face appeared in my mind. I had forgotten her as my conversation with Hunter continued. Not forgotten in the way one forgets an item or a task that must be done. Instead, forgotten as when one recalls an old name or a buried memory—you know, remembering the things we should have never lost. As absurd as it may sound, I always sense that we share the same time together, even when we are apart. As if all of our separate moments come together and form a collective experience. Since the beginning of my talk with Hunter, the connection that joined my time with Emily's time had been weakening. It was lost up until the very moment that Hunter reminded me of her.

"It's you and Emily" he continued, "your love gives me hope. That one day I might find someone with half her grace and loveliness and that our love might be just a fraction of yours. If I could only have it, I would be complete."

I did not know what to say. His words moved me. They made me think on Emily in a different way. A strange sense of shock and shame came over me as I thought of how she had been gone, if only for just a few minutes.

"Tell me one thing, Will," he said, "how did you know? How did you know she was the right one? You've got to tell me."

I thought about his question and then gave the best answer I could.

"It was as if, one day, we each had a sudden realization: that to be without one another was to commit some horrible crime against life. She and I knew it at once, although we were too young to say it with words. We both knew that, even if we were apart, the tie between our lives could never be undone, that there was something pulling us together…at least, that's the way I've always felt."

Hunter was motionless. Soon, his lower lip started to shake. He clenched his teeth together. His eyes looked towards the floor, heavy and sad. I wondered if my answer to his question was just like another one of his books: it described something he knew and pined for, but that something would always be beyond his reach.

"Hunter," I said, "I…I'm so sorry."

He looked at me curiously, like he had not expected my remark. Perhaps he too understood my feelings at that moment.

"Don't be," he said. "It's mine to bear. Mine alone." He sat back in his chair and ran his fingers through his hair. He covered his face momentarily, as if to wipe away the painful emotions that had collected on the slate of his mind.

"Now then, your reward for sitting so patiently. You wanted to know about David and Aaron, didn't you?

13

In the fervor of my conversation with Hunter, I had almost forgotten my sole reason for meeting him in the first place. I was even thankful he had reminded me of my mission.

"Of course," Hunter said, sitting forward, "I'll tell you where they are. But don't you want to know how they got there?"

"What do you mean?" I asked. He lowered his head and was silent. His habit of drawing out an explanation was truly irritating me. He was trying to add to all our lost time. I was trying to make time move faster.

"I've always hated him," he said quietly. He was fiddling with a loose button on the end of his shirt. It hung by one or two threads. He tugged and twisted, until eventually it broke off and fell onto the floor.

"Who?" I asked.

He was looking to where the button fell. "From the moment I met him, I wanted to get away from him."

"Hunter, enough with the pronoun game. Who are you talking about?"

"What?" he asked, lifting his head. He was annoyed at me for breaking his concentration. "David, of course. Who did you think I meant? I assume you know by now that he cheated on Lana. I think we all saw that coming. I had my suspicions. He confirmed them when he did *this* to

111

me." Hunter ran a finger over his swollen lower lip. "The price of trying to do what's right."

"What happened that night?" I asked.

He sighed.

"We were supposed to meet downtown before going to the diner. That was the plan, anyway. But I was sure he was cheating on Lana. I wanted to bring him here. I wanted him to admit it."

Standing from the chair, he slid past the corner of the table. I turned and watched him. He started pacing in a straight line, over the expanse of papers and trash on the floor. At first, he tried stepping around the books. On his way back, he simply walked over them. Compulsively, he brought his right hand to his mouth and bit his nails.

"And he did admit it," Hunter said, deep in thought. "He said it so quickly, so casually. There was no hesitation or remorse. You should have seen him smiling. He knew how much it hurt me. It was delightful to him.

Hunter saw the look on my face.

"Don't think it, Will. I told you, I admire Lana in a platonic way. Truly, I do."

"So what did you do next?" I asked.

"What do you expect? I called him what he is: a manipulative piece of shit. I can hardly remember all the names I called him. *Bastard, scum, and asshole* come to mind. I said he was the lowest kind of low. I told him he was a fool for doing what he did."

"And what did he do then?"

"He laughed at me. Called me queer. He even said that he thought I would empathize with him. Can you believe that? That was the worst."

Hunter finished pacing. Gathering his thoughts, he sat down in his chair again.

"But the next thing I said really shut him up." He smirked. "I told him he was a coward. I said that he was the most scared person I had ever seen. I even told him a prophesy. In short, his life will be long, void, and unremarkable. After school, he'll join a firm that will give him all the false prestige he always wanted. He'll marry— sure, he will. But he'll do it for money and status, not for love. Give it a year, and he will cheat on his wife. Maybe she will leave him, or maybe she will stay. Either way, I feel bad for her, whoever she is. He won't have kids, but he will have a nice car. He won't see his parents, but he will have a big house. He won't have a single real friend, but he will have all the money to buy fake ones. And over time, he will lose it all. The first thing to go will be his body. He will get old and fat. His stomach will turn to rubber. His cheeks will sag and his skin will loosen. His hairline will shrink and his belly will roll over his belt. Then, he will drive away however many people still care about him. He'll turn to whatever ten cent slut he can get his hands on. It will be that way for the rest of his life. The last hour David spends on earth will be the sum of superficial moments and the pain of others. That's his legacy. No one will cry for him at his funeral. No loved ones will carry his memory into the future. With him will be buried the grief of every life he soiled. Fill in the hole. Say a prayer. It's over now. And that will be the end of one of the most astoundingly unremarkable lives there ever was."

Hunter sat forward in his chair. He clasped his hands together and rested his elbows on the table. "As you can imagine, David didn't take my little speech very well. I was not as articulate with him as I am with you, but I think he got my point. I kept talking and, before I knew it, he split my lip. I fell on this chair and he left. Then, you arrived."

I was hunched over, staring at the floor.

"And Aaron," I asked. "What about him? How does he fit into all of this?"

"Well, it's like this. After my night with David, I thought for a while. I knew I wasn't going to let him walk away that easily after what he did to Lana. Someone had to do something. But what could I do? I only have my words. I'm a weakling. But Aaron? He's not like me. He's strong. He can do what it takes to bring David down. And so, I texted Aaron and told him to come here. I convinced him to fight David. The duel was my idea, title and all. Couldn't you tell?"

I thought about what he said. "So you're responsible for the fight?"

"Not exactly. I just gave Aaron the push he needed. You should have seen him, Will. He has such purpose now. He's so determined. This is about more than just Lana. Sure, he's in love with her. But it's also about standing up against all the bad shit that people put us through. Aaron won't let David get away with it. Not this time. There's no reasoning with David. We both know that. The only way to get through to people like him is with force. He's going to learn what happens when we make a game of other people's love."

"Oh stop it!" I shouted.

"Stop what?"

"Stop using that word! *Love*. We're too young for it. We pass it around like handled change. It loses meaning each time we say it. So shut up!"

Hunter was silent. What I said seemed to profoundly hurt him. His eyes stared back at mine and he looked disappointed, not angry. I tried to regain some semblance of composure.

"Tell me where they are," I said again.

"Like it will do any good."

"Hunter!" I startled him. The smirk on his face vanished.

"You're too late…" he said after a short pause. "Look at the time." He took out his phone and held the screen in front of me. "It's already past 8:00. They're probably meeting as we speak."

"Where?"

"In Central Park, underneath the bridge. You know the one. It's where you all went to smoke back in college."

I stood from the chair and went straight for the door. My feet sent the papers and books on the floor into a flurry. I looked back and saw that Hunter had not gotten up from his seat. He was hunched over. I turned my back to him and grabbed the door knob. I went into the hallway. Before I could leave the corridor, Hunter came out of his apartment. He was running after me.

"Wait!" he cried.

I had just reached the first step when I heard him. I stopped and looked back.

"When can I see you again?" he asked plainly.

"I don't know, Hunter."

"I suppose it's silly to ask," he said with a sad smile. "I could tell long ago that you stopped being my friend—that I became too strange for you. You only come to visit when your friends are in trouble, is that it? You never bother over poor old Hunter. Well?"

I shook my head in disgust.

"So that's it. You're going to abandon me like all the rest?"

Then, I said the words which I can never take back.

"You've abandoned yourself."

His eyes were wide. He looked as though he no longer recognized me. Then, he rushed forward.

"Go then! Go with the rest. We were friends once, but you've turned your back on me. If you only knew. If you could only know!"

I closed my eyes, thinking he was going to come at me. I stepped backwards, placing my foot on the next step. There was silence. I opened my eyes. He had not moved. He only stared at me. Those eyes that had been filled with such anger were now sunk with disbelief. I could not stand them any longer. I ran out of the building towards the nearest subway line that would get me to the Park.

14

It was spring and green was back in Central Park. The flowers had blossomed and the leaves had grown. Poet's Way, the Belvedere Castle, even the countless statues seemed to take on a new life with the change in the weather. It was one of the most beautiful times of the year to be in the Park, and as Aaron entered through the North East corner, he could not help but acknowledge so.

It was nearly dark when Aaron passed along the bank of the Harlem Meer. The wind was strong and there were clouds coming from the west. The sun had almost disappeared beneath the gaps of faraway buildings. There was shade all around. The wind blew across the Meer, causing the water to tremble like a sheet. Passing the old boathouse, Aaron noticed the sharp lines of the grey roof top. In the reflection of the water, they were bent and alive. He left the boathouse behind and walked further along the water's edge. On his left, there was an empty playground. He imagined the place not as it was, but filled with children at play: the sound of jeans against a metal slide, the slap of a jump-rope on blacktop. The playground made him sad somehow, so he moved faster and left it behind.

After what seemed like a mile, he reached a section of the path that branched to the right. He followed it, eventually crossing the East drive. He traveled deeper into the heart of the Park. The sky glowed weakly through the trees. Except for underneath the rows of evenly placed lamp posts, the Park was covered in blue shadow. Traveling further into the blue, the number of people Aaron saw diminished. Every fifty steps or so, he looked over his shoulder. At one point, he noticed a man walking several yards behind him. The shadow eventually turned right on an intersecting pathway, leaving Aaron all alone. His hands were buried in his pockets. From inside, he heard the soft ticking of his wrist watch. He forgot he had brought it. Taking it out of his pocket, he slipped the band over his right hand, closing the latch. The metal pulled a few small hairs from his wrist. He had no real reason for bringing the watch along, other than the strange sense of comfort it gave him. It was a memento for mental security that could only help him in the challenge to come.

He walked along the curving road until he came to an overgrown dirt path. It led into a small gully. It was the same path that, several years ago, the group had gone down. Now, Aaron walked alone. He carefully watched his step to avoid any creepers. The thick brush made it impossible to see. He took out his phone and shined it on the narrow path. The surrounding darkness made him nervous. He focused on the noise of the watch. Soon, the path leveled off and the brush started to clear. Aaron stepped onto an old paved walkway, one that had not been looked after for several years.

In the distance, Aaron saw an archway hanging over the gray path. He put his phone away and walked towards it. He recognized the old stone bridge. Beyond it, he thought he heard the muted sound of a saxophone. His mind returned to Amanda's apartment. He quickly realized it was only the wind playing tricks on him. He moved to the mouth of the bridge, eventually crossing directly under it. The air underneath the bridge was heavy. He breathed it in and his lungs became damp and chill. There was no light under the arch. He felt his pocket, trying to find his phone again.

Before he could reach it, a tall figure appeared from the corner of the bridge. It walked towards Aaron, with heavy steps that resonated inside of the bridge.

"Who's there?" Aaron called out.

There was no response.

"Stay right fucking there! Who's there?"

"Shall we begin?" Aaron heard. He raised his phone to the voice, turned on the light, and recognized David. "If you're ready, of course."

"I knew it was you," Aaron said mistrustfully, trying to calm his heartbeat.

"Put that thing away," David said, blocking the light of Aaron's phone. "Someone will see us."

Aaron put the phone in his pocket.

"I'm amazed you found the place," he continued. "It must have taken me three passes before I found it."

Aaron was silent.

"What… doesn't this place bring back old memories for you?" David raised his arms and turned his head to survey the bridge. "I know for me it does."

"I'm going to beat the shit out of you," Aaron said. "How it happens is up to you. You can fight back or you can take it like a man. Either way is fine for me."

"Is that right?" David asked, amused.

He turned his back to Aaron and walked to the mouth of the bridge. He approached the line of shadow that separated the outside from the dark shade of the arch. Standing under the bridge, he looked up towards the sky. There were gray clouds and they were moving quickly.

"Is there anything you want to say?" Aaron asked.

"What else do we have to talk about?" David said, taking his eyes from the night and turning them on Aaron.

"It doesn't matter anyway," Aaron said. "You can't feel regret. It's impossible for you. Maybe, if I just knock your brain a little to the left, you might feel some remorse.

119

But even if you don't understand what's so wrong about what you did, I do. That's why–"

"That's why you want to fight me?" David said, finishing Aaron's thought.

"Yes."

Aaron thought back to his time in Hunter's apartment. He had known since then what he was fighting for. He was fighting for himself, for all those that dared but did not try to stop bad people. He was also fighting for Lana, for all the girls before and after her. For David, words like *character, commitment,* and *trust* meant nothing. For Aaron, however, they were more than just words. They were a code.

"Of course," David said, "but do you think you'll be able to go through with it? I mean, have you ever fought someone before?"

Aaron had never fought anyone in his life. He had seen fights though, actual fights, not like the ones on TV. Real fights were much more uncivilized. Usually, one guy swung his arm and landed his awkward fist into another guy's face. It almost always ended after that. There was no drawn out exchange of blows. There were no dodges or clever moves. The guy who was hit never crouched on his hams, wiped the blood from his mouth, stared at his foe, or stood back up. Real fights were always clumsy and quick. He wondered if that was how his fight would be like.

"That won't stop me," Aaron said. "Besides, I'm a fast learner."

David smirked. "Look, you can drop the act. I know it's hard for you, but do you really think that you're a good fit for the tough guy role? Say what you want, but I know the real reason why you want to kick my ass."

Aaron did not move.

"You're in love with her. It's as simple as that. If you want to be her knight, be my guest. I think I passed some windmills on my way here."

Lana flashed in Aaron's mind. He tried to find the ticking noise.

"But do you honestly think," David went on, "that she didn't know I was cheating on her? Sure, I never told her. All the same, she must have known. Everyone else did. And that means, of course, that she just accepted it."

"Shut up!" Aaron said, losing his composure.

"So why don't you just accept it?" David asked. He started circling Aaron. "Why the hell do you even care? You want her? She's yours. Gratis."

"Fuck you," Aaron said. "You don't just get to walk away from what you did."

"Look, what I did was a shame. Really, it was. But face it: do you really think you can give her more than I did?"

"Shut up!" Aaron shouted. "You don't even realize. It's all your fault. Because of you, I lost my chance to be with her. All because of you! In the beginning, you were the one who told me not to see her. You told me to wait. And so I listened. And what did you do? You took her from me! And despite everything you did, I was still your friend. I was your friend because I–"

"Because you what?" David prodded. He stopped in front of him.

"Because I looked up to you! Because I was too stupid to see you for what you really are!"

"Which is?" David smirked again.

"A betrayer! A damn betrayer!"

"So what are you going to do about it?"

"No more!" Aaron roared. "You can't have her. She deserves better. She deserves so much better. She deserves–"

"You?" David laughed.

"Yes!"

Aaron tore from his spot and lunged at David. He threw a punch with his right hand, completely missing

121

his target. He stepped in and threw his left fist, hoping to make contact. David blocked Aaron's powerful swing with his right forearm. The punch hit hard against David's arm, causing him visible pain. Aaron set up for another hit. Before he could coil his arm, David recovered and grasped the back of Aaron's head with his right hand. Bending him forward, David landed a heavy punch. It hit Aaron in his unclenched stomach. Aaron let out a deep bellow of pain. He clutched the spot where David had struck. Still holding his head, David drove his elbow into Aaron's face. Aaron dropped to the ground. He covered his nose with his hand. After a moment, he took it away and saw a smear of red blood.

"You idiot," David said scornfully, rubbing his forearm. "What did you think would happen? Did you think you would actually accomplish anything? Get up. Come on! Get up, before someone sees us."

David walked towards Aaron. Aaron was kneeling with his head turned down. His eyes were closed and he breathed heavily. His gut burned and half of his face was numb. When he tried opening his eyes, all he could see was red. He wiped the blood away from his face. It dripped onto the ground. He put one hand on his knee and started to stand. David was at his feet.

"Let's go," he said, looking down at Aaron. "C'mon, get up."

Aaron was hunched over, breathing hard. His elbows pressed into his knees and his hair was in his face. David reached out and grabbed Aaron's right hand, covering his wrist watch.

"Come on, that's enough." David pulled harder on Aaron's hand. Aaron would not move. "Get up! You idiot!" David shouted.

Aaron looked up at David's face. He tried to wrench his hand from David's, but he could not get loose.

"Move!" David yelled.

With his remaining strength, Aaron tore his wrist away from David. The force of the pull made him lose his balance. He landed on his back and looked up at the underside of the bridge. He wanted to stay there, but when he heard someone shouting, he lifted his head. David was holding his hand and cursing. When Aaron pulled his wrist free, the latch of his watch tore the skin of David's palm. A dark line quickly spread over the cut.

"You little piece of shit!" David said, trying to stop the bleeding with the bottom of his shirt. "Get the hell up!" He crossed over to where Aaron was lying. He stepped over him and grabbed him by the throat. "You damn idiot! You fucking idiot! I'll make you regret..."

Before David could finish his threat, I ran underneath the bridge and grabbed him by both wrists. Emily got between him and Aaron. Our entrance caught them both by surprise. I pulled David away, until eventually he broke my grip. He backed away, looking at his hand. Emily was behind me. She tried to speak to Aaron who was just starting to stand.

"Look who showed up!" David said. "See what your little friend did to me?"

He held up his hand. Even in the darkness, I could see the line of blood.

"Coward," he said, looking at Aaron. "Do you hear me? That's what you are, a coward!"

Once he finished yelling, David ran from the bridge along the winding path. I started chasing after him. As soon as I came out from underneath the bridge, I heard the leaves all around me begin to stir. It started to rain. I looked ahead and could not see David. I turned back towards the bridge. Emily was holding onto Aaron, trying to stop him from leaving. When I got to her, she let go of him and he stepped backwards.

"...I'm sorry," he said, looking at Emily, then at me.

123

I stepped closer to him. When I did, he ran from underneath the bridge. I went after him and Emily followed. I ran ahead and she fell behind. I tried to catch Aaron, but he was much faster and the rain was getting harder. Looking over my shoulder, I could not see Emily. I slowed down, afraid that I would lose her. Aaron disappeared and I was alone in Central Park, wondering how I had even got there.

Part Two

1

Now was a time of separation. Seven centers of the universe had formed on the island of Manhattan...and in just a sliver of Brooklyn. The fight between David and Aaron marked the unceremonious end to a group of friends that had separated long before then. Only now it was official.

My most vivid memories from the weeks after the fight are a series of daydreams which, surprisingly, occurred most often when I was with Emily. They signify not so much a desire for the return of my friends, but instead, my guilt at having been unable to stop them from harming each other. They always started underneath the bridge in Central Park. Sometimes, I arrived at the inner arch just before the fight. I tried everything I could to stop David and Aaron, but it was all in vain. They started throwing punches and I stepped between them. A fist landed against my face and the scene went black.

Other times, I arrived too late, finding Aaron hunched over David. When I tried to approach, Aaron ran into the darkness. I followed him along a winding road, but as I ran, the jungle of the park closed in. Branches and vines blocked my way. The obstacles increased as I was getting closer. At last, when I could just extend the tips of my fingers to reach his shoulder, the dream would always end.

Whenever Emily caught me spacing out, I gave a tepid smile to stop her from worrying. However, after seven years together, no halfhearted displays went unnoticed. For a while she gave me my space. But even though I pretended to feel better, she sensed I was not well. It started with the little things: uneaten dinners, missed calls, my eyes staring into space while she told me about her day. With anyone else, I would have expected annoyance, even anger. But she never said one inconsiderate word to me. I actually would have preferred it if she had gotten mad. Instead, she waited patiently, assuming time would improve my condition. Her patience is unmatched by anyone I have ever met and, in those times, it was most tiring.

Since the fight, all communication ceased within the group. Calls went unanswered and texts were ignored. *Facebook* had become an asinine and insensitive portal into the lives of those who were once so close. My job at the senator's office was trivial compared to the reality of watching my friends disappear one after another. Eventually, I found out that Lana also had fallen into a state of depression. Emily tried calling her, but she did not answer her phone. David was gone. He broke all ties with us and spent his nights doing...God only knows what.

Then there was Amanda. Something was going on between her and Aaron. My suspicions were confirmed when I learned that she had been secretly visiting him. After he ran from the bridge, Emily and I searched everywhere. We even considered phoning the police, but the next day, Emily spoke with his grandmother. She told Emily that Aaron was at her apartment. At least we knew he was safe.

And what about Hunter? As usual, he was beyond our help. Even now, I replay our scene on the stairs of his building in my head. As with many things in my past, I worry that memory colors the event with more fantasy than fact. He told me to abandon him and I listened. That much

I remember. What was harder to determine is that mysterious force which stopped me from going to see him. It was some feeling of aversion that made me put down the phone every time I tried dialing his number. Maybe I was unwilling to make the overtures to repair our friendship. Maybe I wanted him to suffer for what he did to Aaron. But even then, I think I saw the truth behind it all: reasons led to excuses, making it easier to forget.

The group was in tatters. David left us, Lana was on her own, Aaron was unreachable, and so was Amanda. Then there was Hunter, my former best friend.

Yet although their absence was painful, it alone was not what depressed me. I had resigned myself to the fact that we could never return to our Columbia days, and that was before the failed reunion. Like with old relatives, I was prepared for the death of the group and the end of my relationship with those in it. There was only one person whom I had no intention of letting go of. Now, even that wish was in jeopardy.

Only one question tortured my mind in relentless forms: *what if David is right?* During our lunch, I was appalled by his philosophy of human relationships. But now, after the seeds of his theories had grown, I wondered if I had been too quick to moralize. I considered the evidence. He predicted my friends would grow apart. He said that often the price of change is separation. I'm paraphrasing, but in so many words, that's what he said. His prophesy had come true.

He was proof of how quickly relationships end. I knew what I had with Emily was stronger than anything he ever had with Lana. We made more use of our shared time than they ever did. But that was not the point. David showed me the precariousness of love itself. I was afraid of the sudden and uncontrollable change that he believed could make a person fall in love with another. That same change was not what drove him to cheat on Lana. He was sleeping around for reasons other than love. Even still, his argument had power over me. It was not David whom I was fighting. It was the calculating logic that he used to justify his actions.

Did I have any control over whether or not I fell in love with Emily? *No* is the resounding answer. Our relationship depended on too many factors to conclude that I had any freedom of choice in loving her. Proximity, likes, dislikes, dreams, wishes: I had no control over these commonalities and neither did she. They were what brought us together. Independently, my choice to be with her had very little to do with the equation. As Shakespeare said, we were actors on a stage. We had practically no say in the props we were given, the sets upon which we walked, or the circumstances that drove us forward. The only requirement was to play our parts well.

Could I stop from falling in love with another person? Again, the answer is *no*. I could not expect to have power over love in the future, just as I had no power over it in the past. I was not afraid of committing an affair of passion. I had seen way too many contrived romance movies to doubt my loyalty and fidelity to Emily. But an affair of love? That's what made me doubt myself. Ridiculous as it might sound, I felt I would neither have the ability nor the willingness to refuse some nameless and invisible girl, if only I loved her and she loved me. I feared that no matter how much time Emily and I shared, I would abandon what we had for the guarantee of a more perfect love with another girl. I kept this fear hidden, leaving Emily to guess at the true cause of my depression.

At first, she was content to ride the waves of my unhappiness, hoping they would eventually break. After several weeks with no change in my behavior, however, she took action. I had just come home from the office. I was tired and exhausted, not because of work but because of my anxiety. She began the conversation directly, like she did with any serious subject.

"Did you hear me?" she asked while I grabbed a beer from the fridge. I had not. I was never a big drinker, but it was just one of those days.

"What's with you? You haven't been yourself. What is it?"

I put the cold can on my temple and started walking into the other room.

"Hey!" She reached out her hand and grabbed my arm. "Will, don't walk away. Talk to me."

We sat at our small kitchen table and I made up some bullshit story about problems I was having at work. I said I felt overworked, unappreciated, and that I was thinking about finding another job. Although these were all true, they were not what really upset me. Emily seemed to sense that. Instead of even pretending to believe me, she got up and went into the bedroom.

That night, I climbed into bed in one of my usual moods. I had been making a habit of staying up late in the evenings, doing nothing of real importance. Emily was already asleep on the other side of the bed. When I slipped under the covers, she stirred and rolled towards me. She stretched her arm across my chest and shifted her hips closer to mine. I felt her breath against my cheek and her lips nearly touched my ear.

"I'm sorry I walked away," she said quietly.

I put my arm under her head and brought her closer. Despite all my worries, I could not forget the rare and special happiness that I felt with her in my arms. Although I wanted to keep the moment intact, I felt it slowly slipping. It was being driven away by a creeping doubt. I tried resisting, but the more I fought, the stronger it became. Eventually, out of exhaustion and an absence of willpower, I let the moment go. I could not stop myself from asking: *how long will all of this last?* I fell asleep with a feeling of guilt and self-loathing over just how much of a jackass I was.

2

Flushing the toilet and adjusting her pajama shorts, Lana left the bathroom and entered her adjoining bedroom. It was the same room where she drove Aaron away. She threw herself on the bed and pulled the comforter over her body, leaving nothing exposed. She felt the heat of her breath and sensed the warm darkness around her. With her eyes closed, she envisioned her surroundings from memory.

Above her was the ceiling fan. To the left was the small bathroom. On the right was the bookshelf underneath a window with its blind down. Four off-white walls framed the room. Against the farthest one was a long mirror. On top of the bookshelf next to the bed, there was an alarm clock, a bottle of sleeping pills, and some other incidental items.

She recreated these things in her head. There, they had an existence that shadowed their physical counterparts. She could not recall the particular details of each object and there were many that escaped her memory. Her mental map contained only vague forms of actual things. If an image resembled its object, it was because of all the time she had spent familiarizing herself with it out of boredom. She had no real attachment to anything in that room.

Reaching from underneath the covers, Lana grabbed the bottle of sleeping pills. She struggled with the cap until it finally came off. She poured some pills into her hand. She was about to raise them to her mouth, but she had second thoughts. The trick had worked before, but this time, she was afraid of what would happen if she took any more. Reluctantly, she put the pills back inside the bottle.

It was a Saturday, the second weekend in a row Lana spent lying in bed. She sensed it would not be the last. She only ever got up to go to work, use the bathroom, or get something to eat. Even still, she constantly felt tired and had virtually no appetite. The only time Amanda bothered to check on Lana was when she needed to get her to do the chores that were piling up. Whenever Amanda came into Lana's room, she looked at her like a nanny towards a spoiled child. When she left, she made sure to close the door just loud enough to disturb whatever rest Lana had.

Usually, Lana would not eat until hours after her food was ready. By then, what was hot was lukewarm and what was cold was room temperature. When she ate, she was careless. It was tasteless to her and gave her no noticeable strength. She did not care that she had not washed her pajamas in weeks or that her bed sheets were tossed and messy. She was in an agonizing depression, feeling things that she could neither fully control nor explain.

Lana knew she was depressed, but could not tell why. She was upset at David, yes. But he was only the cause of her depression, not its explanation. The reason eluded her. She had been in relationships before, not many, but enough to claim some experience in love. Why was the end of this relationship so painful for her? She knew that, at some far-off future point, she would likely forget about David. But this knowledge only upset her more. It was like, in her current state, she had access to some hidden reality about love and heartbreak. If she were to wake next morning and dismiss all the thoughts she now had as foolish, she would be denying the truth of her feelings. So instead of wishing the pain away, she thought harder about it.

I know David's hurt me. That asshole. I know it. So why? Why can't I get over him? Maybe, if I talk to him, things will work out. But she knew even before she wished it that the wish was naïve. It was out of desperation. As if to permanently bury the thought, she recalled the events of the past: the failed reunion, her scene with Aaron, the fight. *No. Things can never be the way they were. He's gone. Who would even want him back? I have to think about what comes next...but what's next?*

Faced with this void, she felt like she was going to cry. She restrained herself immediately. Just like the thoughts that provoked them, tears were getting her nowhere.

Rolling to the corner of the mattress, she checked her phone. Like the game of recreating the room in her head, this activity gave a momentary pause to her thoughts. Letting her eyes adjust to the light of the screen, she saw that it had not changed. There were no new texts or calls. She put the phone down and rolled away, tossing the covers as she went.

Why do I bother checking it? She stared at the ceiling fan whirling above her. It creaked and teetered from the spin of the blades. *He isn't going to bother, so why should I...but what if?*

Rolling back to the corner of the bed, she picked up her phone. Nothing had changed.

I knew it.

This time, she dropped the phone over the floor. She heard it land with a soft thud. With this distraction gone, she returned to her thoughts.

She knew one man had cheated on her, while another thought he loved her. Why did she always seem to attract guys like these? Inside, she knew she could never return Aaron's love. And despite what David did, she simply could not let go of him. Even though she was hurt and completely betrayed, she was afraid that, if David walked into the room just then, begging her to come back, she would forgive him of everything. This thought mortified her.

She recalled the fight between David and Aaron. It was Amanda who told her what actually happened. She tried calling Emily to stop it, but that failed. That night, Emily had even called her back and told her where David and Aaron were. But Lana could not bring herself to go to the park. She believed her being there would only make things worse. Then, she thought harder and realized she had lost something greater than David that night.

It was more than just David she lost. It was the time she spent with him. Four years of genuine happiness were eclipsed by their breakup. A slow and drawn-out ending blackened all the good moments they shared. And the memories that, just a year ago, gave her joy now brought her sadness and regret. What was meaningful time had been turned into time wasted.

She thought of a way to salvage the time she had lost, but found no reliable answer. The only silver lining was that she could learn from the experience and let it shape her future. But that was no solace. David stole the best years of her life. Their memory was spoiled by him. In college, she believed that she and David were building something together. Each moment with him was leading to something bigger. Now, whatever they were building had been torn down. Slowly, she began to accept that no matter what outlook she took, she would never be able to recover the time she had lost.

Suddenly, her eyes widened and she became anxious.

This thought. I've had it before!

It was true. Over the last weeks, she rediscovered many old thoughts she presumed to be new. She had lost track of them. What she counted as original was usually something from a forgotten time. She wanted to exhaust a thought to some suggestion of a course of action or of a definite emotion to be felt. Often, she put a thought down when it hit some deeper pain or when she felt too tired to complete it. She tried to mark where she was and told herself she would return to it later. When she tried to resume, however, she never found her place. She was forced to retrace the thought from the beginning, following its contours until she put it down, lost it, and started again.

I'm running in circles. I'm being pathetic. I've got to get up.

She moved her legs towards the edge of the bed. As soon as they got there, she felt the momentary burst of strength fade. She slid back into bed.

Not now. Definitely not now. Later. Later...

Her thoughts fell apart.

In this onslaught of mental exertion, the only comfort Lana found was in elusive sleep. In her dreams, she abandoned the dismal present. There, the worries of life faded and were replaced by fantasy. For the past two weeks, dreams became her reality, while reality became a bleak, bare malaise.

One sanctuary her dreams always brought her was the past. It was her senior year in college. She sat in the diner alone and terribly bored. Suddenly, her friends entered and sat at her table. She started to laugh, but she could not tell why. As she laughed, her six friends joined in. Soon the whole diner was in an uproar. Different kinds of colorful desserts were brought to the table. Without forks or knives, everyone started eating. They used their hands to shovel chunks of cake into their mouths. Lana looked down and noticed she was wearing a red dress, the one from the night of her high school prom. She did not touch the dessert, afraid to spill any on her elegant dress. While her friends ate, she tried to speak to them, but they were too preoccupied by the food. She grabbed them, shook them, and tried to push the cake off of the table. Even still, they would not turn to her. Then, she woke up.

One by one, the objects in the room materialized. First came the end of the bed, then the fan, the bookshelf, the window, and the walls. When she looked down, she saw a red stain on her shirt. Looking closer, she discovered it was red frosting from a leftover cake Amanda had given her hours before. She collapsed in the bed, terrified that her once happy dreams had turned against her.

She looked at the clock on the bookshelf. It showed 12:33. Above it, she realized someone had opened the blind to the window while she slept. It was dark outside and she figured she must have been asleep for a long time.

Did I sleep the entire day? No, that's impossible. When I tried to take the pills it was dark out. Could it have been the afternoon? Oh, who the hell cares!

She threw her head onto the pillow. After a while, she felt drowsy. Before she could find sleep again, the door to the room opened. Amanda entered, carrying a glass of water.

"You were making noises," she said in a voice that did not express any real concern for her guest.

Lana motioned for the glass and Amanda handed it to her. The water was not for her and Amanda became annoyed by Lana's presumptuousness.

"I'm sorry," Lana said. "Bad dream. I'll try to go back to sleep."

"You never leave this room anymore," she said in a matter-of-fact tone. "Maybe you should think about getting some help."

"What's that supposed to mean?" Lana asked, perceiving the hint.

"Nothing. Just, try to get better."

"I am. I really am feeling better."

"Sure." As Amanda was about to leave, she stopped at the door. "By the way, don't forget your sister will be here in the morning."

"My sister?" Lana asked, confused.

"Jacqueline. You talked to her this morning and said she would be here by 9:00. You do remember, don't you?"

"Ah, yes, Jackie. I remember. Don't worry, you won't have to wake me, I'll be ready."

"Good," Amanda said dryly, leaving the room. "Good night."

"Night," Lana answered.

Lifting her hand to the alarm clock, she set it for 8:00 A.M. She fell back into bed, hoping for one happy dream before tomorrow morning's visit. She closed her eyes and, after a surprising lack of struggle, she went to sleep.

3

The next morning, Lana's sister arrived in Grand Central Station. She came on the New Haven line and, to make her train, she had to get up especially early. When she rang the buzzer to Amanda's apartment, Lana was still fast asleep.

Lana was curled in a sea of comforter and bed sheets. There was a trail of dried drool on her cheek. A hard knock came from the door, causing her to jolt from bed. She squirmed from her covers. Out of habit, she began fixing the bangs of her hair.

"Come in," she said as quickly as the knock, rubbing her eyes with her hands.

Amanda entered.

"Your sister's here," she said.

"My wah?" Lana mumbled, confused.

"Your sister! Ugh, I reminded you last night."

"Jackie!"

With speed that took Amanda by surprise, Lana sprang to the opposite side of the bed and grabbed the clock. She realized she must have slept through the alarm. Driving away the tiredness from her eyes, she focused on the face of the clock. It was already 9:00.

"Shit!"

Ignoring Amanda, she jumped out of bed and ran to the bathroom. Amanda watched. The sudden switch between exhaustion and energy supported her theory that Lana was only pretending to be depressed. While she might have been upset, her health was in no real danger. She could have gotten up any time. Amanda saw Jacqueline's visit as a meeting of two princesses who would act out some melodrama. Jacqueline could not help Lana, because in Amanda's eyes, there was nothing wrong with Lana. She left the room, annoyed that she now had to attend to two obnoxious sisters.

In the bathroom, Lana undressed and stepped into the warm shower. The water was revitalizing. She enjoyed thinking how it must have been washing away all her sleepiness and anxiety. While she ran her long hair underneath the faucet, she thought of her sister Jacqueline, who was waiting in the next room. It was Christmas when they last saw each other. Jacqueline lived in California year round, the wife of a wealthy writer who sold most of his work to Hollywood. She loved the west coast, but grew nostalgic for her childhood home. During holidays and on this trip especially, she cherished the chance to see her family that was usually so distant.

Lana turned off the water and stepped out of the shower. She turned on her Avion hairdryer and began tossing her hair with her free hand. She had forgotten the tropical smell of her expensive conditioner. As the aroma drifted through the steam filled bathroom, she thought of how good it felt to be up and moving again. Yet, when she studied her reflection in the foggy mirror, her happy mood vanished.

Just who exactly am I trying to look good for? My sister? She doesn't care. Myself? I don't care either. David?

As his name slipped from her thoughts, her depression returned.

She left the bathroom and threw on some clothes, purposefully selecting an outfit that did not quite match. She brushed her hair and put on a small amount of makeup.

Walking to the center of the room, she turned and stared into the long mirror against the wall. She did not like what she saw. Neither having the inclination to make any changes nor wishing to keep her sister waiting, she went into the living room.

The moment her sister appeared, Jacqueline jumped from the sofa and caught her in a tight hug. Jacqueline almost squeezed the air out of Lana's lungs. After spending so much time in bed, Lana's muscles were tired and achy. Since her phone call with Lana, Jacqueline knew her sister was unwell. Her first clue was the absence of the usual vitality in Lana's voice. It was like she talked to a different person. While they had not spoken of the subject, Jacqueline perceived something was wrong in Lana's world. Naturally, she suspended all her plans and went to the city to find out exactly what condition her sister was in. Judging from her first impression, she was glad she arrived when she had.

Sensing Lana's discomfort, Jacqueline eased her hug. She let her arms fall to Lana's waist, picking up her hands and holding them delicately in front of her.

"How are you!" Lana said first, not knowing what else to say. She forced her lips to smile.

"Lana!" Jacqueline said. "You look marvelous."

She put particular stress on the word *marvelous*, causing Lana some embarrassment. She knew she looked anything but marvelous and that her sister had only said so out of politeness.

"Amanda, this is my sister Jacqueline."

When Lana turned to Amanda, she heard a door open. A stranger in her mid-twenties emerged from Amanda's bedroom. She was extremely pretty and wore a lose t-shirt that fell just above the elastic of her pajamas. She smiled at Lana, staring at her comfortably before looking somewhere else. Lana smiled back, noticing that her face looked familiar. She vaguely remembered the girl, but could not recall where they had met. The girl slid past Amanda and opened the refrigerator door. She took out two pieces of bread and, turning around, she dropped them in the toaster. On her way back, she gave Amanda a soft, quick, kiss on the cheek. Amanda barely turned her head to receive it, refusing to break concentration on the orange juice she was pouring. Then, the girl left the kitchen.

Whether she was straight, lesbian, or both at times, Amanda's sexual orientation never bothered Lana. Love mattered most to her. She always respected and embraced whatever kind of relationship Amanda wanted, so long as each kind was grounded in love. But that was just it. There was no love in what Amanda did. Not even a little. And as she watched the girl disappear into Amanda's room, she wondered, like she had wondered so many times in college, how her best friend could place such little value on the physical and spiritual significance of human intimacy, or on the bright mornings that follow nights of passion.

"We've already met," Amanda said as the girl was leaving.

"Oh, right," Lana said, turning to Jacqueline. "I'm sorry I kept you waiting. I set the alarm for 8:00. I guess I must've overslept."

"Don't apologize," Jacqueline said with a diffusing smile. "I got here early anyways."

In a hurry to get on with the visit, and trying her hardest to keep up with her sister's enthusiasm, Lana crossed to the sofa. She picked up her light jacket which had been tossed there several days ago.

"What do you feel like having?" she asked, sliding the jacket over her shoulders.

"It doesn't matter to me," Jacqueline said obligingly. "You know the area best, I'll let you choose."

"We should try *Térèsa's*. It's new and it's French. I passed it a few days ago."

"Sounds perfect," Jacqueline said, walking to the

front door. "It was nice to meet you finally," she said to Amanda before leaving.

"Likewise," Amanda responded, now peeling a banana.

The two sisters left the apartment building and walked to the end of the street. The weather was gorgeous that day. The soft wind gently rustled their hair. The noise was quiet and there was very little to break the calmness of the street. A heavy set woman waddled along the sidewalk, trying to control two corgis tethered to her hand by separate leashes. The woman stumbled as the dogs swerved like fighter planes, sniffing the sidewalk with their short, tan noses. On the opposite side, a few others were out with their dogs. They hopelessly tried to check their phones or place a plastic bag over a free hand. An occasional car rolled down the street. Nearly every twenty feet, the sisters passed a thin Hawthorn tree. Some were etched with initials or hearts. The light breeze caused the leaves of the trees to sway, producing a faint ruffling. The sound was extremely tranquil and, each time the sisters passed underneath a thin green canopy, speckled with the shifting light of the sun, they were greeted by the rhythmic movement of the leaves.

Despite the serenity of the motion around her, Lana was still melancholy. Stepping outside was like entering some fake world for her. She could not abandon the thought that somehow, the display of life she witnessed was both unreal and unintelligible.

No, this isn't meant for me. I don't know this. This doesn't mean anything to me. She looked at her sister who was just then savoring the aroma of fresh coffee falling from an overhanging open window. *This life is meant for people like her, who can find meaning in it. But for me... this isn't my life.*

As this dark thought ran through Lana's mind, Jacqueline noticed the sudden change in her sister.

"Are you alright?" she asked.

"Fine," Lana answered, using the same fake smile from before. "I'm just tired."

"Well wake up sleepy. This must be the place."

When they came to the corner of the street, they saw a small café with an outdoor seating area. There was a black fence around several iron tables. The sisters approached a wooden podium and were given a table. The café was relatively busy that morning. While it had many customers, most chose to eat their food on the run as opposed to sitting down and enjoying the spectacle of New York life that plays out each morning.

Lana and Jacqueline sat at an outdoor table with an umbrella that gave excellent shade. The waitress took their drink orders: a coffee for Jacqueline and an orange juice for Lana. Given that her sister was not very talkative, Jacqueline felt obligated to start the conversation. She began with California, her husband, and some of his recent accomplishments. When she saw that Lana was disinterested, she tried to coax her out of silence by asking about the family. Truthfully, Lana did not know much about the life of her parents. She knew that they still lived in Darian and that they lived well. Her phone calls to them generally consisted of a few obligatory answers to questions about her life, followed by an awkward request for more money. When Lana thought about how long it had been since she had a genuine conversation with her parents, she felt even more depressed. Seeing this, Jacqueline became annoyed by her own lack of tact.

She was relieved when the food came. It saved her from small talk. She had ordered a light fruit salad with banana yogurt. Lana had the *brouillade de truffes*. Throughout the meal, Lana hardly touched her breakfast. Like when she was a child in a bad temper, she shifted the omelet around with her fork, tossing and poking it. Jacqueline thought better of bringing it to her attention. Eventually, she decided that to keep on pretending like nothing was wrong was impossible. At some point, she had to broach the subject of Lana's health. Seeing her opportunity, Jacqueline began.

"Is something wrong with the omelet?" she asked, cutting a small piece of cantaloupe and placing it in her mouth.

"No," Lana replied, "just not hungry."

"Lana, you have to eat something."

"Thanks for that, mom."

Who's she to tell me what to do? If she knew what I've been through. But she can't understand. She's got a husband who cares about her, a stupid home with stupid things. And I? What do I have?

"I'll eat when I'm hungry," Lana added casually, hoping to smooth over the tone of her last comment. She took a sip of her orange juice. Jacqueline pressed further.

"I only said so because you look like you haven't eaten in a while. I don't know what they feed you here in the city, but you've got to take care of yourself."

"I *can* take care of myself," Lana insisted, looking at her sister indignantly.

Jacqueline's attempt to incite Lana had worked almost too well. Lana's eyebrows furrowed in anger, causing a slight crinkle in her otherwise ski-slope perfect nose. Jacqueline knew this fearsome look of her sister's. She grew up with it. Even though it was months since they had last seen each other, she recalled the look just as vividly as if she were seven years old again.

"So are we going to keep talking about omelets or are you going to tell me what's wrong?"

"Nothing's wrong!" Lana said with hushed anger, not forgetting she was in a public place. She looked fiercely at Jacqueline, but saw that she was busy slicing several pieces of fruit on her plate. "Just drop it. Quit pestering me."

Lana picked up her fork and began scooping bits of omelet into her mouth.

"I wouldn't be pestering you if there wasn't anything to talk about," Jacqueline said, not looking at her sister, but at her own plate. "Clearly there is though. So why won't you–"

"God, why are you doing this!" Lana said, half angry, half disgusted. "What do you want? A heart-to-heart, is that it? Did you expect to take me out for a nice breakfast while I spill my guts? I didn't ask for your help. A lot of good you would do anyway. You've always been a dreamer. *Hang in there Lana! Look on the bright side Lana!* I'm sick of it. You've never understood me. Life has always been easy for you. A nice husband. A nice home. Hell, you'll probably have kids soon. Our worlds are too different. You can't understand me, you can't, you can't!"

Lana sunk into her chair. She breathed heavily and her eyes were red. Her face was flush. She was amazed by what she had said. Although she knew how selfish and hurtful it was, she did not care. If only for an instant, she wanted to release everything she had endured for the past months.

Jacqueline put her fork and knife down and looked at her sister. After calming herself, Lana saw Jacqueline's face. She felt a wave of guilt. She turned her head to the side and, like a frightened criminal, was scared to see the face of the person she just attacked. She brought her hand to her face to cover the tears in her eyes. Jacqueline reached across the table and grabbed Lana's hand. Gently, she brought it down to the cold metal. Jacqueline knew her sister had been hurt. As of that moment, she did not know the details. But the details were not important. After several moments, Lana felt strong enough to remove her hand from Jacqueline's. For a while they were silent.

"Jackie," Lana said, "…I'm sorry."

Lana explained everything to Jacqueline. She in-

145

cluded every detail no matter how small. She took her through the times she and David shared at college. She told her about the group. Then, she said how devastating this past year had been, how her relationship had simply collapsed. Aaron was mentioned, as was the guilt she now felt because of him. She explained that she was to blame for the fight between him and David. She spoke about Amanda and how well she had treated her, when all she wanted was to sleep and forget. Jacqueline listened, letting Lana continue without interruption. At last, when Lana finished, Jacqueline sat silently. She knew the entirety of Lana's depression came down to a single question. She stopped herself, thinking perhaps it would be best to leave the question unasked. When she looked at her sister's guilt stricken face, however, she knew she had no choice.

"Do you still love him?" Jacqueline asked.

Lana expected this. She had been trying to avoid it all this time. It was what kept her restless ever since she found out about his betrayal. There was no avoiding the question and now, with her sister by her side, she answered it.

"I don't," she said. Only afterwards did she feel the weight of her answer. "Not any more. But…"

"Go on," Jacqueline encouraged.

"Without him, what does it all mean? For what seems like an eternity, we've been together. Five years is nothing compared to a life-time, sure. But sitting here, remembering all the happiness we shared, those five years *were* a life-time. And now…that time is gone."

"Lana–"

"And what am I supposed to do now? How do I give meaning to what's meaningless? It's impossible. It hasn't even been three weeks, but I know this feeling will never leave me. It hurts so much, Jackie."

Jacqueline stared into the street, concentrating. Feeling there was still more to say, Lana went on.

146

"If I could just make him care somehow. If only he cared about me as much as I do for him…no, I could settle for less. If his love was just a fraction of what I gave him, then he would know how much he hurt me. But he doesn't care. And he doesn't regret it either!" A flash of anger came over her. "You know, I'd forgive him if he came back to me, begging on the ground. I'd hate myself, but I would do it. But will he ever come back? No. He won't. And don't I deserve better than him? Don't I deserve to be loved like everyone else? That's what hurts the most. It's like the David I knew was a complete lie. Like our history means nothing now. To cheat on me. Not just to cheat, but to not even speak to me. To ignore my existence as if I were just…nothing!"

Lana leaned back in her chair, trying to catch her breath.

"Do you know what the definition of insanity is?" she asked abruptly.

Jacqueline raised her eyebrows. "I suppose it depends on the one who's asking," she replied.

"That's not funny," Lana warned. "Insanity is: *doing the same thing over and over and expecting different results*. Well, lock me up, because I must be the most insane girl there is. David and I had our ups and downs in college. We weren't perfect. But whenever we did fight, he always came back to me and I always forgave him. You see! Now that's insanity. Because each time, I expected something different. I expected change. And for the first time, I see that I'm the crazy one. I wanted him to be something he could never be. I had an image of him, I think, on a pedestal in my mind. Every time he came back, I thought he was becoming more like that image. But I was wrong. And it was wrong of me to want to change him. Either love the man for who he is or else move on. But I can't move on!"

Jacqueline thought of saying something, but Lana continued.

"I wish I could hurt him somehow," she said darkly. "At least then he would be thinking about me. But I can't hurt him. I have no power over him. Listen to me, I'm crazy!"

Lana could not hold back. She brought her hands to her face and turned away, trying not to show her tears.

"Stop it!" Jacqueline said angrily. Lana looked at her, scared and surprised. "This isn't you. This was never you. You're crazy. But not for the reasons you think. You're crazy to blame yourself for giving him another chance, for thinking he would better himself. Everyone has flaws, but that doesn't mean we have to stand by and accept them blindly, especially the flaws that can't be fixed."

"So what then?" Lana asked spitefully. "Should I just go back to David and forgive him?"

"No!" Jacqueline answered. "Aren't you listening? Whatever problems this David kid's got, they run deeper than you. What I'm saying is: it isn't your fault for wanting to make him a better man. But this guy…he's got some kind of issue that's beyond your help."

Lana thought. She stared at the remains of her half eaten omelet. Then, she looked at her sister.

"You would think we've made progress in the last one hundred years, but everything's still the same. To David, I was only as good as what I gave him: stability, comfort, sex. But when I stopped giving, he stopped caring. I thought we were settling down. I thought, finally, here is a guy I can be myself with, someone who can put aside all that fake bullshit and really see me. But men only see what they *want* to see in us, you know? David, Aaron: it makes no difference. I give them the body and they fill in the rest. They're looking for their own ideal, just like I did. I thought David was different, but in the end, I was wrong. Don't you get it? Whatever girl they need in the moment, that's what they expect us to be. Rich girl, poor girl, pretty girl, sad girl: whatever suits them best. When will I find a guy who loves *me* for me?"

Jacqueline lifted her coffee above the table.

"Cheers to you and Eve both."

"You're hilarious," Lana said, taking a sip of her orange juice.

"Look," said Jacqueline, "whatever happens to you and your friends, and especially this David, it won't change the past. That much is true. I know you're hurting now, but believe me, things will get better soon. Just don't let these experiences make you give up on love, or friendship, for that matter. And if you decide that you would be better off going separate ways, never seeing him again, remember, whatever you do…don't hate him for it. No matter how much he deserves it, don't hate him for what he's done. It might make you feel better at first, but in the end, it will only hurt you more…understand?"

Truthfully, Lana only understood half of what her sister said. She knew that she should not allow this experience to ruin her ability to love or care for others. This she wholeheartedly rejected. But the part about not hating David she didn't get. It all seemed so patronizing and Lana wondered why her sister had even bothered to say it at all. Despite being confused and tired, she nodded at Jacqueline, giving her a look that seemed to say she understood everything.

Eventually, they left the café and returned to Amanda's apartment. On their way back, Lana started to feel better. While she talked with her sister, life became palatable again. She could not explain how, but at some point between breakfast and the walk home, a new kind of endurance had taken hold of her. She was not happy, that much she knew.

Even if I don't have happiness, I can still go on. That, in the end, has to be worth at least something.

Although she was decidedly unhappy, her health improved and her depression was over. That was enough for both sisters. As they said goodbye to one another, they looked forward to a time when they would see each other again. For Lana, that time meant a great deal. It signified a distant checkpoint on a new and unfamiliar road. She knew she would reach it. But as for what kind of person she would find there, she could only hope and move forward.

4

Shortly after Lana and Jacqueline left for breakfast, Amanda picked up her designer purse and started towards the door. As she was turning the knob, she heard a voice.

"Where are you going?" It was the same girl from before. She had put on jeans and a navy blazer. "You haven't finished breakfast."

Amanda turned and faced her. "I'm going shopping," she said. "I'll be back in an hour."

"Must be a long way away," the girl said disappointedly. "What are you doing tonight?"

"Tonight?" Amanda thought. She looked down and smiled. "Tonight I've got plans."

The girl looked at her, confused. "Well, text me if anything changes."

"I will," she said. She left the apartment, leaving the girl alone.

Amanda stepped out of her building and began her usual route towards the C-line. When she got to the stairs of the station, she saw a homeless man lying on the ground by the green stairs. On top of him was a bull dog, brown spotted, lying with its head on its master's stomach. By the dog's mouth was a collection bowl and a cardboard sign written in black sharpie.

Reaching into her purse, Amanda pulled out a twenty dollar bill. She dropped it into the plastic bowl.

The dog's eyes looked up at her.

"Oh, God bless you!" the man said, tipping the rim of an imaginary hat.

"Make sure you save some for him," Amanda said, looking at the dog.

"Always," the man said. "I always do."

Amanda left the duo behind and went down into the station.

She did not believe in true acts of altruism. Behind every act is an ego, she thought. Anyone that insisted they were acting selflessly, she either considered naïve or idiotic. In college, she avoided volunteer work of any kind. Although her generosity was rare, she always gave much. She also gave spontaneously. She didn't do it for the sake of the recipient. Actually, she could have cared less what twenty dollars meant to the homeless man. She did it only to prove to herself that she was not as rotten as, deep down, she sensed she was. She gave to compensate for all of her past and future faults. Incidentally, she also had a soft spot for dogs.

When the train arrived, she stood to the side to let the people off. She got on and went to the middle of the car. Holding onto the metal handrail, she looked at her reflection in the window. It was all that separated her from the tunnel wall. The train started to move. She looked at her reflection closer, studying it. Tilting her head, her face fell to its most flattering angle. The slight ridge in her nose disappeared, along with several other imperfections.

Her mother always told her that a person's beauty lies in their peculiarities. Amanda never believed her mother. She knew she was attractive and that, if she could just make some minor changes, her looks would achieve perfection. She turned her head from one side to the other, keeping the angle just right. She followed the eyes of the near-perfect image. Having had enough, she looked away.

At the next stop, a woman with a stroller got off

and Amanda took her seat. Pretty soon, she got bored. She took out her phone, put her ear buds in, and started listening to some music. She skipped the first song. Once the second one came on, she started to relax. She tapped her foot in sync with the base line and let her thoughts wander. Like always, her mind quickly turned to Aaron. He was the one waiting for her at the end of the tunnel.

As far as she could recall, she had never wanted anything in her life as badly as she wanted him. If there was something else, she had forgotten it years ago. Her desire for him had not happened overnight. It took time to grow, gradually becoming more and more aching. At a certain point, it crossed a threshold. It was a time when another atom of want caused her desire to overflow. From then on, she could never contain it. The only solution she saw was to possess him and, by possessing him, put an end to her longing.

Everyone she had been with before Aaron meant nothing. Her memories of them were murky and forgettable. Everyone since she found Aaron was merely a substitute for him. They only gave her a fraction of the sensations she imagined that Aaron would give her. People tried to love her, but simply found they could not. She would not let them in. While her body was open to everyone, her heart only wanted one person. She burned to share her life with him. And once she had him, she would never share him at all. To be with him was enough. To occupy the same space was a victory.

In her recent visits with Aaron, she admitted that things were not exactly ideal. Since the fight, he had become more violent and lost than ever. He stayed in his room practically all day, brooding and moping. He felt he had to avenge himself after what David did. But it always happened that, after one of his tantrums or flashes of anger, he felt that much more distant from Lana. No matter how many times he begged Fate to intervene, he saw no scenario that brought him and her together. Amanda tried to get his mind away from Lana, but she had no effect on him.

As for Lana, Amanda was waiting for the day when she could get her to leave the apartment. Despite the extra cash from her rent, Amanda could not stand having her around, especially since her depression started. Only one thing stopped her from going back to the apartment and kicking Lana out right then. She was practically the only thing that tied Amanda to Aaron. Without her connection to Lana, Aaron had no reason to see Amanda. Even now, he only accepted her visits to get the latest information in Lana's life. Amanda knew that, before she could get rid of Lana, she had to find some way of breaking Aaron's obsession over her.

Amanda was not bothered by Aaron's indifference to her company. She accepted her role, hoping that soon Aaron would come around and reciprocate her desire. Men like him need time, she always said to herself. Once he was over Lana, she was certain his affection would pour out.

I've thought a lot about Amanda's fixation with Aaron. I've tried to trace the calculating logic that drove her to obsess over him with such blind conviction. Although I've tried many times, I have never understood her rationale. What made her think that, by throwing herself blindly at Aaron, she could win his love? For as much as she obsessed over him, she hardly even knew him at all.

He was only an idea to her. Besides some morsels of genuine conversations, she had no real understanding of what he was actually like. His favorite plays, his greatest hopes, his most secret fears: she knew none of these things. To compensate for these gaps, she filled them with her imagination. She never considered that, in her attempt to win him over, she would change him for the worse. And would their union give her the satisfaction she so desperately craved? Maybe for a while. Over time though, not even the real Aaron could help the emptiness she was trying to fill.

At Fulton Street, she got off the train. Within ten minutes, she was inside Aaron's building. She stepped into the wood paneled elevator that had become so familiar to her in the past few days. She got off at the seventh floor. After a short walk along the right-hand corridor, she arrived at Aaron's door. She gave three short knocks. After no more than fifteen seconds, Aaron emerged.

"You have to be quiet," he said in a low voice. "My grandmother is sleeping."

Amanda walked into the living room and tossed her purse on an armchair. When it landed, it hit the tail of Aaron's sleeping cat. The cat hissed. It jumped from the armrest, nearly hitting Amanda's face. She flew backwards. Drawing in several sharp breaths, she sneezed. Both Aaron and the cat turned and gave her an angry look.

"Sorry," she said, wiping her mouth with the sleeve of her shirt.

Aaron walked slowly into the adjacent bedroom.

She followed him into the room, closing the door softly. Now they were alone. Aaron sat on the edge of his bed, chest bowed. He leaned his elbow on his knee, holding the weight of his head. He pressed his forehead into the palm of his hand, massaging his temples with his fingers. Amanda did not know whether to approach him or to stay put. After a minute of silence, she took several cautious steps forward. Placing her hand on his shoulder, she sat beside him. Her gesture went unacknowledged. Aaron kept his head lowered to the floor. Amanda was stunned by his coldness. For a moment, she even thought that her attempt to win his love had decidedly failed. But once Aaron tilted his head towards her hand, allowing her to feel the softness of his hair, she knew her goal was still within reach.

"How do you feel?" she asked softly. She ran her narrow fingers through his hair.

"How I always feel," he answered.

Amanda playfully twirled the locks of his hair, testing how far she could go. Soon, Aaron turned his head away. She pulled her hand back and placed it on her lap, like a child caught reaching for candy. She studied the side of his face. She tried to anticipate his next move.

Aaron stood up. With his long powerful legs, he began pacing around the bedroom. Like the charged atmosphere before a storm, Amanda sensed his anger. She looked around at the numerous bedroom objects strewn across the carpet. They were the remnants of one of his previous fits of anger. She saw the look on his face as he tried to keep calm. Like a loaded gun, all Amanda needed to do was apply a little pressure.

"I can't imagine how you must be feeling," she said with hidden satisfaction.

Fire.

"I can't imagine you would," he said scornfully. He held his hands up to his face, as if looking for fresh wounds. "What can I do now? What's left for me? I've failed. I couldn't stand up to him. When the time came for me to be strong, all I could do was…"

He felt hot tears seething in his eyes.

"All I could do was lose!"

He slammed his fist on the wooden table against the wall. Several objects, including a packet of gum, some pens, and his wrist watch, jumped in the air. A loud crash filled the room. The sound reverberated until everything was still again.

He shoved his hands into his pockets. Amanda knew he was afraid of himself. He was afraid of the new-found rage that caused him to swear and strike. He was terrified by the violent tendencies that had been happening more and more often. With every fit, a red haze blanketed his mind. It caused him to forget who he was and even the source of his anger. He continued to walk circles around the room. His head faced the floor. Amanda rose from the bed and walked to him. She stopped in front of him. He looked at her, confused.

"I can't stand to see you this way all because of *her*," she said.

When she mentioned *her*, Aaron's face twisted in visible agony. He could not keep Lana out of his head. Shame and disappointment weighed down on him. Kneeling to the floor, he sat on his hams and lowered his head.

"Don't talk about her," he said, looking at the ground. "I failed her, don't you get it? Everything is ruined. She hates me. If I go to her, she'll look at me like I was the one who hurt her!"

This particular thought was especially painful for Aaron: the idea that, with each outburst, he somehow grew more capable of hurting Lana. Their scene in Amanda's apartment frightened him. He tried to repress the memory as best as he could, but the image of her in bed, arms back, hair across her face, gave him a kind of shame that he could not exactly describe. He preferred not to think about what had happened. He was afraid to probe too deeply into his mind.

"Tell me what to do," he said after a short pause, looking up into Amanda's face.

It was the first time he reached out to her. She was surprised, having grown accustomed to only his rage. She smiled inwardly, savoring the moment as the one where she finally gained ground in the battle for his heart.

"There is something I've thought of," she said softly, baiting Aaron.

"Did you talk to her?" he asked desperately.

"No, she doesn't want to talk to anyone. That won't work. But there's another way."

"What is it?" he begged. "You aren't making any sense!"

"Calm down. There's a way to make all this trouble go away, everything that's happened up until now, all of it, *un mot*, gone."

"Amanda!" he yelled, losing his patience.

"Two weeks from now," she began, "it will be Lana's birthday. I've been toying with the idea of throwing her a party. Seeing you like this, I'm convinced I should."

"A party? What does that have anything to do with me? That's when she should be the happiest. Why would she want to see me?"

"I can't tell you that yet. The only thing that matters is that you come to the party. If I told you the reason, you'd just get worked up over it. Then, the plan would fall through. Just make sure you come to the party."

Aaron looked at her completely confused. He could not tell if she was planning some kind of cruel trick or if she truly had a way of bringing him and Lana together. Amanda read the doubt on his face.

"Look," she said plainly, "you're just going to have to trust me. If you want to see her again, come to the party. There, everything will work out fine. But it won't work if you don't trust me. You do trust me, don't you?"

She crouched to the floor, bringing her face level with his. Aaron stared at her apprehensively.

"I do," he said at last.

"Good," she smiled, standing up. She reached out her arm for him to take. "I'll let you know the details later on. It will be at my place."

"One more thing," Aaron added, looking at her hand.

"What is it?"

"Will and Emily have to be there."

She thought for a moment.

"No."

"If they don't go, I don't go," he said.

She thought again.

"Fine. Just make sure you wear something nice." She bent down, grabbed his hand, and started to help him up.

"You really think it will work?" he asked.

"Without a doubt. Now get some rest."

Pretending to lift him, she enjoyed every muscle of his body she managed to touch. He brushed her away and walked to the bed.

"I have to trust you," he said pensively, sitting down. "I have no choice. I just need a chance to speak with her. That's all. Just a chance to explain myself. Please, whatever it is…make it work."

"I promise," she said. Her look did not altogether reassure him.

Amanda pressed Aaron's hand warmly and gave him a soft kiss on the cheek. The kiss took him by surprise. He suddenly recalled the previous kiss she had given him during his last visit to her apartment. He had somehow forgotten it. He was going to say something to her, but when he looked up, he realized it was too late. She was already at the door to the bedroom. He lay back down on the bed. He closed his eyes.

"Hey," Amanda called from the door. He thought she had already left.

"What?" Aaron asked, lifting his head.

"What are you doing tonight?"

5

"Are you even listening to me?" asked the voice of Tasha Thomson.

"Huh?" David uttered, lifting his eyes to her soft brown face. He had been looking across the red restaurant, staring into space.

"I asked if you were listening to me," Tasha repeated.

"Haven't missed a word, love."

"Sure. Anyway, I was just…"

Tasha went on to tell some funny story that happened to her while performing in the New York Ballet. While she spoke, David studied her. He was deaf to the words that flowed from her pink lips. He tried to recall the subject that had occupied his mind before she interrupted him, but the longer he looked at her striking body, the more he felt the strand of memory disappearing. At last, it faded completely.

His date wore a shade of silver eyeliner that showed-off her deep brown eyes. Her tiny earrings were also silver. They worked well with the blush on her round cheeks, like pearls on the tongue of an oyster. Her hair was pulled back in a tight ponytail, accentuating her slender neck. As David leisurely finished his tour, he tuned into the conversation. She was in the middle of her story, raving about some distant friend. The sound of her voice, while pleasing in moderation, was spoiled by excessive talking. Losing interest in her story, David went back to examining her body, until that became boring too.

His eyes lowered to his half eaten filet mignon. It was steeped in red juice, with strands of parsley pushed to the corner of the plate. He prepared to take another cut with his knife. Before he could sink the tip of the blade into the meat, a tiny fly landed in the red pool covering the bottom of the dish. With his fork, David brushed the fly away. It spiraled around the plate, eventually flying past his ear and away from the table. He returned to the meat. He tore a piece from the whole and guided it into his mouth. The cut was medium rare, just how he liked it. To prevent his date from discovering yet again that he was not paying attention, he occasionally threw in a gruff *yup* or *huh* into the conversation. It took him only several grunts to realize he should probably say more.

"That's interesting," he dropped in the middle of one of Tasha's sentences.

She did not notice David's absent mindedness. She went on talking in her smooth, flute like timbre, leaving his mind free to wander.

Although David admitted there was something truly captivating about this ruby of a girl, he could not stand how she betrayed her voice with endless chatter. Whenever he tried to join the discussion, he managed to get out one, maybe two sentences before Tasha ran him over with words. He learned to speak only when absolutely necessary, that is, when awkward silence threatened to spoil the evening. After some thought, he decided he really did not mind that his date was so talkative. All it meant was that the use of flattery and prolific compliments was no longer necessary. His only requirement was to sit and smile as Tasha went on and on. He checked his phone periodically, counting the minutes until they would be alone in her apartment. He felt himself slowly drifting into the familiar fantasy of being alone with a beautiful girl. Then, he caught himself before fantasizing too much.

It'll have to wait. Right now, I have to endure this dinner for a little longer...oh no, she's spotted me!

"David!" Tasha lashed out, more annoyed than last time.

"I'm listening, I'm listening! Your friend rolled his ankle and couldn't perform that night. Go on."

By sheer luck, he avoided yet another regrettable scene. As she went on with her story, David cautiously let his eyes wander, trying to alleviate his boredom.

Across the room, he saw a blonde girl about his age eating a salad. She delicately skewered the green leaves with her fork, raising them to her lips and sliding her white teeth along the four tines until at last, she closed her mouth with poise. Finishing her bite, she ran her tongue along the skin of her top row of teeth. Her mouth curved into a full smile and her eyes shifted effortlessly from one guest to another. David sat admiring this woman from across the room. He wondered what secrets she kept behind that unassuming smile. Before Tasha could suspect anything, he let out some *uhuhs*, reassuring her that she held his attention. Seeing he had bought himself more time, he continued to look around.

He admired the flowers that were placed on each table. The soft flicker of candle light illuminated their petals in a very poetic way, he thought. An expensive carpet covered the floor. It had rich designs that added a level of depth to the room. Two potted ferns flanked the entrance of the restaurant and on the ceiling were several small chandeliers. The place was more expensive than some of David's other reliable evening establishments. However, as he checked Tasha one more time, he decided that the fruits of the night would be worth the extra cash.

Since his night in Central Park, David had seen many of his usual girls. They were a welcomed distraction from the frustrating memories of his past, memories he hoped to erase soon. The main reason he had accepted Aaron's challenge was out of principle. He refused to walk away from a fight. Aaron had proposed it, not him. To decline would have been an admission of weakness, a violation of one of his basic life codes.

That the fight was carried out for Lana's sake was irrelevant. He had no intention of going back to her. Although he had beaten Aaron very badly, it was not out of any feelings of jealousy or spite. In fact, he did not care either way if Aaron loved Lana. To him, Aaron's act signified the ridiculous wish of a desperate boy. At one time, he admired Aaron for his overwhelming natural strength and resolute character. From the moment they first met in their Columbia dorm room, David sensed Aaron was a man of principle. However, when he learned just exactly what that principle was, he began disliking him more and more. He had no tolerance for misguided notions like honor. To fight for something so intangible amounted to a pointless battle. From what he had seen recently, it also clouded Aaron's judgment. It made him weak and vulnerable. So what use did David have for such a dated concept?

He inspected the long cut on his hand from Aaron's watch. It made him feel sheer indignation for his former friend. He spurned the thought that a weak kid like Aaron had wounded him, even if the wound was accidental. With his opposite hand, he ran his index finger along the fresh white skin that had formed over the cut. Then, he turned his palm over. He could not stand to be reminded of the mark left by a love-struck fool.

As for the complete termination of his relationship with Lana, he felt no remorse whatsoever. While dissatisfied by the tone of their breakup, he was not responsible. He saw other women because the one he had could not satisfy him as he deserved. He met all the expected requirements of the breakup and had even tried to let her down gently by simply easing out of her life. Yes, once he may have been contented by a stable relationship with Lana. Perhaps, on some delirious nights, he had even imagined sharing a future with her. But those thoughts were from a mind far more naïve. Whatever possessed him to want a committed relationship, it was gone. And while he may very well lose his job at the law-firm due to his severed relationship with Lana and, consequently, her father, he remained unphased. He could easily find someplace else to work while he finished his law degree.

As for the loss of his friends, he could easily make new ones. Maybe, given time, he would grow beyond the need for friendship. Even in the company of Columbia students, he always imagined himself on some higher plane. His classmates, including his closest friends, could never match his intellectual caliber. Of course they could not understand why he did what he had done. They were not burdened by the weight of a superior intellect. And just consider the lives of history's most distinguished men. They did not achieve immortality by settling for mediocrity, that's for sure. They climbed ever higher, with one eye on the present and the other on the future. And how many would-be stars had been extinguished by a quiet life with a regrettable spouse? That's the real trick to life. Treat the present like quicksand. Step lightly. Avoid the step that stops you in your tracks. Yes, all was truly for the best. He would exist independently from everyone else, deriving pleasure the only way he knew how.

The check came. As usual, David paid. He ushered Tasha out the door, slipping her black jacket over her smooth dark shoulders. Unwilling to walk on a full stomach, the two shared a taxi back to her apartment. For David, that's when the real evening began. He had his way, just like with all the others. He said all the right words and made no slips. Tasha was overwhelmed by the sense of mystery in him. She hoped to decipher the riddle of David's soul, to know the complexities of his character and, in knowing them, to prove herself worthy of his love. She, like many others, realized too late that there was no profound enigma. There was no key to unlocking his compassion. It was all a charade he had been carrying on for years. He never changed, because the disguise always worked. And as he made love to Tasha in the high New York City apartment, he was satisfied once more.

6

Hours later, David lay awake in bed. He had one arm around Tasha who slept at his side. They were underneath a large comforter. Despite several unsuccessful attempts to shift to the left, David could not move without waking her. He looked for his phone and realized he had placed it on the bedside table. Extending his arm as far as it would go, he tried to reach it. Tasha kept his other arm pinned underneath her head. Eventually, he gave up. With nothing else to keep his mind occupied, he looked around the apartment. He started to wonder how a dancer like Tasha could afford such an expensive place.

First of all, the apartment was just off of 36th and Broadway. Then, there was the interior, decorated with fine furniture and artwork. The walls were light tan, with white trim along the corner moldings. The floor was solid black oak, covered by a white area rug. On the opposite wall facing the bed, there was an electric fireplace with a marble boarder. Two thick columns separated the bedroom from the rest of the apartment. Between them was a wooden beam with curtains suspended from metallic loops. The curtains were purple and, when hit by the light of the moon, they doused the nearby walls with the same color.

On the mantle above the fireplace were three antique African masks. Each was painted in a different earthy hue and their mouths gaped in grim expressions. On the left wall was a knotted walking stick. It was bent and soft like a piece of drift wood. Above all the other pieces, David admired the solid elephant tusk that stood alone in the corner of the bedroom. The tusk was extremely old and its yellow ivory was engraved with scenes from some old story from African folklore. The bottom of the tusk was covered in a rim of silver that was also engraved with markings. Although it was not to his taste, David appreciated Tasha's little art collection.

She really is a gem. If only she didn't talk so much!

Shortly after David finished scanning the apartment, his stomach became uneasy. He slipped his arm out from underneath Tasha's head and placed his hand on his stomach. The feeling caused him to roll over in pain. Sliding out from underneath the cloud-like comforter, he hurried to the bathroom. When he returned, he found Tasha sitting up in bed, looking at him with her rich, silver-rimmed eyes. She smiled, yawned, and then stretched her arms in the air like a cat.

"Are you feeling alright?" she asked, admiring his muscles. She liked his sculpted stomach, following the *V* of his lower abs until the rim of his underwear blocked her view.

"Just felt a little queasy," he answered casually, running his hands through his hair. "I feel better though."

"Good," she said. "Come back to bed."

David did as commanded. Settling under the sheets, he was surprised by the serenity of Tasha's voice. She had said very little, but there was an air of calmness to her body, suggesting that she too savored the stillness of the evening. David was pleased by the change. He thought how, if only she were like this during the day, she might be more bearable.

"Where would you like to have breakfast tomorrow?" she asked unexpectedly. "There are so many good places to eat in the area, you can't go wrong. It's your choice, I insist."

David rescinded his previous thought. Her presumption annoyed him very much, especially since he already told her he would not be staying for breakfast. Of course, he had nowhere to be. He had purposefully told her during dinner so she could not refuse to spend the night with him. But it was the principle of the matter. To avoid a scene, he kept his casual tone.

"I told you, I can't stay for breakfast, I have class in the morning."

"You never told me that," Tasha responded, sitting up straight with her back parallel to the headboard.

"I did to," David insisted. "I said so at dinner."

Seeing that Tasha was unconvinced, he moved closer and began slowly running his fingers along her arm.

"Please don't be angry," he said playfully. He looked up to gage Tasha's reaction. "I don't want to leave you. I wish I could stay, but if I miss any more tort classes, I'll fail the course. Don't be angry." He touched his lips to her brown skin. When he kissed her, he felt the tiny hairs on her arm stand on edge. "I didn't think. I thought I told you, but I must have forgotten. Is there anything I can do to make you forgive me?"

He looked into Tasha's strong face. Desperately, uselessly, she tried to keep her austere expression. As he moved further up her arm, her resolve became weaker and weaker. She collapsed her head to the pillow. With each kiss, she forgot her anger.

"This is a start," she said, eyes closed. She smiled as he tickled her neck with kisses.

Eventually, she brought David's lips to hers. She held him tightly. Once more, Tasha let go. Once more, David was satisfied.

It was later that night. While Tasha slept on her side of the bed, David was still awake. His mind was restless, just like when he slept with Carrie. This time, his discomfort was increased by the churning and rumbling of his stomach. He rolled to the left, then to the right. He curled his knees to his chest, then lay flat on his back. He heard his grumbling stomach, bubbling like boiling water. He pressed a pillow against his front, trying to smother the feeling.

Suddenly, he heard a sharp noise dart past his ear. He turned his head in the darkness, trying to see the source of the noise. Moments later, the sound came again. It was louder and closer than before. He grabbed his ear and started to pull. He began swatting in the air, trying to drive the sound away. For a second, it disappeared. Lowering his guard, he returned his attention to the pain in his stomach. Just as he repositioned his pillow underneath his head, the sound returned.

Soon, he felt something crawling on the lobe of his ear. He realized it must have been a small fly. He swatted his ear again and it flew away. It was persistent though. As soon as David dropped his hands, it resettled on his ear. He could only hear the fly, having to guess its proximity from the buzzing of its wings. Each time it landed, David swatted ferociously in the darkness, hoping to kill it. His efforts were in vain. He stuffed his head between two pillows. Even still, he heard the fly circling overhead, waiting for him to reappear.

It was impossible to destroy it. He crawled further inside the covers, hoping it would eventually leave him alone. He closed his eyes and tried not to focus on the fly or on his miserable cramps. Eventually, he felt the pain in his stomach start to go away. Running his hand along the tight muscles of his abdomen, he was amazed at how quickly the feeling had vanished. He lifted his head out from underneath the comforter and, to his further surprise, the fly was gone. He rubbed his ears once, then twice, checking to see if it had really vanished. He stopped moving completely, listening in the dark. Some time passed and the room held its quiet stillness. When David was sure that the fly had left, he relaxed his head onto the pillow. He took several cleansing breaths. Closing his eyes, he fell asleep.

Moments later, he was awakened by the return of the fly. It swirled around his head in fast circles, landing on the rim of his left ear and crawling on its folds. He tried to slap the fly away, but he could not hit it. Sitting up, he shook his head to the side. The fly would not come off. He looked over to Tasha and saw she was still asleep. He tried to wake her, but the buzzing of the fly got louder and he clasped his hands over his ears.

He felt everything. The fly's six legs moved in spurts of rapid energy. Its body ran over his ear, zigzagging until suddenly it stopped. David was still, thinking that the fly was finished. Then, he felt it begin to crawl through his ear. Its wiry legs travelled deeper inside him. He tried turning his head to drive it out. The fly scrambled in his skull. Its buzzing shook his bones.

The fly droned inside him, scampering through the passageways of his head until it reached his mouth. He felt it land on his tongue and tasted its putrid body. The fly ran down his throat. It cut through his chest and into the flesh of his shoulder. It traveled through the shoulder and down the entire length of his arm. He saw it crawling underneath his skin, passing through blood and sinew. He felt it stepping on the tissue of his muscles, pausing periodically to take small, fierce bites with its sharp mandibles. The fly gnawed through the column of his arm, running along his veins and past his wrist. It crunched through the thick jungle of meat and gore. It came to the palm of David's hand. It stopped underneath the cut of Aaron's watch.

The fly pushed against the line of fresh skin. It ripped through each layer of flesh. David tried to scream for help, but he could not make a sound. It drove harder and harder against the underside of the wound, beating its wings in heavy strokes. Under the bubble of skin, the fly shook and writhed. Finally, it burst free. It broke from a thin crevasse in the cut. As it crawled out, its red eyes stared murderously into David's. He looked helplessly at the fly. Fighting to regain control of his body, his eyes opened wide and he let out a piercing scream.

David jolted up in bed. He held his hand tightly to his chest. His heart raced and he realized it was a dream. He had a cold sweat and he breathed rapidly. Tasha, who screamed herself, sprang from the bed and stared wild eyed. He brought his palm closer to his face and inspected Aaron's cut. It was just as it had been hours before. There was no break or tear.

"Are you alright?" Tasha asked breathlessly.

David could not hear her. He was fixated on his hand. Before he realized it, the pain in his stomach returned. He became extremely nauseated. Jumping from the bed, he frantically gathered his clothes that were scattered around the room. He fumbled with his socks and struggled with his pants.

Just then, a sound came from the front of the apartment. Both David and Tasha stopped what they were doing and looked in the direction of the noise. They heard a door close and a light came on in the kitchen. David looked to Tasha, who was still staring ahead.

"Fuck," she whispered.

Suddenly, the pain in David's stomach spiked. He groaned, bending over and grasping his front. There was the sound of footsteps approaching the bedroom.

"Hide!" Tasha said desperately, "you've got to hide! He isn't supposed to be back."

"Wha?" David slurred, looking up at her. Before Tasha could say it again, a man entered the bedroom. He stopped in-between the two white columns.

"What the fuck is this?" the man asked. He wore white pants with a tight black Henley shirt. He looked at

171

David. "Who the hell are you?"

"I-I'm," David stuttered, "I'm leaving."

"And I'm kicking your ass! Get the hell away from my wife!"

"Sam, don't!" Tasha yelled.

"You're married?" David asked, shocked and confused. He looked at Tasha as if he actually expected an answer. Before she could say anything, the man lunged at David. Grabbing his shirt from the floor, David rolled over the bed. He ran out of the bedroom and opened the main door of the apartment. He looked back and saw he was not being followed. Running into the hallway, he pressed the elevator button as quickly as he could. After a few agonizing seconds, it came and he stepped inside.

7

David ran out of Tasha's building faster than he had ever left a place before. On the sidewalk, he groped the rough wall next to the entrance to keep from falling. He opened his mouth once, then twice, trying to force the foulness inside him to come up. When that failed, he doubled over. He clutched his belly and cursed the pain. With his head bent forward, he looked at his feet. He realized he had forgotten his shoes.

"Damn it!"

Staggering from the side of the building to the corner of 36th and Broadway, he saw there were still many people in the street. Rounding the corner, he was struck by the lights and sounds of the city. Broadway was awake—the pulsing artery of New York.

What are they all doing? It's too late for any shows to be getting out and the restaurants are closed by now, aren't they? Pah!

He spit onto the concrete, as if spitting into every face that blocked his way. The flash of streetlights and the noise of the cars caused the pain in his stomach to increase. Stumbling up Broadway, he kept close to the glass storefronts. He used his right arm to propel his body along the buildings. Periodically, he caught his reflection in the glass. The sight only made him feel worse. Fumbling to the curb, he waved his arms desperately, trying to flag down a taxi. After several unsuccessful tries, he pushed on towards Times Square. He was looking for the 2-line that would carry him back to his apartment.

Deliriously, he thought about going back to Tasha's. When he realized just how stupid the thought was, he walked faster. He considered which was worse: his nightmare or being caught by Tasha's husband. All he knew was that he had to get away from that dreadful place. Suddenly, he felt the feeling of the fly crawling beneath his skin. He clenched his scarred hand, trying to suppress the wound. Normally, the journey from midtown to his apartment would have been an easy one. However, his illness caused him much pain. It forced him to stop almost twice every block to regain his strength.

David staggered up the chaotic street, thinking of only his home. He could almost feel the warmth of his mattress, its softness that was well accustomed to his size and shape. In order to get to it however, he had to travel through Times Square.

As a native New Yorker, David avoided Times Square like the plague. The sight of senseless tourists, walking with their bright clothes and their dumb smiles, repulsed him. It was not so much the relentless swell of movement or the voluminous amount of bodies that bothered David. What really drove him mad was the sheer amount of economic excess that accosted him everywhere he looked. When he visited Times Square as a boy, the colorful images and wonderful attractions left him in awe. But when he got older, the allure of 42nd street was replaced by the prevailing sense that everything around him was one piece of a giant universal sham, constructed not to cause him joy, but instead, to take his money. Now, as he approached Times Square, this same thought returned, causing the putrid feeling in him to grow.

The closer David got to the high buildings that bordered Times Square, the sicker he felt. He slipped his hand underneath his shirt, tightly grasping the muscles of his stomach. He felt the hard ground beneath the thin layer of his socks. He sensed that everywhere, people were staring at him. He moved his free hand to his throat, trying to loosen the top most button of his shirt. When the collar broke free, he ran his hand along the back of his sweaty neck, massaging the skin with his fingers. His chest was heavy. On the verge of passing out, he stopped underneath a newsstand on the corner of 38th Street. Looking over his shoulder, he saw the lacquered glow of Times Square.

David took a deep breath. He crossed 39th, then 40th, until at last, he was in the heart of the world. Walls of intense light surrounded him. The brightness hurt his eyes, causing him to look towards the ground. Night turned to day. All around, swarms of people travelled in dense clusters. Everywhere there were people: thick, thin, gazing, gawking, goggling and ogling. To the north, a construction crew was tearing up asphalt. The sound of a jackhammer thudded through the air. David covered his ears with his hands, but he could not stop the roaring noise. As the crew broke through each layer of ground, a rancid smell leaked out into the street. The hole in the asphalt hurled out a funnel of grey steam. Around it, men dug and tore. David's senses were scrambling.

He passed a large peanut cart with a smell that, mixed with the construction site, became noxious. On top of the cart was an old radio, blaring out a strange and incoherent sound. Above and around him were billboards. On them were girls with unimpressed faces. They looked down on him with their tawdry mouths. David gripped his throat tighter, struggling for fresh air. Sweat gushed down his back. He wanted to get away from it all. He searched for an escape, but everywhere he looked, he saw only a haze of color and light.

It was disorder. It was a circus. It was some eerie unreality. Street performers in wild clothes flashed in front of him. Twisted caricatures clung to metal fences along the sidewalks. Bursts of purple spray-paint clouded his vision and crowds of slow-moving people blocked his way. At last, he saw his way out: a subway station in the center island. He crossed the street and saw a small police station next to the subway entrance. He was just a few steps from the stairs to his salvation, when he had a menacing thought.

But what's down there? The roar of subway cars? The den of trash and filth that the homeless call home? And the rats! The rats! Finger like tails, squirming and writhing. I can't make it, I'm going to...

David could not complete his thought. His head began to spin and everything spiraled into a sickening blend of sound and sight. His knees became weak. Just before he reached the green iron of the subway stairs, he lost his step. Barely grabbing hold of a nearby trash can, he fell to the ground.

With his remaining strength, David lifted his head above the can. With one quick spasm of his head, he vomited. He heaved again and again, gripping the sides of the garbage bin and throwing his shoulders inside. He tried to pull himself away from the smell of the can, but when he lifted his mouth too high, the sickness came up and, mechanically, his head fell back inside. Each time he came up for air, he took quick breaths that seemed to gradually restore life to his body.

A large police officer, seeing David vomiting in the trash can, approached him from behind.

"Sir, are you alright?" she asked, keeping her distance.

It took David a few seconds to realize that someone was talking to him. Having guessed the reason, he waved the stranger off with his hand.

"I'm fine," he answered weakly, spitting into the garbage bin. "Just leave me."

Although his strength was gone, the vomiting had

purged the sickness from his body. His senses returned slowly along with his taste for the cool night air.

"You don't have any shoes," the officer observed.

"Look, just leave me alone!" David lashed out.

He turned around to see who dared confront him in his vulnerable state. Seeing that it was a police officer, he quickly changed his tone.

"I'm sorry for yelling, I didn't know. Look, I'm alright. Really, see?"

He held his arms in the air as if to show he was not carrying a weapon.

"What's your name?" the officer asked sternly.

"Byron"

"What did you say?"

"Dorian"

"Have you been drinking?"

"No officer, I haven't. If you'll excuse me, I have to get going. It's very late."

Not in the mood for conversation, David turned and left. The officer did not try to stop him. She simply watched as he went down into the subway station.

It took David twenty minutes to get from Times Square to his apartment. When he unlocked his door, he was greeted by the familiar scent of his living-room. He peeled off his dirty socks and threw them into the garbage. Finding the bedroom, he felt the softness of the rug between his toes. He fell face down onto the bed, landing his head on the cool pillow. He took a relieved smile, reflecting on the chaos of the evening that he had somehow overcome. He was thankful that his journey was now over. For the rest of the night, he slept soundly, without any nightmares or stomach pains.

8

Over the next few days, David could neither leave his apartment nor go on a date without being followed by nausea. It was the same illness that had started on his night with Tasha. And despite the fact that it was most likely caused by a bad piece of filet mignon, David could not get over the bug. Each time he went onto the street to go to work, school, or to buy some food, the sickness returned. In a very short time, every aspect of the city became repulsive. As the temperature increased, the odor of the air became fouler. Pedestrians eyed him suspiciously when he ran down the street, covering his nose with the collar of his shirt. They avoided him as though he were deranged. Only when he returned to his home fifty-three stories in the air did his senses recover among the everyday sights and smells of his apartment.

He tried seeing girls like before, but each time, the reaction was the same as when he walked the city. He had not grown less fond of women since his evening with Tasha. His desire went unchanged. What did change was the sensation he experienced with these girls. He simply could not reach the same level of pleasure and gratification that they once brought him. On every date in every moon lit bedroom, he became confused and even frantic. He tried to put these infirmities behind him and carry on as usual. But by the end of every night, he felt the same sense of dissatisfaction weigh him down.

At first, he tried blaming Tasha.

I had an unlucky night. A lousy meal and a lying girl are to blame. It's only natural I feel this way. My system is trying to recover. A few days in bed are all I need. I'll have some rest and eventually it'll pass.

After nearly a week, nothing changed. He scheduled a visit to the doctor, but the session proved fruitless. After some blood work and a few taps on the stomach, he was given a pill for the nausea and was told to monitor his diet. The pills did not help and he could not monitor what he did not eat. He began to suspect the cause of his illness lay deeper than just his night with Tasha.

His hypothesis was confirmed when he reached out to Carrie and some of his other usual calls. Under normal circumstances, David preferred to start and stop his amours without any overlap in-between. Once he finished with a girl, he moved onto the next without any consideration for the one he left behind. He kept in touch with his scraps, only restarting his relations after some time had passed. It was better that way. By keeping his relationships tidy, there was little chance any two girls would meet, thus averting a big mess.

Of course, the one exception to this rule was Lana, who he held onto only until recently. Now, however, in his moment of weakness, David went on a spree. For a while, the sheer variety of women, accompanied by the lift to his ego, seemed to cure him. He tried a number of different medicines hoping one would be the cure. But as more time passed, he felt the euphoric effects of his liaisons wear off.

I've heard stories about prisoners who, convicted of their crime, go for days, sometimes even weeks, in complete and total disbelief. They tell whatever loved ones they have that the sentence cannot possibly go through. In a matter of days they will be free, they insist. It's only after some time has gone by that they realize they are trapped.

That's the way it must have been for David. While seeing girl after girl and forgetting each face with the arrival of a new one, he was in denial. At every turn, he rejected the truth that something was changing in him. Whenever he felt the truth approaching, he ran from it. He plunged deeper into the old habits that had consumed him for the past years. He immersed himself in the behavior that had once given him such thrills. And despite the overwhelming evidence, he still would not admit the change. To do so would have been to compromise himself, to go against everything he held sacred.

At the time when he felt his entire world was under siege, David looked for a friend. That friend was Roy Lipton, the waiter and senior at Columbia. He and David had good times in college. They did not have a normal kind of friendship. Instead, what kept them together was a tie between two young men sharing a common appetite for evening fun. While we didn't know then that David was seeing other girls, he and Roy often went to different parties in the city. And while Roy never saw him make any serious moves at other girls, he sensed that David could not be bound by one for long. David liked having a wingman and Roy enjoyed the role of mentee he assumed so well under David's leadership. Only when the doubts in David's heart began to grow more powerful did he seek out Roy. Through his old friend, he hoped to rid himself of those inhibitions and reclaim his lost fulfillment in life.

The two boys met at *The Silver Lime*, a bar they had visited many times in college. On his way there, as he tried to suppress the pangs of nausea, David imagined his upcoming visit with Roy. It was over six months since they last saw each other. At that time, even though they spent no more than a couple of hours together, David was still able to appraise the character of his old friend. In that visit, it reassured him to see that Roy had not changed from the way he remembered him. He found Roy to be his usual, life-embracing self. He was enthusiastic and adventurous as he had always been.

Roy did very well in college. Not as well as David of course, but well enough to graduate with honors. For his intellect, as well as his mocking indifference towards everything other people held dear, David liked him very much. In keeping with his own moral outlook, Roy held similar views when it came to the nature of women: that every girl is replaceable and, despite differences in the body, is singularly identical with respect to the mind. This unified belief made the two boys natural friends. Although separated by time and distance, they could always reunite in their shared belief. Shaken by his illness, it was exactly this thought that David hoped to validate. In Roy, he saw his former self. Roy was the way he had been in college and the way he would have been now, were it not for certain unforeseen and unpleasant circumstances. As he approached the bar, he recalled his memories of Roy and of nights gone by.

This is what I need. After all this nonsense, I need to be reminded of how good my life is. Roy is just the person.

David entered the bar and was struck by the smell of sticky beer. He grabbed his stomach and leaned against the door frame. In the farthest corner of the solid brown bar, sitting next to a man with ruddy cheeks, was Roy. He held a half-finished *Samuel Adams* in one hand and his phone in the other. As David approached, a feeling of comfort washed over him. He smiled slightly.

It's true, he hasn't changed at all.

Trying to contain his enthusiasm, which he made a point of always doing to not seem un-dignified, he crossed behind Roy and slapped him on the back.

"Still going strong, I see!" David remarked, noting the bottle of beer.

"I was beginning to think that I'd been stood up!"

Roy exclaimed, matching the excitement of his friend. "I thought I was in for a surprise a month ago when everyone came to the diner. I should've known better than to think you would make an appearance."

From the very first words of their conversation, there were several things David found surprising in Roy. First, he disliked the casual way in which Roy had greeted him. While they were only separated by a year's difference, David operated under the notion that he was the teacher and Roy the disciple. That was the way it had always been. Now, although it had only been a brief instant, David knew that dynamic was no longer intact. Second, whether intentional or not, Roy had flushed out the memory of the unfortunate evening David had spent in Hunter's company.

Does he know what's happened between me and Lana? He searched Roy's smiling face for an answer. *Maybe he does, maybe he doesn't. But who cares either way? It makes no difference.*

"Have you been waiting long?" David asked, just as he always did whenever he arrived late.

"I've had a beer, but not too long, no. How've things been with you?"

David proceeded to tell Roy just how things had been. Naturally, he omitted all the disagreeable aspects of his life, including his recent illness and troubles with women. When he told Roy about his work, school, and social life, he became painfully aware of the fact that his description seemed incomplete in one way or another. With each story he told, he invented some false ending that he knew would appease the expectations of his friend. After a few minutes of small talk, David posed the same question to Roy. While Roy spoke about how things were going, David nodded his head, letting out short *uhuhs* and even throwing in a couple of complementary questions. Suddenly, David caught the words *graduate school* come out of Roy's mouth. For the remainder of the conversation, he

182

gave him his full attention.

"I never thought you were one to go hiding in grad school," David said, motioning the bartender for a beer. "But I guess it won't be an entire waste. Where do you plan on studying?"

"London," Roy said with pride. "I got a scholarship that will pay for nearly the whole thing, three years and all."

David was again surprised by Roy. He somehow forgot about his old friend's academic prowess. With Roy's impressive scholarship, David was again confronted by the possibility that there was still more to Roy that he did not yet know.

"How exciting," David responded in his typical tone, trying not to appear too impressed. "You've got to let me know where you're staying. I've always wanted to spend more than just a few days in England. Maybe we'll do a tour of Europe, who knows. What will you study?"

"Economics," Roy answered.

"Ah, how fitting. Maybe, after you save Europe from crisis, you can work your magic in America"

"Maybe, it's in the cards…but there is something else."

"What's that?" David asked, taking his bottle of beer from the bartender.

"Jennifer is coming with me."

David looked up from his drink and into Roy's face. He was confused at first and it seemed to Roy like he had not heard him at all.

"Jennifer is coming with me," he repeated.

"Who's Jennifer?"

"Haven't you been listening?" Roy asked with a laugh, not allowing himself to become irritated. "I've been seeing her for over a year now. You've met her, don't you remember?" As much as he tried, David could not remember any such person. "I can't believe you don't remember her. You must have seen her at least a dozen times. Oh well, it doesn't matter."

After a moment lapsed, David picked up the conversation again.

"So this Jennifer, she's going to Europe with you. For how long?"

"She'll be staying with me while I'm at school," Roy replied.

A smirk spread across David's face. Roy knew it well and was prepared.

"Don't look at me like that," he added with a smile. "I know how it sounds, but trust me, I know what I'm doing."

"I've heard that before," David scoffed. "So what, she's going to follow you to London? It looks like you've got trouble, my friend."

"Why do you say that?"

When Roy asked this question, David looked at him in slight disbelief, as if the fact that he was in trouble required no explanation.

"Because you've got a dog biting at your heal and it won't let go! On second thought, it might be nice to bring a comfort along from the States." There was silence as Roy chose not to respond to David's comment. "Maybe I'm being too harsh," David added to smooth things over. "After all, I don't know her. So you're in England with her, that's fine. But what's she supposed to do while you're at school?"

"She'll find a job," Roy answered.

"Doing what?"

"Whatever she can find that she likes."

David said nothing. He just smiled at Roy with his usual smugness. He saw that his smirk angered Roy, so he covered his lips with his beer.

"What's so funny?" Roy asked.

"You are," David answered.

"Why am I funny?"

"Because this isn't you!" David laughed. "Getting a scholarship and going abroad is one thing, but taking a girl with you? What happened to the guy I spent all those nights with in Brooklyn apartments? Do you remember that night in Williamsburg?"

"That was ages ago," Roy said with knowing embarrassment.

"Not by my count it wasn't. If anyone else told me what you have, I'd believe them. But coming from you, it can't be true."

"And why can't it be true?" Roy asked.

"Oh come on, stop. Let's not spoil the evening."

"No, I want to hear what you have to say," he insisted.

"You know why," David said, becoming increasingly annoyed by his friend's persistence.

"What? Why is it so ridiculous that I go to London with the girl I love?"

"Because it's all fake!" David said seriously.

"What's fake?" Roy asked, confused.

"Stop…please. I feel si–"

"What's fake?"

"Everything!" David roared, beating away the nausea. "You and this girl, how pointless it all is! It's all a great joke. You and your love…what nonsense. You say you love this girl. You say she means the world to you and you'll follow her to the end. But you don't have any idea what it means to say it! It all seems so poetic at first. They'll tell you that you're different. They'll tell you how much they care about you and how they were dead before they met you. In the dark, it'll all seem like a dream. But in the light, you'll be horrified! You'll be faced with the terrible reality of it all: that the one you love is really nothing special, that, in point of fact, she's something quite ordinary. Then what will you do? When the masks come off?

185

Drop the act already! I wish it weren't this way, I really do. But that's the reality we must face. You'll leave her and she'll leave you. That will be the end. It's all nothing but a sham, a great phantom of the ideal we chase all our lives. You'll run until your legs give in and your heart stops. In that moment, you'll realize you were better off single all along. That's the true test of a man, whether he can be alone, faced with the single commandment: *Exist!* So spare yourself the trouble. I've ran the distance and I can tell you for sure, no woman will ever make you happy."

"Where did this come from?" Roy asked, astonished. "Is this really you?"

"Why does everyone keep asking me that! How could I be anyone but who I am? What have I done that's so terrible, tell me! I hurt one girl along the way. Who hasn't? And aren't I doing the right thing? Isn't it only fitting that I, who has hurt this girl so much, should never want another relationship for as long as I live? How can I be blamed? I'm not guilty. It's everyone else that's guilty. They're the ones who are too stupid to realize that love only brings pain, and that the only way for a man to have any happiness in this world is by avoiding it altogether. They're the ones who will suffer, but not me! Not me!"

David was finished. His breathing was heavy and his throat was dry. He reached for his beer, but then withdrew his hand to his stomach. Roy stood from his stool. David's outburst had drawn the attention of many in the bar. Roy saw no point in going on with his friend.

"Where are you going?" David asked as Roy started to move.

"This is too much," he said without looking at David. "I'm going home now."

"Wait!" David commanded. He grabbed the sleeve of Roy's shirt. "Don't leave me, please. I don't know what came over me. I've been very sick lately, but now I'm better. Honest."

Roy gently pulled his arm away from David's. He looked towards the exit, then at his friend.

"Look, I'm sorry," Roy apologized, "but it's getting late. I really have to go."

David turned away in disgust.

"Fine," he let out bitterly. "Go if you want. Leave me and we'll never see each other again. Just, tell me, please. What's so wrong about what I've done? I may drive you away, maybe even the whole world, but tell me, give me an answer."

"David, I honestly don't know what the hell you're talking about. I think you need help or something."

David looked at Roy's face. He recognized it immediately. It was the same face he had carried in the past few weeks, due to his insuppressible revulsion towards his surroundings.

"Enjoy England," he said, letting Roy go.

He watched him leave. Turning to the bar, he lifted his beer to his lips. As the smell drifted from the neck of the bottle to his nose, his hand convulsed and the beer fell to the floor. After apologizing to the bartender and taking out some money, he left the pub.

On his way home, David sunk into a deep depression. It was a kind he had never experienced before. The evening could not have gone any worse. Within just a few months, the Roy of his memories had been replaced by a new one. What caused that sudden change? What compels a person to leave their former self behind and embrace another? Was this change something voluntary or did it occur against his will?

"But it's all useless!" David exclaimed after suffering these questions. "I've been through it all. I've gone through these stages before. What Roy is feeling now, I felt years ago. I've felt it all…but if there's nothing left for me, then…my life is…nothing. Agh! I can't think!"

He walked angrily towards the stairs of the downtown subway. As he approached, he began to smell the hideous stench flowing up from the dirty tunnels. He stopped in his place, looking left, then right. Seeing a yellow taxi cab approaching, he flagged it down and gave his address.

As the cab glided down the avenues and cross streets of the West Side, David's temper cooled off. With sad eyes, he looked out the glossy window of the cab into the darkness. Turning his head towards the sky, he watched the overhead streetlights shoot by in rhythmic time. The light soothed him and he leaned his temple against the cool window. Looking down, he watched the streetlight wash over his upturned hands. He stared at the cut on his palm. It was just a faint line across the surface of his skin. The scar appeared and then disappeared in the light. There and gone. There and gone.

Eventually, he got tired of the vanishing act. He returned his attention to the street. He must have passed hundreds of New Yorkers enjoying the spring night. As the cab neared 70th street, the traffic signal turned red. The car slowed to a stop and the noise in the backseat lowered to the hum of an engine. Watching from behind the glass divider, he saw a couple start across the crosswalk. Their hands were joined and their bodies pressed tightly against each other's. He watched them not as a man, but as a ghost, an empty spirit in the back of cab 7C43. And as the couple made it to the other side, that emptiness inside him grew. Turning away, he looked at his reflection in the car door window. Then, like someone had whispered in his ear, his mind went back to his night with Carrie. It felt like it was years ago. He tried to remember what she told him while in bed.

About wanting to feel important, that's what she said. No, not just that, there was more to it than that. Even if she didn't say it herself...why can't I remember?

His memory failed him and he became even more lost. He remained in that state for the rest of the evening.

Not even the comfort of his own home could break his misery. He climbed into bed exhausted and limp.

Everything's changed, but I'm still the same. I can't go on living the way I am, but to change is impossible. And life—that daunting cloud that hangs over my future—what will tomorrow bring? So I'll be like this for as long as I live, and in that life, I'll live only for myself. But without anyone, with only myself, without progress, change, or perfection...without love...what will...what will my life...?

His thoughts became jumbled and incoherent. He struggled to stay awake, to complete the puzzle of words that had led him to *life*. But like a man who sees the opening of a well shut above him, constricting the light and leaving him in the dark, David fell asleep. He would have to wait until the next day in order to regain his thought. And even once he found it, there would be more struggle, defiance, and rejection before he could finally get his answers.

9

It was the next morning when David, with a crooked tie and a crumpled collar, boarded the 3-train at 72nd Street. His nausea was bearable and it was only a twenty minute ride to the office on Fulton Street. He got on immediately, going against the current of people exiting the train. He sat as close to the doors as possible, leaning his head against a framed subway map. He closed his eyes and tried to sleep, but the jerks and twists of the train kept him awake. His eyes were bloodshot out of tiredness. His jaw had patches of stubble from where the razor had missed. He did not shower that morning and the part in his hair was unkempt. With the sound of a racehorse, the train passed the 50th Street Station. When the car screeched into Times Square, David opened his eyes.

34th Street? No, Times Square. There are too many people. How long have I been on this train?

A crowd stood impatiently on either side of the doors. When one exited, the other entered. Among those boarding was a young African American girl who could not have been older than ten. Her hair was braided. At the end of several locks was a column of plastic beads—pink and green mostly. She wore a school uniform with a white button down shirt, tight stockings, and a plaid green and blue skirt in-between. Holding onto the straps of her backpack, she slipped past the others and sat next to David. Once the doors were clear, the train started to move.

Just then, on the other end of the car, a man nobody recalled having entered the train woke up. He had been sleeping in the farthest corner, occupying the entire row of seats with his long body. Several newspapers were spread on the seat from beneath his feet to his shoulders. He wore tattered grey sweatpants and a black hoodie. Judging from his vinegary smell and raggedy beard, he had not bathed in weeks. There was a black brace wrapped around his right hand. He kept it tucked beneath the folds of his sweatshirt. He sat up quickly, startled and confused.

"Wha," he slurred, looking out the window. Bursts of sparks flashed against the tunnel wall. "What stop was that? Hey, don't you hear me? I said, what stop was that?" His eyes were focused on a Korean man wearing head-phones.

"Times Square," the man answered, momentarily pulling a bud out of his ear and then putting it back in.

"God damn it," the bum let out. "That was my stop. Now howm' I supposed to get back? Hello?" Seeing he no longer held the man's attention, he reached across the aisle to grab him. Before he could touch him, the man got up and moved to another seat.

"Well fuhhck you!" the bum said, waving him off. He collapsed into the bench and began muttering to himself. He folded his arms and let his head droop forward. Strands of drool dribbled down his lower lip and into his messy beard. Nearby, a woman in running shorts had heard his predicament. She turned to help him.

"Just get off at Penn Station," she said to the bum, trying to offer some charitable advice.

"Can't they just turn this train around?" the bum asked with a laugh.

The woman did not answer. Her eyes darted away and she became tense. She started to move, when suddenly, the bum began tearing through his pockets. He twisted his body and stretched his legs out, digging further and further. Losing his patience, he pulled out both pockets. Lint and loose change spilled into his hands. He began counting the coins frantically.

"Twenty, twenty-one, twenty...ah, damn! My metro card! Where's my metro card?" He fell from the orange seat onto his knees. He started groping underneath the bench. With his right hand pressed against his belly, he searched the dirty floor. "Where is it? Where! How'm I supposed to get back without it?" He looked up towards a business woman crossing to the middle of the car. "Did you take it?" he asked, pointing his mangled finger at her. "I bet you did, you slut."

Avoiding eye contact, the woman moved to the center door. As the car pulled into Penn Station, she left along with a flood of others. Once the new passengers were on, the train started to move again.

"Oh what's the use!" the bum said to an insurance ad. "If I can't find my card, then I can't get off. I'll ride the rails until dark and...oh, my wrist! I can't get off, I can't..."

The bum's voice trailed into spurts of incoherent rambling. Those near him became nervous. One after another, they began moving to the front of the car, away from him. The bum seemed not to notice and continued mumbling to himself. He rocked back and forth on the bench.

Meanwhile, in the very front of the car, David was inert in his seat. He pressed his head against the cool metal handrail and covered his face with his palm. When he felt the tread of footsteps coming his way, he lowered his arm and opened his eyes. Looking towards the other end of the car, he saw the bum doubled over. When the train pulled out of 14th Street, the bum snapped out of his trance. He stood up slowly.

"Excuse me ladies and gentlemen," he announced. "May I pardon the interruption? I'm homeless and I'm hungry. I have no money to get back, see?" He pulled out his pockets. Some left-over pennies fell onto the floor. "I had a metro card, but I lost it and...I need some meds for my wrist." He held up his braced hand. "I broke it and I spent all my money to fix it. But the doctors fucked me and now they won't give me my God damn meds! Can't anyone help?"

The car came into Chambers Street and people began to move. They formed small, tight crowds near the doors.

"Anyone? Anyone at all?"

The bum touched the shoulder of a larger, much younger man.

"Watch it asshole!"

The man jerked his arm away. The bum fell backwards onto the row of empty seats. His legs flew up and his head crashed against the hard plastic.

"Fuck you, ya bastard!" he cried. "You try that shit again and I'll..."

The young man was already gone and the doors of the car were closed. The bum regained his balance and began muttering under his breath again. His elbows fell to his knees. His head sagged and wavered. He let out a string of curses, stomping his bare feet and tossing his shoulders back. Then, he raised his right hand and pounded it against the bench. He moaned loudly, grabbing his injured wrist with his free hand. He cursed even more.

The atmosphere in the car was charged. The passengers were fastened to their seats. They were afraid to draw the bum's attention. Their eyes were glued straight ahead, occasionally dashing to the side to check on him. David, now fully awake, watched a young boy on the other bench pull at his mother's shirt. He asked if he could take a picture of the crazy man. The mother agreed, on the condition that he take it when the bum was not looking. Two old ladies in the front corner of the car were openly cursing him.

Then, when David turned his head toward the bum, he noticed the little girl with the beads in her hair was still beside him. Looking closer, she seemed to be the most nervous of all the passengers. She held a children's book in her hand, but watching her eyes, David knew she was not reading it. Her arms started to tremble. The pages of the book began to shake.

The car left Park Place. The bum moaned and bellowed, gripping his wrist and swearing loudly. David took his eyes off him and watched the girl again. She was not even pretending to read anymore. She took off her backpack and held it firmly in her little hands. The car neared Fulton Street. She stood from her seat. David's eyes followed her in disbelief.

What's she thinking? She's going right towards him! Isn't anyone going to do something?

He started for the girl, but before he could reach her, she was already at the bum's feet.

"Mr.?" she asked, tugging his sweatshirt. David, the young boy, his mother, the two old ladies, and everyone else in the car were still.

The bum raised his head slowly. He stared behind blue eyes. Reaching into the front pocket of her backpack, the small girl pulled out a *Ziploc* bag. She opened it and held out a ten dollar bill.

"Here," she said to the bum, handing him the money. "So you can get home."

The bum's eyes began to water. His lips started to convulse along with his feet and leathery fingers.

"God bless you child!" He rose and took the money with his callused hands. His arms trembled and his knees shook.

"Go," said the girl. "You'll miss your stop."

The bum staggered to the center door.

"God bless you! God bless you! I'm gonna find

you one day. That's a promise. I'll repay the kindness you did me. I won't ever forget. But wait, what's your…"

The car doors closed and the train moved on. David, who had been standing the whole time, sat down slowly. He stared at the girl as she returned to his side. His eyes were wide. Before he could open his mouth to speak, one of the old women spoke up.

"That was a very nice thing you did little girl," she said.

The girl nodded with a smile, her mind in some other blissful state.

"You must be a Christian," the other insisted.

The girl shook her head *no*.

David wanted to say something, anything to the girl. He opened his mouth, but soon closed it. He knew anything he could possibly say would be woefully inadequate. Suddenly, it dawned on him that he had missed his stop. At Wall Street, he left the train. As soon as he stepped out, he was struck by a deep pang of regret. He turned back and, through the window, he saw the face of the girl. With her arm outstretched along the bottom of the window's edge, she looked at him over her shoulder. She smiled at him. Dimples spread on her coffee colored cheeks. Then, she turned around and the train went on. He never knew her name.

10

Happy Birthday to you,
Happy Birthday to you,
Happy Birthday dear Lana,
Happy Birthday to you...

Lana's party was already three hours underway. Things were not as she had imagined. The music was deafening. The low light made it impossible to see. The alcohol kept everyone stupid. Worst of all, she was surrounded by total strangers. The only friends she recognized in the hoard of people gathered in the cramped apartment were me, Emily, Aaron, and Amanda. In the sea of faces, she saw several strays who had visited the apartment in the past weeks. They were acquaintances that seemed to come and go without any consideration for Amanda or her home. Their only goal was to get drunk off of warm beer, cheap wine, and what little hard liquor was in the cabinets. Together, they formed a single orgy of inebriation. Occasionally, Lana tried to speak with one of the strangers. But when the music got louder and the people got drunker, she gave up on talking. She decided to sit silently instead.

It became increasingly obvious to her that the guests had no intention of celebrating her birthday. That made her feel even worse. She tried convincing herself that the date of her birth was really something unimportant.

It was a day just like any other. She was wrong to expect anyone would show appreciation for her existence. When I saw how upset Lana was, I motioned to Emily and crossed to her. Before I could reach her, Amanda appeared and led her away.

"Some party!" she shouted over the music. Placing her hand on Lana's back, she led her towards the window.

Amanda held a *Miller Light* in her hand, using the other to fix her hair which had become messy from her pass through the crowd. Lana, although she tried not to show it, could not help but feel betrayed by her friend. They had never spoken about a guest list, but she knew that what was happening was not what was intended. She also knew Amanda must have known that.

Maybe Amanda just has a different notion of 'party' than I do. Maybe I said something to make her think that this is what I wanted, or maybe she thought this would cheer me up somehow.

Behind all the *maybes*, Lana avoided the truth that her friend was not really her friend at all, that she had only thrown the party to hurt her in some way she could not see. But Lana kept these thoughts to herself. In the confusion of throbbing sounds and swelling motion, she even felt guilty for thinking such things about her friend.

"What did you say?" Lana asked Amanda, not hearing her through the pulsing music.

"I said, this is some party!" Amanda repeated. Lana did not reply. "Why don't you get up and dance a little. There are plenty of guys here. They've all been asking about you."

"Not in the mood," Lana said, seeing no point in keeping silent.

"You've got to lighten up. Here," Amanda offered Lana her beer. "Want a sip?"

Lana took the bottle and smiled gratefully. Amanda, counting the accepted offer as a sign of peace, returned to the other side of the room. As she went, she glanced over her shoulder towards Emily and me and smiled. When she turned her back, Lana placed the beer underneath her chair. Then, she looked at me. She would have rather been any place in the world except that room. Acknowledging her, I tilted my head and gave a dumb smile. It's a stupid habit that happens when I want to say: *Yes, I understand you're upset. But what can I do?* Confused by me, Lana returned her attention to the mass of people in the center of the room. They were dancing to the music and pounding their feet against the floor.

After she handed Lana her beer, Amanda weaved through the center of the room. She went to the table where the drinks were. She picked out a red solo cup and poured a rum and Coke. Then, she looked for Aaron. He was sitting on a nearby sofa with his body bent forward. A beer dangled from his fingertips, but he had not taken a sip. He did not see Amanda approach. When he felt her hand on his solid shoulder, he looked up towards her.

"What did she say?" he asked softly, so soft that it was impossible for Amanda to hear.

Guessing his question, she leaned closer to his ear.

"Nothing. I mentioned you were over here, but she didn't say anything."

Aaron looked down. He had a headache from the boom of the music. His eyes had bags underneath them from a lack of sleep. By the window leading to the fire-escape, a group of kids held a lighter above a bowl of pot. Some of the smoke drifted into the apartment, irritating his tired eyes.

"Should I talk to her?" he asked, rubbing his eyes with both hands.

"Not now. Just wait. You've got to relax. Here, drink." She reached out and took his bottle of beer. She handed him the red cup.

"What's in it?" he asked.

"What?" Amanda said, leaning in.

"Forget it." Reluctantly, Aaron took a large gulp.

His disappointment formed a throbbing pain in his chest. This was the night that was supposed to change everything. It was the night that he would finally be able to explain himself to Lana. At least, that's what Amanda told him. He got up several times to leave, but each time, Amanda coddled him back to his seat. Now, terribly aggravated and embarrassed, he only wanted to go home and forget about the night. Seeing him like this, Amanda drove away a couple that was tangled on the cushion beside him. She sat down in their spot.

"Please don't let her upset you," she said. "It'll take time. You should enjoy yourself for now."

"Impossible," he said without lifting his head. "She's gone, and with her, my only chance for happiness"

Still looking down, Aaron felt Amanda's hand on his knee. Her touch took him by surprise, melting his guard like a flame.

"It isn't so impossible," she said softly. Somehow it rose above the music. "You worry about things too much. Once in a while, you just have to let go."

"What do you mean?" Aaron asked.

"I mean, if you can't have her, there will always be someone else."

"Who?" he asked, feeling her hand traveling up his leg.

She leaned in towards him. He smelled the spice of her red hair and felt the glow of her skin.

Amanda is all that's left for me. You've always known it. If I do this, the pain will go away. If I do this, Lana will go away. I have to. I have to do this. I...

Before Aaron could finish his thought, the moment was shattered by a loud crash from the entrance of the apartment. Amanda rose immediately, trying to see the cause of the noise. She looked intensely as if, by her eyes

199

alone, she would obliterate whoever ruined her moment. She stared through the crowd and saw someone waving a bottle in the air and stumbling into the room. The stranger began pushing against everyone in his way, demanding to be let in. From where I stood, I heard the slurred and garbled speech of a familiar friend. Through the forest of faces, I recognized Hunter.

He pushed his way inside. He thrashed like a fish on a boat, knocking into the walls and causing anyone within his reach to back away. Taking large swigs from the bottle in his hand, he barged forward. He swung his arms carelessly, crashing into several people. He tried to get the attention of a girl in a blue dress. When she saw him, she laughed and ducked into the crowd. Hunter became agitated. He threw his hands up in the air, spilling his bottle. I moved forward and grabbed his arm. He reared his head back. Before I had time to say anything, he leaned forward and kissed me on the lips. Instantly, I shoved him away. I spit the taste of whisky from my mouth.

"Say," Hunter said, looking me over. "I know you!"

"Hunter!" I shouted, grabbing him again. "It's me, Will!"

"Hmm?" he said blithely, looking everywhere except in my eyes.

I did not have to repeat myself. He recognized me and the usual grin appeared on his muddled, unshaven face.

"Will!" he let out. He wrapped his arms around my chest, whacking a few people in the process. "I'm so glad you could make it."

His voice was clumsy and his eyes were drunk. His nose was flush and he reeked of alcohol. He wore baggy jeans, kept around his waist by a warn leather belt. His white shirt was covered in stains both old and new.

"L-listen," he stammered, "before you say anything, I...I want you to know how sorry I am about our little tiff from earlier. I treated you very poorly, I did. You were right to go, I...I was wrong to yell and, well...aren't you going to forgive me?"

Before I could ask what he was doing at the party or why he was drunk, Amanda came forward. She walked with controlled ire, looking at Hunter like an unwelcomed rat. Without acknowledging me, she spoke directly to him.

"What are you doing here?" She folded her arms contemptuously. "You weren't invited. And you're drunk. You're pathetic. Totally pathetic."

When he saw Amanda, Hunter turned his head gradually and gave her a dumb smile.

"Yes, here I am," he said, letting his eyes find her face. "I didn't want to seem rude, but I didn't want to drink the jungle juice. So I brought my own." He waved his bottle in her face, almost hitting the tip of her nose. "Or are you serving Kool-Aid tonight? I never know." Before Amanda could think of a reply, Hunter turned to me. "But I didn't come to see either of you," he said plainly, as if trying to offend us. "I came for the birthday girl. So where is she? Aha!"

Through the thin wall of people, Hunter saw Lana. He left us and faltered towards her.

"Surprise!" he said to her with outstretched arms. "Happy birthday birthday girl! We never speak much and, well, I can't tell you how glad I am to see you." He leaned forward and threw his arms around her. He pushed so hard that Lana's chair rocked back onto two legs.

"It's good to see you, Hunt," Lana replied with a smile. She patted his back and tried to guess just how drunk he was.

"So are you happy?" he blurted out.

"Am I what?" she asked, confused.

"Are you deaf?"

"What?"

Hunter burst out laughing. He stumbled to the wall.

Everyone in his path backed away and laughed. Running to his side, Emily grabbed his arm to stop him from falling. I followed behind her, trying to see what had happened in the thundering music and low light. Amanda was next, followed by Aaron, still holding his drink. He had just found out about Hunter's arrival.

"Ah, there's the man," Hunter said, forgetting Lana and moving towards Aaron. "And how've you been, my friend? Not so good, eh? I bet not. But don't worry, she'll keep you in good spirits. Isn't that right, Amanda?"

"Go home Hunter," she said angrily. "You're drunk. You weren't invited."

"Say," he said to Aaron, ignoring Amanda entirely. "I heard about you're little mishap with...well, I won't say his name. I wanted to come here to apologize to you in person because, well, you understand, it's all my fault." Aaron looked at Hunter, puzzled. "No? You don't know? But you must have told him, Will?" Hunter looked at me with his large dark eyes. They were more pronounced from the alcohol. "No? Ah, well, it doesn't matter now anyway. In time! Don't worry, all in good time as they say..."

He spoke in quick bursts of energy. His sentences were long and jumbled and inevitably trailed into senseless rambling. Just like when I spoke to him on the night of the fight, he seemed to have something terribly important to share. It was clear he wanted to keep it a secret for as long as he could.

"It's true, of course," he went on, "I am pathetic. And I'll go soon, I promise. You see, I didn't have the strength to come see you all without a little liquid encouragement and, well, of course..."

His words became inaudible and soon he quit talking altogether. Emily pulled up a chair for him to sit down. He took the seat gratefully.

"Thank you, thank you. I'm sorry. I'm such a burden, really I am."

Losing control, tears swelled in his eyes. He was crying. He threw his head down and bent forward. He was in hysterics. No one knew what to do or how to make him stop. After several minutes, he calmed down. He choked on large gulps of air as he tried to inhale.

"Oh, how embarrassing, really, I'm…I'm so sorry."

"It's alright Hunter," Emily said, kneeling beside him. She rested her hand on his back. "Just try to calm down."

"Calm down? How can I?"

He started to cry again. He lost all composure whatsoever. As soon as he was done, he wiped away the tears with his fists. He fumbled for his bottle. When I saw what he wanted, I took the whisky from underneath his feet. He quickly forgot whatever it was that made him cry.

"Give that back!" he demanded. "It's mine, I bought it. You can't take it from me. I'll fight you for it!" Amused by his own choice of words, he broke out into a stretch of laughter. "Aha, oh, but really, how pointless it all is. You know," he said to Lana, shifting in his chair to get a better view of her face, "I don't see what everyone's on about. You're not so pretty after all. Parts, maybe. Oh, but I shouldn't have said that. What am I thinking? I'm an idiot after all. I didn't mean it Lana. Please believe me Lana. You do believe me, don't you, Lana?"

Lana did not know what to say to Hunter. She just nodded her head, hoping it would appease him.

"Ah! How good you are. An angel, really, that's what you are. Thank you, thank you. And what are these, hmm?"

He turned his attention to several rows of books on white shelves above his head. He got up and tried to stand on his chair. It teetered back and forth. Grabbing hold of one of the shelves, Hunter found his balance. He looked closely at the books.

"Ha-ha! I thought I was the only one who kept

a filthy apartment. Look at all this trash, trash of human knowledge. I'll take it all out!" He pulled some large biography from a shelf and opened to a random page. *"And at such and such time in my life I spoke with Monsieur so and so who said to me…* oh I can't go on!" Laughing even harder, he threw the book on the floor. It fell like a stone, hitting the wood with a loud smack. The crowd behind us started to cheer. They were egging Hunter on. "Let's see what else you've got."

He tore through each of the books on Amanda's shelf. He opened one, then another, until he simply began pulling them all. They fell like an avalanche, crashing to the floor and forming a pile of mangled spines and creased pages.

"Let them fall! Let them all fall!"

Everyone around us laughed and cheered. A girl stepped out of the crowd and went up to Hunter. It was the same girl from before, the one in the blue dress. Holding out her arm, she invited him to take it. With an ecstatic smile, Hunter took the girl's hand. He jumped down from the chair. I tried to grab him, but the girl held onto his hand and dragged him to the center of the room. They started dancing to the music. Everyone else started to dance around them. Slowly, I pushed my way towards Hunter and the girl. When I got to them, Hunter was spinning her underneath his arm.

"Hunter!" I shouted. "You've got to stop. I'm going to take you home." I put my hand on his shoulder and started pulling him away.

"No, no," he said defiantly. "I want to stay."

"C'mon, let him stay," the girl in the blue dress said to me, laughing.

"I don't even know you!" I said to her.

The music stopped. I felt my ears pulsing and my head seemed lighter. The crowd stopped dancing. They started to mumble and look around.

Amanda had turned off her *iPod*. With tremendous anger, she crossed to the center of the room towards Hunter. She got to him and pushed his chest.

"Get out, get out, get out!"

She pushed harder and he fell. He landed directly on his back, with only a Monet book to break his fall. Emily ran to him. He was stunned at first and did not know what had happened. When he saw Amanda standing over him, however, the same wide grin spread across his face.

"Ah, it's you," he said, squinting to get a better look at her. "When did you get here?"

Amanda bent down and grabbed him by the collar of his shirt. She twisted the cloth in her fist, bringing his face to hers.

"Listen to me you little faggot," she said. "You've caused enough trouble already. Leave now and don't come back here."

"But how can I leave?" Hunter smiled. "After all, didn't you invite me?"

Amanda was irate. She tightened her grip and brought him closer to her face.

"If you don't leave now, you'll regret it."

"And why will I regret it?" he asked delightfully. His lips quivered as he tried to suppress his laughter. He clumsily brushed her hand away from his collar. Placing one arm on his knee, he tried gathering some strength in his legs. Before he could stand up, he lost his balance. He stumbled forward towards Aaron. He reached out his arms and Aaron stepped backwards. They collided. Aaron dropped his drink and stopped Hunter from falling. Hunter leaned against Aaron, holding onto his shoulders.

"Let go!" Hunter said, making no effort to mask his breath. "Let go of me." He pushed off of Aaron and stumbled back to his chair. Exhausted, he sat down and threw his head between his legs.

Aaron straightened his shirt. Reaching down to the

floor, he grabbed the red solo cup he had dropped. Then, in the pool of rum and Coke, he saw something. It was an un-dissolved white pill. Picking it up between his thumb and his index finger, he felt its chalky sliminess. He stood up.

"What the hell is this?" he asked, holding the pill for Amanda to see.

"It's..." she stumbled, "it's nothing. I don't know how..."

A sharp slam rang through the room. Amanda stopped talking. She looked towards the entrance where the sound had come from. Everyone else followed.

"Ah!" Hunter shouted, "so the gang's all here!"

Standing by the door of the apartment, still holding the handle, was David.

11

David's entrance caused all the noise in the apartment to stop. With steps that were sobering in the absence of sound, he crossed to the center of the room. Amanda, taking his presence as a challenge, met him there.

"What are you doing here?" she asked, trying to keep cool. "You weren't invited."

Without acknowledging her, he looked around the room. His silence provoked her even more.

"I said, you aren't invited here. Leave!"

He tuned Amanda out and kept scanning the room. His eyes met mine, then Emily's, Hunter's, Aaron's, and at last, Lana's. Since his arrival, she had become completely still. The moment she had both dreaded and anticipated had finally come. He was here. Since her meeting with Jacqueline, a part of her had a strange curiosity as to what it would be like to see David again. She was not curious to see how he would react. It was her own reaction that she doubted. She knew no matter how many times she ran the scenario of their meeting in her head, only the singular and tangible event could determine whether the principles she used to build herself up in his absence were based on truth or delusions.

Turning away from Lana, David looked towards Aaron. Just like her, Aaron had foreseen this moment in his imagination. He had even seen it in his dreams. He thought that, when he saw David for the first time since the fight, he would be angry. He had prepared lengthy and powerful speeches to justify his retaliation. He did not know what he wanted from David or how things could ever be right between them. All he felt for certain was that he had to act. But now, staring into the face of his friend turned enemy, he knew that, if more violence had to happen, he would not be the one to start it.

David walked to us. I looked at Emily, who had the same apprehensive expression.

"The man himself!" Hunter exclaimed. Rising from his chair, he tried to approach David. After the first step, he lost his balance and stumbled backwards. I caught him and lowered him to his chair. His head tilted to the side and he began to groan. Emily motioned to me and I ran to the kitchen. Grabbing the garbage bin from under the sink, I brought it back to Hunter. He took it instinctively, threw his head inside, and began to vomit. David looked at him with pity.

"You can all relax," he said. "I didn't come here to fight." He came closer to where we were, resting his eyes on Lana. "I came here to speak and, above all, to say what needs to be said to *you*."

David followed her eyes as they rose to meet his face. They were green, causing him to recall in one instant every time he had seen them. To keep the moment, he kept still. Having taken in all he could, he turned to Aaron.

"There's something I need to say to you first," he said to him.

David stepped closer and stopped just inches from his forehead.

"I have betrayed you," David said at last. These were words that Aaron did not expect. He searched David's face, wondering if he had heard him correctly.

"You were my friend," he went on. "You were my best friend. And for the past five years we've known each other, I've abused you. I was around when I could use you and I left when you needed me most. I stole what you wanted. I counted your talents as my own and undermined you at every opportunity. And although you followed me through it all, never giving up on me or letting me drive you away, I still thought you were the lesser man. Well, now and forever, you're a better man than I'll ever be. You're good natured and honest. Your anger is not your own. I took you down with me, and if you want your revenge, know that, whatever you do, I am the cause of it. I injured you and, in injuring you, I hurt myself. I've learned the horrible fate that follows a man who insults another, but all the lessons in the world won't ease the pain it took to learn them. And so, before I forget the guilt I feel now, I have to try and make right what can never be right between us."

He embraced him. "I am so, so sorry for what I did to you. My words, though I say them with sincerity, seem hollow and unapt. But they're everything I have left. You have to choose whether or not you accept them."

Without waiting for an answer, he turned to Lana.

"What I said to Aaron is the same for you. Still, you have to let me say more. I hurt you more than any man ever dared. I scorned your love, that love which countless men and women would lose themselves for. From the moment I met you, you were only a pabulum to me, something to be devoured without remorse. You loved me and I made you believe that I loved you back. Worse than not loving you, I made your love a game. I lied to you. I used you for profit. I didn't just fool you. I lied to your family and friends: all those who care about you the most. I slept with other girls. Worse still, those girls were good people. If you knew them, you would call them your friends. Don't blame them in your thoughts, blame only me."

His face lowered.

"When you met me, you said I brought you back to life. You said I restored your hope in this world, your desire to lead a life for love. When I told you that I thought the same, I lied. The truth is, even though I may have brought you back to life…I was still dead. I've been dead for a long time, living without purpose or meaning. I want to change that now. I want to be better than I am today. Here, in this moment, I'm trying to start something new. And it starts with you."

He stepped forward.

"I am so sorry for what I've done and for who I am. I don't want forgiveness. I'll never earn it. I don't, nor will I ever, deserve you. All I want is for you to understand what I'm doing here. Even though you can't forgive me, you must believe me." He looked into her eyes. "You'll never see me again," he managed get out. "It can never be the way it was between us. For you to take me back would undo everything that needs to be done. If you forgave me now, I would forget the past. That can't happen. I'll leave you, and you'll leave me. We can't see each other, not for a long time. If I'm going to change the way I am, I must remember you as you are now. I'm so sorry you had the misfortune of meeting me when you did. If it brings you any comfort, know that through you, I've been taught what it means to live again. But at what price?"

Tears began to form around his eyes. Seeing that he had said enough, he began his farewell.

"If we do meet again, I hope you will meet a better man than the one who speaks to you now. I hope that neither of us forgets one another and that, no matter where we are or who we are with, we will never lose our memory of the time we shared. Other couples might have the luxury of calling those times *happy*, but it won't be that way for us. Instead, I'll remember the way things could have been between us, the times we could have shared, the man I could have been, the love I *could* have given you…that love I'll dream of, but never realize. I hope it will be the same for you. Goodbye Lana."

12

Once David finished what he came to say—a speech that appeared in reality just as in his imagination—he stepped closer to Lana. He was waiting for her to say something.

There was so much she wanted to say. She wanted to tell him just how much she hated him at that moment. She wished she could gather all the words from his speech into a ball and shove it down his throat. She was certain that everything he said had nothing to do with her: it was only an attempt to save his conscience. After everything he put her through, he had the arrogance to show up like this? She wished he would have stayed away. She wished he had never bothered to say anything at all.

Suddenly, she felt something. It was a kind of lucid joy. It was a freedom that she had not experienced before. She realized she was so far beyond him that anything she could possibly say would be superfluous and futile. She checked her memories of David and found that, now, there was no pain in them. All the possibilities of her future were too great to let him affect them. And if he gained some kind of magnanimous comfort from his attempt at redemption, it really made no difference to her.

Lana reached out to David and embraced him. He was stunned at first and, when he realized what was happening, he hugged her tightly. He pressed his head into her shoulder. She let him keep the connection for as long as he needed. David brought his head back and looked into her eyes. Then, Lana stepped away. David turned and started towards the door, resisting the urge to look back. On his way out, he passed Hunter.

"I had a speech for you too," he said to him, "but you probably wouldn't remember it anyways."

Hunter's head was still buried in the garbage can. Out of the corner of his eye, David looked at me. I waited for him to say something, but before I could stop him, he was gone.

My mind returned to underneath the bridge. He had run from me then and he was running again. He was going to leave without so much as a final word to me. I could not let him go. I told Emily to wait in the room while I went after him.

Running out the entrance of the apartment, I saw the elevator doors close. Finding the stairs, I hurried to the lobby. When I exited the building, David was already on the other side of the street.

"David!" I shouted, drawing the attention of those on the sidewalk. He stopped underneath a street light and turned.

I ran from the front steps and across the street. If I had turned my head, I would have seen the white truck accelerating towards me. The driver blasted his horn and drove by, shouting inaudible curses through the open window. Bringing my hand to my heart, I crossed through the thick smell of exhaust to the other side of the street. I worried that the momentary separation of sight caused by the truck would allow him to slip away. But he was exactly where I had left him in the yellow circle of light. He smiled at me with a strange mixture of amusement and disappointment.

"You shouldn't have come," he said, his eyes glistening from recent tears. "You almost lost your life."

His joy confused me and, after catching my breath, I asked the only question I could think of.

"David...why?"

"Why what?" he asked.

"What you said back there to Aaron and Lana, did you mean it?"

"Every word," he said, no longer smiling.

"But why? Why do you have to leave? Where will you go?"

"I'm not going anywhere," he answered, as if my question was something completely ridiculous. "I have school in the morning."

"But you said that–"

"I can't see Lana anymore, or any of you, for that matter."

"But that isn't the way!" I shouted, losing my temper at his indifference. "If you've changed, if you've really changed, then why do you want to leave her? If you love her?"

He sat down on the curb, placing his feet into the grey street.

"A person like me doesn't know what it's like to love. Not yet, anyways."

I remained standing, looking down at his profile.

"You aren't making any sense," I said, frustrated. "You show up out of the blue, admit that you've wronged her and then, just like that, you want to leave?"

"It's for her own good," he said.

"But where did this come from? Why now?"

"Ah!" he said with wonder, "that's the question, isn't it? I don't know where it's come from. Maybe it's been inside me all along. Maybe someone put it there so that, when I was broken, I could be made new again. All I know is that something's happened to me. A new idea has taken hold. It's breathtaking, Will. If only I could describe it."

He looked up at me. His eyes invited me to join him, so I sat down.

"These past few weeks have been the strangest of my life," he said, looking into a sewer grate. "But, through it all, I realized something. My life was purposeless. I didn't care for anyone but myself and, even though I cared for myself, I had no meaning, only emptiness. I want to change that."

"David I–"

"I want to change," he said with determination. "I see the way I could be, and that possibility drives me forward. I want to perfect myself. I want to love those around me. I want to know what justice is and fight for those who don't have it. All the possibilities! But I'm so far away. And there's still so much I have left to learn. I've wasted so much time already and only now can I begin to live for what's good. It's time that I can never get back, memories that will only cause me regret. My one condolence is that I've seen what happens to those without purpose. Hopefully, that will be enough to drive me forward. Now do you understand why I can't be with her? All of this is so new that, with one false step, I'll slip back into my old ways. I have to do this alone. Here, a new David Clay is born."

I stood from the curb and started walking. I thought I would keep walking until I stepped right into the river, but I turned after only a few steps.

"What about what you said?" I asked.

"What I said?" he parroted.

"At Gabriel's. Our lunch. Nothing's been the same since then. Emily and I, we've been fighting like we never have before. The worst is when we keep silent. I…"

He rose and looked at me sternly.

"You've got to forget it, Will," he said, bracing my shoulders. "Forget everything I said."

"But you were right!" I said hopelessly. "I can't look at her the same way. You said things would change and they have. I'm waiting for the day I'll lose her. You may say it's a self-fulfilling prophecy—that I think I'm driving her away and so she goes—but it'll still come true! And…"

While my mouth ran, I felt a warm slap across my cheek.

"Snap out of it," David said, drawing his hand back. "What you have with Emily is precious. It's probably the most precious thing in the world. So protect it. You hear me?"

"But I…"

He raised his hand again and my mouth closed instantaneously. I broke away from him, running my hands over my face.

"You've got some fucking nerve," I said, turning back with hot tears. He looked at me blankly. "It's all so easy for you, isn't it? Did it ever occur to you that Lana doesn't need your goodbye? What, you think that just because she has your permission, she can move on? You're a selfish prick, David. You hurt everyone around you, then you spout some bullshit about change, and suddenly we're all supposed to believe you?"

"I'm trying to change," he insisted. "You have to believe me. Yesterday, on the subway, I saw–"

"Just go," I said. "I don't know why I bothered to chase you out here. You wreck a person's life and you think you can just walk away?"

"It's the only chance I've got," he said sadly.

"Just go," I repeated, refusing to listen.

He came closer, forcing me to look at him.

"You've always been a good friend," he said to some future part of me. "It'll be hard to lose you. But fate will bring us together again. I'm sure of it. Promise me one thing. Look after Lana. Make sure, whatever she does and whoever she's with, that you're watching her."

Even through the rage and misunderstanding, I

215

nodded my head yes. He started to turn away, but stopped himself.

"Oh, and next time we meet, remind me I owe you a lunch. My treat, any place you'd like."

It was hard not to like him. Maybe it wasn't for others, but it was for me. I tried not to think about how this might have been our last meeting. He seemed to guess what I was thinking. Instead of leaving just then, he wrapped his arms around me. After a moment, I pushed him away and stepped back. He turned around and, giving me one last treasured image, he turned his head and smiled. Then, he turned completely and started to walk. He kept walking along the street, past the eye of the lamplight until at last, he faded into the backdrop of the city.

After I ran out of the apartment for David, conversation and laughter slowly returned to the room. Everyone began talking to each other. No one could understand the meaning behind the two visitors. One was completely plastered, while the other had been all too sober. Eventually, someone turned the music back on. The crowd started dancing again. All this time, Amanda had been silent. She was looking around when Aaron stepped in front of her. He stared down at her.

"What was in the drink?" he asked.

Amanda said nothing.

Aaron went back to Hunter, who was recovering in his chair. Lana came to Aaron's side and, with Emily, they tended to him. Amanda crossed to the four of them.

"Get out now," she said vehemently. "Get out, all of you!"

Although her words were not meant for everyone, a stream of people began leaving the apartment. More started to go, until eventually a large column formed at the exit. Lana, Aaron, and Emily looked towards Amanda with mutual resentment. She returned their looks unashamed.

"I won't say it again," she threatened.

"Oh, but really, there's no need," Hunter drunkenly blurted out. He teetered on his chair like a small child. Occasionally, he lost his balance, nearly falling off. "All she has done has been for love, it can't be helped."

He gave a twisted smile to Amanda, which only encored her wrath. She crossed to him.

"You've ruined me!" she yelled. "You're pathetic! You know that, fag? Does that hurt? You haven't seen anything yet. I'll get you for this, just wait, I'll make…"

Before she could say more, Aaron stepped between her and Hunter. She stared at Aaron and did not know what to say or how to act.

"Haven't you done enough?" he asked. Amanda heard a change in his voice. He was no longer afraid or uncertain. He seemed to look at her with pity. He did not pity her, exactly. Instead, he pitied the circumstances that drove a girl to do all she had done for the sake of a false notion. Amanda hated this new person. She knew he was now far beyond her.

"So you won't love me?" she asked softly.

Aaron said nothing.

"And you'll never…"

Amanda waited, but he kept silent. Her face began to tremble. She clenched the folds of her dress with her small fists. She did not think about Aaron or the fact that her chances with him had come to an abrupt and unexpected end. All she could think about was the drunken idiot who ruined her one and only hope of obtaining what she wanted most.

Although his senses were impaired, Hunter felt the sting of Amanda's eyes. Instead of being intimidated, her look seemed to only amuse him more. He tried restraining his smile, but it soon broke into a wide grin.

"How can you look at me like that?" he asked. He shook his head with disapproval. "Ah, so what if you hate me. I love those who hate me!"

He was becoming increasingly agitated. Emily, kneeling at his side, tried to calm him.

"I don't need your consolation," he said to her. "Not you or anyone else can blame me for what I've done. Oh, but if you only knew how much I admire you!" he said, returning to Amanda. "How can you hate the one who admires you? You've made me realize something and I'm so thankful for you, really I am."

Hunter stood from his chair, lost his footing, caught his balance, and then stumbled towards Amanda.

"All my life, I've lived with certain principles. These principles were my Gods. Through them, I tried to live. Strive for virtue. Have temperance. Be mindful of the faults of others…temple of the body. What madness! No, you've shown me the way. My principles are killing me, can you see that? They'll be the death of me unless… unless I do something!"

He ran to the exit with large, uncontrolled steps. On his way, he knocked both Aaron and Lana, causing them to nearly fall. He caught the frame of the door and stopped. All eyes were on him.

"If I keep my oaths, I lose myself. So I forsake my oaths, to save myself!"

His words died into silence. He looked around the apartment, out of breath. He stared at his friends, as if trying to discern what they thought of him in that exact moment. It was impossible for him to keep his eyes fixed on any one person for too long. Without saying anything else, he opened the door and ran to the elevator. Emily followed him, then Aaron, then Lana. Amanda stayed behind. When Emily entered the hall, she saw the elevator doors closing with Hunter inside. He was with a group of people leaving the party. Just as Emily arrived at the elevator, the doors closed. She found the stairs. She went to the lobby with Lana and Aaron. As they exited the main door of the building, there were still many people from the party going out into the street. Emily tried to get through, but the people slowed her down. She pushed her way to the curb and looked around. Down the street, she saw a yellow taxi cab. Hunter was getting inside. There were already several people in the cab. The last one to get in was the girl with the blue dress.

I watched from the other side of the street. Through all the people, I could barely see what was happening. Before I crossed the road, the cab drove off. Emily ran into the street and stared towards the back of the car. I ran to her and asked what had happened. She explained everything.

13

With my mind still in a haze after Lana's party, I walked along Convent Avenue towards Hunter's building. After all my visits to him within the past weeks, I had grown accustomed to the area. It was early in the morning and the shops were just opening. On my right, I passed a pharmacy with scuffed windows covering some neon beer signs. A brown Pontiac puttered down the avenue, crossing in front of the Church of the Annunciation. It made a wide right down 131st Street and disappeared. The sky was grey that morning. Behind it was the dim glow of the sun. I passed an old woman pushing a metal shopping cart with all her strength. She bent her head and locked her elbows forward. The cart was piled with black garbage bags containing empty aluminum cans. Its worn wheels thumped along the concrete. As I stared towards the grey sky, I imagined myself standing on the bank of some far away river, staring at colorless water that appeared to extend forever. It seemed a strange thing to imagine, so I quickly returned my focus to the sleepy avenue.

Two men rounded 133rd Street and were coming towards me. As they came nearer, I began to decipher strands of their conversation. Occasionally, they were interrupted by a passing car. The two spoke with animate faces, describing some event they had just seen. The taller one made large gestures with his smooth tan hands, running them in circles as if he held some invisible ball. I passed them and turned down the same street they had come from.

Last night, after watching Hunter disappear in the taxicab, Emily, Aaron, and Lana explained what had happened in my absence. When they spoke about Hunter's reaction to what Amanda had said, I became worried. You often hear that, when a person's drunk, they take off the mask of everyday life and reveal their true selves. But when I heard about Hunter's drunken tirade, I knew he had not been true to himself when reciting those horrible thoughts. He had abandoned everything that was once sacred to him. In a moment of delirium and intoxication, he threw himself away. It was all too much for him to take. I was scared for him. But why hadn't he answered my calls to let me know where he was? After setting up Lana in our apartment, Emily and I went to Hunter's. We rang the buzzer many times, but there was no answer. I had to try again alone this morning.

In the middle of 133rd Street, I was almost at Hunter's. Above the wall of buildings to my right, a thin black cloud came overhead. It hung in the air like a ghost, looking down on the neighborhood. It rose slowly, ascending into the sky. I intuitively recalled the Boy Scout lessons of my grandfather: black smoke meant trouble. As I rounded Amsterdam, I started to run. When I came closer to the black cloud, I saw the flashing red and blue lights of police cars. There was a small traffic jam. Yellow caution tape stopped bystanders from getting too close to the source of the smoke. Behind the tape, firefighters casually walked back and forth. They were rolling up their long hoses and hanging their tools onto the side of the fire engine. They talked with one another, stripping heavy oxygen tanks off of the backs of their partners.

I ran towards the crowd and realized the smoke was coming from Hunter's building. Stopping at the caution tape, I scanned the front wall. The smoke was coming from

Hunter's apartment. Panic set in. The blood shot out of my arms and legs, leaving them weightless and cold. I became frantic, desperately trying to make my way through. I ducked underneath the tape. Before I could even process what I had done, I was almost to the door of Hunter's building. A tall red haired man, still wearing his black and tan overalls, grabbed me. He backed me away. I realized he was trying to speak to me.

"Whoa, easy kid," he said. He gave a look to his fellow firefighters to show them that the situation was under control.

"I've got to get through!" I cried, not really knowing what I was saying.

"You can't go in there, it's not safe."

"But my friend, my friend's in there!"

"Oh God, what a shock! Relax, kid, your friend's going to be fine."

"I've got to get through!" My mouth fired while I attempted to pass the man in vain.

"Easy, easy, he isn't in there. Don't worry, he's safe. We pulled him about twenty minutes ago. He was right next to the door when we came in. I almost tripped on him. I couldn't see anything."

"He's…he's ok?" I asked, feeling the blood return to my arms.

"Yes kid, don't worry. He took in a lot of smoke, but he'll be fine."

"H-how?"

"The idiot. He must've left a cigarette or a match by the bed. That's where the fire started. I figure he was sleeping in bed when the fire started, but he panicked and didn't know what to do. So he ran around the apartment, trying to gather his things, but inhaled too much smoke. I've seen it before."

"Where is he now?" I asked hurriedly.

"New York Presbyterian, Washington Heights. The

ambulance took him about ten minutes ago. Hey, where are you going?"

Without even giving the command, my legs took off up the street. I could hear the firefighter calling me from behind, asking where I was going. I ran with a dead *iPhone* and an obscure inner compass for my guide. After what must have been three blocks, I felt my knees begin to hurt and my throat became sore and prickly. I would have run the entire length of Manhattan up and down if it meant I could find the hospital. After several taxis passed, I flagged one down and told the driver my destination.

When I got to the hospital, my entire head was covered in sweat. Running through the sliding glass doors, I looked around the main lobby. I was looking for anyone who could help me. It seemed like the entire hospital staff was on call that morning. Everywhere I turned, I saw thick clusters of men and women dressed in scrubs and white coats. I crossed the white tiled floor to the reception desk and asked if they knew where Hunter was.

"What's the last name?" the woman behind the desk asked, looking down at her keyboard.

"Ricci, R-I-C-C-I. He came here this morning. He was in a fire."

"Here he is. He's on the second floor, room B-203,"

After entering my name, I took an elevator to the second floor. As the doors opened, I smelled the sterile air of the hospital—a blend of disinfectant and lime. I went down the right-hand corridor, carefully following the posted room directories. Eventually, I came to another desk where I was required to give over my name. The man behind the desk told me I was not allowed into Hunter's room without permission. When I explained I was only dropping off some personal belongings, he let me through. I kept walking down the corridor, passing opened doors that let me glimpse into the fragile lives of the sick and dying. An elderly man with bandages wrapped around his legs hobbled down the hall. He was trying to keep both feet within the thick blue line on the floor. A woman in maroon scrubs kindly held his elbow, giving him strong words of encouragement as he went along. Soon, I took a right and noticed the room numbers were going down. I was getting close. I became nervous and my heartbeat raced as I tried to imagine the scene that was about to take place. At last, I arrived at room 203.

From the small window slit in the door, I saw the inside of the room. Light poured in from outside, a momentary break in the grey sky. There was two of everything in the room: beds, chairs, tables, television sets. The occupant of the first bed was ancient. In the bed by the farthest wall, I saw a lump curled against the metal railing underneath a white blanket. I could not see his face, but I knew it was him.

I placed my hand on the handle of the door. At that moment, it flew open from the inside. In front of me was a little nurse wearing blue scrubs. She was holding a wash basin. I had not seen her while looking into the room and she caused me to step back in surprise.

"Oh I'm sorry, sir," the nurse said in a gentle voice. "I didn't see you there."

"It's fine, can I go in?"

"Who are you here for?" she asked. I pointed to the mass underneath the sheets.

"I wouldn't go in. He just got to sleep. He's resting now and shouldn't be disturbed."

"If you don't mind, I really would like to see him. When do you think he'll be awake?"

"Hard to say," she said, pulling a cart from the room and placing her wash bowl on top. "He's had quite a scare. His burns weren't too bad, but the smoke caused a little damage."

Seeing her words worried me, she reassured me that he would be fine. Then, she started pushing her cart down the hall. Just as I was about to open the door to the room, she stopped me again.

"I'm sorry to ask, but you're name isn't Will, is it?"

"How did you know?" I asked.

Her face became grave. She looked around for a moment. She reached her hand into the deep pocket of her uniform. She pulled out a couple of ragged pieces of paper, folded into a small square.

"I think you should have this," she said, handing me the papers. "It's against hospital policy, you know. But I figure this is an extreme circumstance. I had to read it, I hope you don't mind. I'll have to report it, because it isn't safe for him to be in that room. I just saw the letter was addressed to you and, well, I thought you should have it."

The nurse anxiously walked away, pushing her cart with quick, short strides. She rounded the corner and looked in my direction before moving on to the other rooms.

I unfolded the crisp papers. The corners were chard and the blue lines of the pages were warped and faded. I held it up and realized it was a letter, written by Hunter and addressed to me. The writing was uneven, drifting over and under the blue lines. There were black scribbles in many places, indicating words that had been crossed out. Blots of dried water stained the pages and, in some places, had smeared the black ink of the letter. I held it closer and started to read.

Dear Will,

I hope this letter makes it to you. Once you're finished, I ask that you destroy it immediately, without showing anyone. You've seen the fire and know my fate. By the time you finish reading this very sentence, I will be gone from this world. I can't begin to tell you what an insane idea that is:

225

that the mind that drives my hand to scribble these thoughts onto paper will, in a very short time, cease to be. It's like death himself is here beside me, guiding my pen without any effort of my own. But enough poetics.

I've composed this letter for one person only, and that person is you. You, who know me better than anyone else and who have been my friend, even when all others ignored me or thought me too strange to bear, this letter is for you. I write it so you can see the world as I do now and so you can understand why I did what I have done. Hopefully, in the end, you'll realize the succession of thoughts that has driven me to this point. I tell you this not to frighten you or to provide you with a document that signifies a last act of vanity. In writing this letter I hope, from it, you'll gain a complete comprehension of my character. I hope it will make you remember me not as a coward who made a regrettable choice, but rather, as I truly am, without any labels attached.

I've always thought it strange how we consider suicide an act of cowardice. For some scoundrels—the mass murderer who kills dozens and then executes himself before caught—suicide is certainly an act of fear. However, these are rare examples. In general, I think the majority of suicides in our society do not result from any fear or frailty of spirit. Instead, I suppose these decisions are made in a state of pure knowledge, when a person realizes the horrible truth that confronts him and can therefore never return to the way things once were. They say that suicide is a permanent solution to a temporary problem. Well, I'm sure you realize, my whole life has been nothing but one great problem.

Surely it's not a coward who writes these words. The people who call me a coward do so fallaciously. They turn their backs on me in gross indifference, too ignorant to step across the threshold of my mind and see reality from my perspective. They're the cowards. They refuse to acknowledge that, at any moment, a person can encounter things in this world so horrific, that to go on living would be to commit an injustice against life itself. Life is not meant to be lived in suffering. For the man who suffers constantly, life is not for him. It's my body, after all. It's my right.

For those who will condemn my decision on the grounds that I am unworthy of my suffering, I have a few choice words. Misery, by its very nature, is meaningless. On this, we all agree. But what's equally true is that any meaning I fabricate for my misery must also be meaningless. Life is indifferent to our existence. It expects nothing of me and, if it did, I would spit in its face. Long ago, I stopped answering the call of the future, which begs us to achieve some finis. Hope is the anesthetic for the present. It dulls our perceptions while deceiving us into thinking our suffering will soon be over. It's only just begun.

In the five years we've been together, you've never known me to be a religious man. Considering how, in these final moments, I am perhaps the closest person on earth to testing this two thousand year old hypothesis, I think it fitting to tell you that my thoughts on the subject of God have not changed. When I die, I won't go to heaven. No angels will welcome me as an arbiter of a great cause, nor will I be sung as a martyr of my generation. I won't go to Hell either, though

I would truly welcome such a place if it existed.
There is no afterlife, because when I die, I won't
survive my death. Despite the works of some well-
meaning but misinformed transcendentalists, there
are two empty peripheries of our existence: before
life and after death. Why should the latter not
follow directly from the former? Indeed, I don't
know anything that can survive its own death.
The soul is a fallacy, the resurrection a myth, and
reincarnation a good laugh.

   Here you will say that I've lost my way.
You will say that I'm suffering from a crisis of
faith. Let me tell you what faith is. Faith is the
acceptance of a conclusion in the absence of
evidence. No rational human being accepts the
conclusion of an argument that's devoid of evi-
dence. Why then do we accept the argument for
God? They say He is elusive, that stemming from
His very nature and a certain nasty fall, we cannot
know Him. So they've taken away the evidence.
But, at the same time, they say we must trust in
His word, believing in His providence through
what shreds of proof are available to us. Do you
not see the contradiction here? Oh, if only I could
avoid the accusation that I'm merely a disbeliever
operating in a divine framework! What will it
take for you people to see that the world of God
is as alien to me as the moon? I'll show you a
new world, one that rejects Him altogether. If I
must jump from this world to the new one, then I'll
jump!

   What amazes me still is the way we intel-
lectuals treat the problem of evil. Our theodicies
no longer satisfy us. We fear that any explanation
of evil is a betrayal of the facts. We've abandoned
the ideas of original sin, the devil, or liberation

228

theology, because, to the mother who's lost her child in war, our explanations aren't worth shit. But when I hear that God has given mankind free will, and that our free will explains all the evil in this world, I can't help but turn my head in disgust. The free will defense is just the latest theodicy to rise to popularity. In time, it too will be cast aside.

Yes, in my final hours, I see the world as it truly ought to be seen: with divine indifference, as that Frenchman in the Facel knew all too well.

I write with full sobriety, without any doubt or hesitation. Although the horrible nightmare of last night's events still lingers in my head, I want you to know that it alone was not what pushed me over the edge. Instead, it was the simple chain of cause and effect that has formed my predetermined fate since the day I was born. Don't blame yourself for what's happened. You and I are blameless. Everything has already been decided. There's nothing you could have done to stop me and I refuse to mar you any longer.

When I was young, I took great pride in the knowledge I consumed. Through study, I sought to climb above the rest so that I might discover some higher truth in this world. In that state of existence, I was in the darkness. I was in the cave. I lived like a blind-man, crashing and colliding with other blind-men, trying to find an exit. When I looked up, I thought I saw a light. Groping my way towards the cold wall, I started to climb. After much struggle, I arrived at a ledge. Taking a moment to regain my strength, I looked down on the herd of the blind from which I had risen. A deep satisfaction filled my soul. Seeing them in the darkness, I smiled. But when I raised

*my head to survey the ledge on which I stood,
a horrifying site filled my eyes. On both sides,
countless figures stood in the darkness. I looked
above and, to my fright, I saw the faces of all
those who had climbed higher than I. They smiled
at me, just as I had done at those below. I climbed
higher and higher, hoping to rise above them and,
by doing so, catch the light. But, at every ledge,
though the number of shadows decreased, I still
couldn't reach the end. It wasn't long before I
realized the obvious truth: the light I sought was
only an illusion. There is no exit, only more darkness. We are the blind men, climbing and crawling our way out of the cave of our lives. The cave
is endless. The cave is life.*

    *I must be going soon, the sun is rising. I
originally supposed my exit would be something
silent, something quick and easy that wouldn't
make such a mess. A gun shot. A few too many
pills. But, the more I think about it, the more I
realize a smooth death doesn't suit me. I despise
this life, this apartment, and most of all, this body.
I want it all to burn. I will die, having had my
purity stolen from me by a girl I can't even remember, but whom I'll never forget. Although I really
shouldn't say it was stolen from me. I gave up on
my principles long before last night. I'm sorry we
couldn't say goodbye in person, but this letter will
have to speak for us both. It's about time for me to
be going. The sun is almost here.*

    *Goodbye my friend. Live well and enjoy
your life. You must go on to find the happiness
that I never could. For me, all that's left is the
dream of every atheist: a death happily met. No
more anything. No more dreams. No more me.
No more...Goodbye Will.*

My hands trembled and the letter slipped between my fingers and onto the white floor. I bent down to pick it up. When I did, tears fell from my cheeks onto the wrinkled pages. I wiped them away with my sleeve, picking up the pieces of paper and folding them into their original square.

The inside of Hunter's room was now covered with sunlight. I peered through the slit in the door, but the glare made it nearly impossible to see. I placed my hand on the metal handle, feeling its coldness against my warm skin. My body was stone. I wanted to turn the handle, but some force stopped me from opening the door. Suddenly it occurred to me, not by any great revelation or profound insight, but by the power of ordinary objects on forgotten memories, that the force that prevented me from entering Hunter's room had been at work in each forgone visit and delayed phone call. I thought back to college and realized that my quiet aversion to him had been present even then. And soon I felt a profound sense of guilt and shame, as I knew a part of me had wanted him gone all along.

I stood for what felt like an eternity, unable to go forward. The sun fell behind the grey sky and the light vanished from the room. Through the slit in the door, I saw him lying in the farthest bed. His head was above the sheets now, turned towards the window. He was there, alone and very afraid. It was life that scared him. He was probably staring out that window at the brick wall of the building next-door, trying to imagine what was beyond it. Maybe he was not awake at all. Maybe he was asleep, far away in some happier place. Either way, I could not tell.

With my hand still clenched to the handle, I was motionless. Just when I was ready to release it, I felt another hand cover mine. It was warmer, much firmer and far more beautiful. I turned my head to the left and saw Emily.

"What are you doing here?" I asked, surprised.

"I couldn't let you go alone," she said. "I've been

231

trying to call. I went to Hunter's to look for you. I saw the smoke. What happened?"

"It's Hunter, he's…"

Reaching into my pocket, I took out Hunter's note and handed it to her. She started to read. After the first few lines, she knew what it meant. She pushed the note back to me. With the same hand, she covered her expression of shock and disbelief. After a moment, she grabbed the handle of the door again.

"Together," she said with determination. "We go in together."

We went inside.

14

The sunlight was back inside the hospital room. It reflected off of the clean white plastic and framed pictures. Emily walked towards the window and lowered the blind. I looked at the elderly man lying in the bed next to Hunter's. He was sleeping with his arms folded neatly on his stomach. An IV line was tapped to the inside of his forearm. An oxygen tube ran from his nose to a tank beside his bed. Each breath he took seemed like the roll of dice in a game rigged from the start. Out of the corner of my eye, I saw the sheets on Hunter's bed shift. I crossed to the other side to get a better look. His long black hair was spread over his forehead and across his cheeks. Beneath it, I saw his eyes.

When he saw us, a look of terror and shock spread over his face. His lips slowly began to move, but neither one of us could understand what he was saying.

"Hunter?" Emily asked, reaching her arm towards him. His head snapped up.

"Leave me!" he screamed. His eyes were wide. Grabbing anything within reach, he began throwing things at us. He tore the pillow from behind his head and hurled it at Emily. I stepped in front of her and caught it. He continued to scream and writhe.

"Get out!"

Grabbing the television controller, he threw it at me. I dodged and it crashed against the back of the room.

Reaching for the metal lamp on the bedside table, he fell off of the bed. We rushed to help him, but he waved us away violently.

"I said get out!"

Just then, a pair of nurses came into the room. They must have heard Hunter's screams. They each took one of his arms and lifted him back into the bed. As they raised him, he kicked and screamed defiantly.

"It's my right! It's my right!"

I tried to go near him again, but one of the nurses stepped forward and blocked me. She escorted Emily and me out of the room. As we were leaving, I looked over my shoulder and noticed the old man in the other bed was still sleeping. Once we were in the hallway, the nurse closed the door behind us. We were back to where we had started. Looking through the window-slit, I saw Hunter was still fighting back.

"Well," Emily said after a few seconds went by, "what do we do now?"

We stayed in the hospital for the rest of the day. At noon, we returned to Hunter's room to see if his condition had improved. We found him sleeping underneath the white sheets of the bed, just like that morning. His lunch had been placed on the side table. At first I thought he was only pretending to be asleep, but when Emily pointed to his twitching eyelids, I knew he must have been dreaming. We let him sleep.

In the evening we came again. This time he was awake. He was sitting up in bed, focusing on the brick building just outside the window. When he heard the door open, he turned his head towards us. Seeing our faces, he immediately returned his attention to the brick wall. I tried to think of anything to say that would break the silence. Despite my efforts, the room remained quiet. What could I say after reading his letter? Where could I begin? While these questions kept me still, Emily crossed to the chair next to his bed and sat down. I followed her and soon fifteen minutes of silence had elapsed.

Some visitors came to see the old man who shared Hunter's room: a married couple and their three children. From what I gathered, the old man was very close to death. Trying not to disturb us, the daughter of the old man drew the hospital curtain, dividing the room. Although I could not see the family, I heard them crying. The son-in-law said some words of encouragement, but they seemed to offer little comfort. I tuned the sounds of the family out and watched Hunter more carefully. He sat up-right in bed, periodically shifting his eyes from the window to the black television on the opposite wall. He was avoiding eye contact.

After more time, a nurse brought in his dinner. She handed it to Emily who removed the plastic fork and knife from their wrapper and unfolded the napkin. She gave the meal to Hunter, placing it delicately on his lap-tray. Hunter's eyes followed her. Eventually, he began to eat. We stayed with him for as long as we were allowed. Although we spent several hours together, he had not spoken to us.

Instead of returning to our apartment, Emily thought it would be best to visit Hunter's burned out room. We hoped to salvage whatever precious belongings we could from the fire. The trip from the hospital to his apartment took only twenty minutes. When we arrived, the fire crew was gone and the tenants had begun their usual evening ritual of microwave meals and television. The only sign of a disturbance in the life of the building was the blackened hollow that Hunter once called home. Climbing the four flights of stairs, we found his apartment. The door had been broken in and was now boarded over with a thin layer of plywood. I began pealing back the board, but my struggle caused the resident of a nearby apartment to come out and inspect the noise.

"Hey!" a stout old woman shouted, "what do you

think you're doing?"

"We're with the health and safety department," Emily said. "We need to check the apartment."

"Let me see some I.D. then," the woman responded.

"Fine." Emily began searching through her bag. "If you know the gentleman that lived here, you wouldn't mind coming down to our office to answer a few questions about the fire, would you?"

The old woman was taken aback by Emily's question.

"Just…just don't make such a racket!" She turned quickly and went back inside her room.

After prying the board off, Emily and I went inside. The fire had destroyed nearly everything in the apartment. Most of the large furniture, including Hunter's desk and armchair, had been thrown away. Whatever papers and books that had been spared by the flames were now piled in the farthest corner of the room. I went to the pile, while Emily continued to look for anything salvageable. Lifting several pieces of charred paper, I made out the covers of Hunter's most prized books: a copy of *Hamlet*, an annotated version of Goethe's *Werther*, and a torn paper back of *The Sound and the Fury*. I left them where they were. While I dug through another pile, Emily entered the small kitchen.

"Will," she called out, "come over here." I left the living room and followed her into the kitchen. "Look…"

In her hand she held a picture that had been tapped on Hunter's refrigerator. It was an old Polaroid, the kind that develops immediately after being taken. The picture was of the entire group on the day we visited Coney Island. In the background the sky was overcast. We were leaning on the railing of the pier, our backs turned to the sea. Farthest to the left, Emily and I stood holding hands. Next to us was Amanda. In the center, Lana stood embracing

David. Aaron was next, his right arm hanging around David's neck. Finally, there was Hunter, smiling to the camera. Written on the bottom of the picture in black ink was the date: *11/20/12*. I must not have noticed the photo on my last visit to the room. Emily gave me the picture and I placed it in my pocket. We left Hunter's apartment soon after.

Early the next morning, Emily and I returned to the hospital. We arrived at the earliest opportunity, before the sun rose. We went to his room, B-203, but he was not there. I asked an attendant at the help desk and she told me he had been moved to the seventh floor, where he could be monitored more closely. Apparently, the nurse who found Hunter's note kept her promise. We went to the seventh floor and found Hunter's new room. I opened the door quietly, but without hesitation. There was Hunter.

He was out of bed and resting on a nearby chair, an uncomfortable one, by the looks of it. Unlike yesterday, he acknowledged us by turning his head and staring at us. He said nothing and only kept his look as if to show he was not afraid. The room was very dark. The blinds were down and the sun was just coming up. There were no sharp objects in the room, no string or cord of any kind.

He followed us with his eyes, watching as we entered and closed the door in our wake. His fingers squeezed tightly against the ends of the arm-rests and his entire body was rigid. Emily crossed to his right and kneeled next to him. He was too busy watching her to notice that I had done the same. With my head lowered, I began searching through my pockets. I found the picture we took from the apartment and handed it to him. He looked at me it for a moment and then accepted it.

Just like last time, his lips began to tremble. Emily and I leaned away from him, expecting another outburst. I closed my eyes. But instead of screams, I heard a soft whimper. I opened them and saw he was crying. His eyes were shut and small streams of tears fell onto the square photo. It shook in his hand. Soon, his entire body began to heave. He bent forward, throwing his hands over his head while still holding on to the picture.

Emily wrapped her arms around him and I did the same. We stayed like that for a long time. I don't remember exactly how long it was before we let go.

15

By 9:00 A.M., we left the hospital. It was a week day after all. We each had places we had to be. Work needed doing. Lives needed resuming. I remember it was particularly sunny that morning. We passed people wearing sunglasses and *Yankees* hats. When we descended the stairs of the downtown 1-train, the air got much hotter. The heat irritated my eyes and I wanted to return to the street. I passed the turnstile, swiping my metro card without breaking my stride. Four minutes until the train.

There were several clusters of people waiting on the platform. I walked towards the center of the station, moving faster than Emily. She was a few steps behind me, watching to make sure I did not get too far ahead. I crossed between the people, trying to avoid a collision. I hit against one guy's shoulder and knocked his headphones off. Emily apologized for me. Then, I saw what I was looking for. Against the wall of the station, next to a shiny wooden bench, there was a black trashcan. I walked up to it and reached into my back pocket. I pulled out Hunter's note which I had kept since the day before. I held the wad of mangled pages in my fist. I clenched tighter and several bits of charred paper broke off and sprinkled onto the floor. Standing over the can, I tossed the crumpled ball inside. It fell slowly, suspended by a blast of hot air moving through the station. At last, it landed in a forgotten pool of glittering soda cans and yellow metro cards. The pause gave Emily enough time to catch up to me. Then, I walked away from her.

I looked around and what I saw was chaos. The station was in constant change. People passed in front of one another, some collided, others dodged. Like a river, they moved in rapid succession. I soon realized that I was caught in the current. I looked across the tracks towards the uptown side and saw the same thing. A homeless man begged for God and quarters. A church group read from the gospels. In the corner of the station against a dirty wall, a man played a few lines from *Lean on Me* with his guitar. Two minutes until the train.

I thought about the change I saw and found I could not stop thinking. I knew it would never stop and, years from now, time would have altered everything. I could not stop the world from spinning. All I could do was watch it go around. In front of me were the faces of friends I would never meet, lives that would intersect only once, in this station. I looked back at Emily and realized she would also change. Then, I heard a voice.

There is a downtown one train to South Ferry approaching the station. Please stand away from the platform edge

The location made no difference. I walked towards the edge of the platform. Emily followed. I crossed the bumpy yellow tiles which warned my feet that they were very near danger. When I looked down the tunnel, I saw the faraway light of the train.

An insane thought had taken control. It began as a spark, faint and unsure of itself. It grew brighter with each second. A strange anticipation swelled inside my chest and the sounds of the outside world became dim. I thought it would devour me until at last, I kneeled on the ground. Then, I felt the eternal question flow effortlessly from my lips.

"Emily Foster," I shouted with all my voice, "will you marry me?"

Her eyes widened. In them was my future. There was her and only her. No subway, no city, no time, no death. Two children in a crowded world, one with an outstretched hand, asking the other to follow. Her lips parted and a breath escaped, deciding my fate forever.

"Yes!"

The subway roared past us.

Epilogue

1

The wedding is in May, just under three months from now. As the countdown continues, the days get longer and my hours of sleep get shorter. Yesterday, it was a visit to the florist. Today: the caterer. Tomorrow: the photographer. And in spite of all the matrimonial minutiae, Emily seems less concerned with the particulars of the wedding than I am. While some girls fret and fantasize about their wedding until the honeymoon is over, with Emily everything is easy. Gold or white place settings, Beach or Vintage invites: she never bothers with the small stuff. For her, I think a sunny river bank and a clean grassy slope would make her the happiest girl in New York. Even still, it's best to be safe and spring for the chateau and band.

I suppose I'll always get the same sarcastic smile whenever I tell someone I married the love of my life at twenty-three. I'll be classified as one of those rare and dying breeds of half naïve, half miraculous children who keep their childhood love. And, in a way, I've gotten what I always wanted: to end where I began. And no trivial job or fleeting sense of worldly wealth will ever make me trade the blissful anticipation that I have of waking up with Emily each morning or of holding the hands of our children as I walk them to the bus on their first day of school. But these are chapters in some future story.

I think things worked out as best they could have

for Hunter. After a four month stay in Ohio, he came back to New York, got out of Manhattan, and moved to a nice neighborhood in Queens. It's a good thing too. I don't know what I would do without my best man.

As for Amanda, no one has heard from her since the night of the party. After several unsuccessful attempts, Aaron landed a part in a feature film shooting in Toronto. With the money, he'll be able to move out of his grand-mother's apartment and find a place of his own. Before going out west to stay with her sister, Lana went back to Darian. She didn't say goodbye when she left Manhattan, but somehow, I don't think she ever needed to.

There's still one person who requires a few more words. I have not heard from David since our curbside farewell. He deleted his Facebook and he probably would not answer my texts even if I sent them. I was angry when he told me he had to leave. I didn't understand his decision then and I barely understand it now. Part of me thinks David was looking for the quickest road to a new beginning, and so he took the first and easiest one that came along. But another far more delirious part of me thinks David was chasing what only a few run towards and even fewer catch. It's the promise of perfection, the knowledge that each moment can transform us into a person far greater than we were in the last.

The ones we love—the ones we lose—we carry them with us long after they are gone. We hope we will see them again, but memory alone can sustain us. And so their absence becomes less-painful, less-hurtful, until we realize they have never truly left us at all.

The End

Brandon is an undergraduate at Fordham University working towards a degree in politics, economics, and philosophy. Outside of class, he enjoys spending time with his family in Westchester, practicing judo, and reading Russian literature. This is his first novel.